TRAVELERS

Books by Ruth Prawer Jhabvala

Novels

TRAVELERS
A BACKWARD PLACE
GET READY FOR BATTLE
THE HOUSEHOLDER
ESMOND IN INDIA
THE NATURE OF PASSION
AMRITA

Short Stories

AN EXPERIENCE OF INDIA
A STRONGER CLIMATE
LIKE BIRDS, LIKE FISHES

Ruth Prawer Jhabvala

TRAVELERS

Harper & Row, Publishers

New York • Evanston • San Francisco • London

FIRST U.S. EDITION

Designed by C. Linda Dingler

Library of Congress Cataloging in Publication Data

Jhabvala, Ruth Prawer, 1927–
   Travelers.
   First published in England in 1973 under title: A new dominion
   [1. India—Social life and customs—Fiction]
I. Title.
PZ7.J573Tr3   [Fic]   72–9765
ISBN 0–06–012193–9

---

part I
DELHI

Lee Travels

Lee spent a good deal of time on buses and trains. She liked traveling though she wasn't much of a sightseer. She sat and looked out of the window. It was always the same countryside. Intrinsically it was boring, but to such an extent that the boredom became interesting. It was always the same and one could see that it had always been the same. The land was usually parched and ugly except where there were fields. When there were fields, there were peasants in them and these too were always the same: drab bodies in drab loincloths. They drew water from wells or guided bullocks drawing plowshares. The wells, the bullocks, the plowshares, the dry land, the everlasting sun: they continued mile after mile, day after day, while the train traveled on.

Inside the buses or trains it was also always the same. But whereas outside it was empty and silent, inside it was just the opposite. The public transport was always overcrowded. Crammed to bursting point. Everyone was traveling. They went to attend weddings, join pilgrimages, visit relatives in distant places. They brought many children with them, and some livestock, and a variety of shabby bundles. Many of these bundles held food: much eating had to be done in the course of the journey. Journeys were always long, for, in order to get from one place to another, great distances had to be traversed. Everyone accepted the overcrowding and the ensuing heat, smells, and discomfort without question.

Lee also accepted them. She was happy traveling this way. She felt she was no longer Lee but part of the mass of travelers huddled and squashed together. And when she looked out of the window, and the hours passed, and nothing ever changed out there, then too it was easy to forget about being Lee. That suited her very well. It was what she had come for: to lose herself in order—as she liked to put it—to find herself.

Raymond Writes to His Mother

Raymond had come for different reasons. Here he is writing to his mother; he writes to her about three or four times a week. They had always shared everything.

". . . Bought another handloom rug. I know I'm overdoing the handicrafts and I'm sure I shall soon be quite sick of them but in the meantime they're nice. It's getting very snug in here. Actually, I feel as if I've been living in this flat for ages. I'm already familiar with the exact daily routine of my neighbors. E.g.: at seven every morning the householder from downstairs sits in his courtyard to be shaved. He sits on a chair like a king and the barber scrapes at his cheeks with some great cutlass— a murderous-looking instrument which, however, he wields very tenderly. In the next courtyard regularly at the same time two women fight with their servant, a pock-marked old man who fights back, and in the courtyard next to that another woman fights with *her* servant, who doesn't fight back. He is an undernourished boy who looks eight but is probably twelve.

"Yesterday I looked up another of my New Delhi contacts (uncle of Surinder who is a friend of David Manse, who was at Cambridge with me). They asked me to dinner. I'm getting quite blasé about accepting sumptuous hospitality from strangers for no merit of my own except that I happen to know someone who knows someone they know. The food, as always, was superb and excessive. Everyone here eats excessively—those that do eat, I mean. There were the usual questions which I'm getting adept at answering though never to anyone's satisfaction. They're all sure I'm hiding something. I notice that people find it hard to believe that anyone should want to come here of their own free will and on no particular business. Certainly, all the Indians I meet seem, most of them, intent on getting out. Quite a few of them have recently been. I'm shown the ice-cream mixers and tape recorders they've brought back with them.

"But now I too am entertaining. Great excitement: Shyam keeps popping in and out to show me dishes and trying to decide which will do for sandwiches, which for cakes. It seems none of them will do for anything and we shall have to acquire an entirely new set. Shyam also thinks it might be necessary to outfit him with a new uniform consisting of a high-collared coat with gold buttons. He points out that some American ladies equip their bearers with white gloves for the purpose of serving guests. I retort that my guest may not have as high standards as the guests entertained by the American ladies. Then Shyam becomes suspicious and, pressing inquiries, discovers that my guest is in fact an Indian, and a mere student at that. I'm afraid this entirely destroys Shyam's pleasure. But I continue to look forward to my guest. He seems a pleasant boy. I met him at that wedding I wrote you about. His name is Gopi."

Asha Is Bored

Asha lived in an apartment in Bombay. It was a beautiful apartment in a very modern block and she lived right on top, from where she had a wonderful view over the sea. It was the rainy season and the sea was in turmoil and huge waves rose up like sea monsters and flung their spray far over the land. Usually

Asha loved this sight—she adored things fierce and passionate because she herself was so—but now she was bored with everything. She moved from one room to the other and out onto the terrace where she leaned on the parapet to look with moody eyes over the heaving sea. This palled quite soon and she was back inside, fiercely kicking at things that got in her way and quarreling with Bulbul, her old woman servant. Bulbul retreated into the kitchen where she winked at the other servants and told them that it was going to be a rough day today.

But she was wrong. Instead of tempests, there was an unnatural silence shot through with Asha's heavy sighs. She drank some vodka, which, however, made her feel worse. Then she began to telephone various friends, hoping that they would come and visit her and cheer her up. But either they were not at home or they were not free to come. This made her feel she had no friends. No friends, no lovers, nothing, no one: only Bulbul and the other servants who would have left her tomorrow if they got a better chance elsewhere. Especially Bulbul, who pretended to be so devoted, just because she had seen Asha born: she would be the first to run off if there were anyone else to give her money the way Asha did and saris and blouse-pieces. Just as Asha had reached this point in her thoughts, Bulbul came up behind her and began to massage her temples in the way Asha usually loved. But today Asha flung her off and told her to keep out of her way for the rest of the day and preferably forever; that would be the best, if she could pack up and leave and not show her ugly old face here again. Bulbul took it all quite calmly and said her baby, her sweetheart, was out of sorts today, and then she went off into the kitchen and made a nice meal off some leftover fish curry and a piece of pickle.

The way a finger probes a wound, the tongue a hollow tooth, so Asha sought to aggravate her aching soul. She did this by looking at herself in the mirror. Yes, then indeed she had cause for pain. However, as she looked—fascinated in spite of herself, drawing back from the mirror and looking from the best vantage point from over a shoulder proudly turned—she began to find that there was after all still something left to admire. Her eyes burned with fire, her bosom heaved; her hair was still as black as ever, and what did it matter that this effect was achieved with the help of a tiny bit of art. Not a young woman but, she found, a handsome one: and she was about to cheer up when it struck her that, however handsome she might be, who was there to admire and appreciate her the way she needed? She took up the framed photograph of her husband that stood among the gold and crystal vials on her dressing table; she pressed her face against the cold glass. But that too was no satisfaction: not only was he dead, but the memory of him alive was not all that pleasant. She had had a lot of trouble with him.

The telephone rang and she pounced on it greedily. With what joy she greeted her friend Tara Bai! They talked and soon Asha was quite cheered up. Tara Bai had rung up to tell her about a dinner dance she had attended the night before and what a scandal had been created there by one of those new little starlets. Only she couldn't tell Asha over the phone because— well, it was so *dirty,* said Tara Bai giggling madly, she would have to wait till they met. At once! Asha commanded, they must meet at once, they would have lunch together, perhaps drive out to the restaurant on the beach and eat steak and watch the waves. But Tara Bai was busy for lunch, she was going to meet —guess who, and she giggled again in a sly way so that Asha knew it was one of those young men she was always taking up with. "Wish me luck," said Tara Bai and smacked loving kisses into Asha's ear before ringing off.

Asha felt disgusted. It *was* disgusting, the way Tara Bai carried on; at her age. But then, what could you expect from someone like Tara Bai, a film actress, and everyone of course knew what to expect from film actresses. What were they but glorified prostitutes? In some cases, Asha thought, turning down her mouth corners, not even glorified. Asha's family were quite right when they told her not to take up with such people. They weren't worthy of her. She went back to the mirror and looked at herself again with pride; and now it was pride not only in her looks but in her birth too, for whereas Tara Bai sprang from an unrelieved line of prostitutes, Asha had royal blood in her. She was a princess and that still counted for something.

Gopi Comes to Tea

"Is it imported?"

Gopi asked this question several times and was each time disappointed. Raymond had brought nothing with him but had furnished his flat with local handicrafts. Nevertheless there was a foreign atmosphere which simultaneously thrilled and intimidated Gopi. He sat stiffly with his arms pressed to his sides and his eyes lowered.

Instead of relieving his guest's discomfort, Raymond aggravated it by a certain tea-table formality that came instinctively to him. He loved teatime, especially he loved guests at teatime, and he loved to have everything just so. He poured the tea and heard himself say in the rather fluting voice his mother adopted on such occasions, "Milk? Sugar? How's that for you?" Raymond had always lived with his mother and an aunt, and both these ladies had enjoyed having other ladies and elderly bachelor gentlemen to tea.

Shyam, the servant, was being uncooperative. He made it clear that he was not used to serving people like Gopi. Gopi felt this and resented it and sometimes he raised his modest eyes and resentment flashed out of them. At the same time, he was as afraid of being seen to do something wrong by Shyam as by Raymond. He was usually a graceful boy but his fear made him clumsy. He crushed the delicate bread and butter in his hand and dropped a spoon and finally even, in setting his cup and saucer on the table with an unsteady hand, spilled tea on the tablecloth. Shyam stood and sneered.

At last the tea ceremony was over and Raymond could relax

and attempt to make his guest relax too. But the first question he asked him, which was about the college Gopi attended, was not a welcome one. Gopi's college was not very good—in fact it was distinctly third-rate; it was run by private enterprise in some outlying suburb for boys like Gopi who had not scored high enough marks to get admission into a better place. Gopi was ashamed of going there and he replied to Raymond in an indistinct mutter.

"Oh, yes?" said Raymond with encouragement. He waited for Gopi to say more, and when he didn't, continued. "And what course are you doing?"

Gopi muttered again. Raymond remained bright, smiling, and encouraging, but he did not succeed in making Gopi easy. He was saddened to see his guest sitting there, opposite him, hunched up in the tall canework chair with his gaze obstinately lowered. He was also saddened by the way Gopi had dressed himself up so carefully for the occasion, thereby almost obscuring his good looks. He wore a transparent shirt of some thick synthetic material, and overtight trousers, and his hair was smothered in oil.

Shyam was clearing away the tea things. He did it with maddening slowness. When he came to removing the tablecloth, he bent over the stain caused by Gopi's spilled tea; he shook his head over it, then pointed his finger at it.

"It won't come out," he prophesied.

"Never mind," Raymond said.

"Our new cloth."

"Never *mind.*"

Raymond was a friendly and indulgent employer but he could be sharp. Shyam saw it was time to remove himself and he did so, though with a superior air.

Gopi raised his eyes and looked after him with the same smoldering glance as before. But then, instead of concentrating on the floor again, he looked for the first time directly at Raymond and his eyes were still smoldering. He said, "You have a very bad servant."

"Oh, I don't know," Raymond said. Actually, he didn't feel like defending Shyam, who *had* behaved badly, but he didn't want to drop the subject either because at last here was Gopi showing some spirit. "Shyam's not such a bad chap really. He just has moods."

"No," said Gopi, "he is a bad chap. We would not keep such a person in our home."

He was still looking at Raymond. Gopi's eyes were full and dark and at this time they were burning with a splendid fire. There was a cake crumb on his upper lip, and Raymond wished he knew him well enough to point this out and perhaps even wipe it away for him with his handkerchief.

"He is only a servant," Gopi said. "He should not be allowed to behave in any way he pleases."

Raymond began to protest, but in the mildest manner possible. Perhaps it was this mildness that inflamed Gopi—at any rate, his anger mounted, he said many things. He said that Shyam was of a very low caste, that such people could never get employment in a Hindu family, and that was the reason they fastened themselves on to foreigners whom they fleeced mercilessly and behaved with them in the shabbiest manner and insulted their guests. . . .

"Well, I'm sorry," Raymond said in the middle of this. Gopi was brought up short: he stared at Raymond in surprise.

"Why?" Gopi asked. He laughed. "Why are *you* sorry?"

He laughed more: in surprise but also not unflattered to be apologized to by this Englishman who was so much older than he was—Raymond was at least thirty—and well educated and cultured and probably rich. Suddenly he relaxed. Still laughing, he bounded up from the chair into which he had been hunched ever since he came, and sat on the floor. He began to ease himself out of his shoes. Evidently they were hurting him and had been doing so all this time; they were ugly, tight, black shoes. His socks followed and he wriggled his toes and breathed "Ah" in relief. Raymond watched with pleasure. Gopi's feet were narrow and had delicate bones.

"You see, I'm quite at home," he said, smiling up at Raymond who said, "Good," and then added, "Lovely," he was so pleased. Gopi patted the floor so that Raymond slid off his chair and sat beside him. Gopi nodded in approval. "It's our Indian way," he said. "We don't care for chairs—all this furniture, what use is it when we can be most comfortable on the floor itself?"

"Quite," agreed Raymond though he did not look comfortable. His joints were not as flexible as Gopi's, and his knees stuck up into the air.

"You didn't bring any with you?"

"What?"

"Furniture from England."

Raymond explained how he had brought nothing because he wanted to be quite free and also he didn't know how long he was going to stay, though he hoped it would be for some time. Gopi was a little disappointed that Raymond didn't belong to an embassy or some international organization, but he was intrigued by Raymond's reasons for coming at all. He didn't quite believe him and felt there was something more which Raymond was hiding.

Raymond was already used to this reaction but with Gopi he took more trouble than usual to explain himself. He said, "My family has always had connections with India. One of them was in Delhi in 1835, the year when William Fraser was murdered here. He was a friend of Fraser's and wrote long letters home about the case. We still have them. And there's a great-uncle buried somewhere near Meerut, he was killed while he was out pig-sticking. . . ."

Raymond saw that Gopi's attention was beginning to wander and guessed at once that he would be more interested in practical matters; so he told him how he had taken a year's leave from

11

his job—which was in a publishing firm owned by his uncle—
and that he intended to spend that time living in India.

"And money?" Gopi asked, with a shrewd, inquiring gesture
of rubbing two fingers together.

"Well . . . there was this little legacy my aunt left me—"

"How much?"

Raymond was taken aback for a moment and then said, rather
cautiously, "Not all that much. . . . But enough for me to take
some time off and experiment."

"With what?"

"Myself."

Raymond smiled in embarrassment. He heard himself sounding pompous. But in any case Gopi's eyes had again begun to
wander around the room. Raymond watched him and after a
while he said, "There's something on your lip." He took out his
handkerchief and said, "No, here," and wiped it skillfully away.

After a pause Gopi said, "You don't look like other English
people. No, you don't," he insisted. "Your face is not red."

Raymond was as a matter of fact unnaturally pale. His hair
had a reddish tint in it and he blushed very easily.

Now Gopi was tired of sitting on the floor and making conversation. He bounded up again and began to walk around the
room, picking things up here and there. He also went into the
bedroom. He didn't much like the bedcover, he said. It was not
very bright. He said he liked very very bright things. "Are there
any more rooms? Only these two?" He added, "There is only
one bed." He asked, "You're not married?"

When Raymond laughed, he said, not without reproach, "In
India you would have been married long ago. . . . Will you have
friends to stay with you?"

"I hope so."

"Do you like friends to stay with you?"

"Some friends, yes," Raymond said. He added, "Very much."

But Gopi had already moved over to the wardrobe and
opened it and was critically studying Raymond's clothes. Al-

12

though they were not very bright, Gopi liked some of them. He fingered the material, with approval and desire.

Lee Among Hindus and Christians

Lee had no fixed itinerary. She got on a train and got off when she felt like it. Usually she met people on the train who urged her to come and stay with them, or gave her the address of relatives who would put her up. She had begun to take such hospitality for granted. She was also beginning to find her way around the small towns where she so often landed up. They were always the same. There was a bazaar down the center and, branching off it, a network of lanes which got narrower and narrower the deeper one penetrated into them. But Lee no longer got lost among them, and she had no hesitation in making her way through the most intricate alleys or disappearing inside the darkest doorways.

But once something went wrong. She found the address but the place was in commotion. Women were screaming inside and outside the house while a crowd stood and watched. Lee couldn't get through and had to crane her neck to see what was going on. Some men were arguing and giving each other contrary instructions, and after a time several bent down to heave something up and place it on the shoulders of several others. Then the women redoubled their cries. Lee saw that what they were carrying was a body on a plank. It was wound in a red cloth and secured to the plank with ropes; the face was uncovered and was that of a young woman. All the men fell behind the pallbearers and they walked away in procession. Lee joined them. They walked for quite a way, chanting as they went. In between chanting they carried on fairly normal conversation with each other. Lee was asked who she was and where she had come from and what she was doing in the town. She explained how she had been given this address to stay at. One of the men said that now that would no longer be possible because of the death in the family and so she had better come home with him. Lee said all right. They got to the river and there the body was placed on the pyre and a priest said prayers and the fire was lit and the body began to burn. Lee's new host said that it would take a long time to burn, and that they had better leave now and go home for their evening meal.

This new house was, like the other, in a lane off the bazaar. It was reached through a dank brick passage that opened out into a spacious courtyard. Here Lee sat crosslegged on a string cot to be served with food. She was hungry and ate a lot. Meanwhile people kept coming into the courtyard, and there was an air of excitement, of turmoil even. They were discussing and arguing with passion. Lee couldn't follow what they were saying, and when she asked, they wouldn't tell her. But the excited talk continued, and she began to realize that it was something to do with the death. She asked, "What did she die of?"

At first no one would answer. She understood it was something mysterious and frightening and looked from face to face.

At last they said, "They say she was poisoned."

Lee recalled the young woman's dead face; also the pallbearers and the chanting and the women wailing. Then she recalled the flames that had been lit and had crackled and begun to rise above the body; by this time the body would have been mostly consumed. "And the inquest?" Lee asked. "The police?"

She was agitated but her hosts remained calm. They shrugged. "What can be done? It's too late." They shook their heads in sorrow. It was such a pity. She was young, she had only been married seven months. But her dowry had not been very big; her father had not been as generous to the son-in-law as he might have been.

Lee asked, "Is that why they poisoned her?"

They said, "Such things happen"; they added, "Who knows what goes on?"

When she left that small town, Lee went to Delhi to stay in a Christian mission run by an English missionary lady called

14

Miss Charlotte. Lee was very glad to be there. She stayed in a room with whitewashed walls which were bare except for a small icon of Christ on the cross. Another girl shared the room with her; she was called Margaret and was also traveling around India on her own. Meals were included in the price of the room and they had them in the dining room together with Miss Charlotte. There was a very old Christian bearer to serve them and the moment one meal was finished he laid the table for the next. He set out three crockery plates on the oilcloth, turning them upside down so that they wouldn't catch the dust. When it was time for a meal, he rang a gong and Miss Charlotte came bustling in and stood behind her chair and briskly said grace. The old bearer shouted "Amen" the loudest, and when Miss Charlotte and the two girls had sat down and turned their plates the right way up, he went round the table serving them.

Miss Charlotte had been in India for thirty years. Her mission house, a large rambling bungalow, was in a poor state of repair but she managed to keep it going and to fill it with worthwhile activity. One of the rooms was used as a school for the children of sweepers, in another girls of poor family were taught to knit and sew; a corner of the back veranda was used as a part-time dispensary. This last activity was not quite legal, for Miss Charlotte was not a qualified dispenser and could not afford to hire one. Once or twice government inspectors had come and looked grave. Altogether Miss Charlotte did not have an easy time: questions were often asked in Parliament about proselytizing missionaries, and Christian missions of varying denominations were being closed all over the country.

The food Miss Charlotte and the two girls ate was boiled, meager, and English, except on Sundays when there was rice and curry. The dining room carried the congealed smell of a long succession of such meals. It was a cheerless place but, thanks to Miss Charlotte's serene high spirits, their mealtimes were not cheerless. Although she was completely wrapped up in her work in India, she had not lost interest in what went on at home. By no means. Her first love was literature; her favorite novelists were George Eliot and Thomas Hardy, both of whom she read over and over again. She also had a passion for the theater, although she had never really quite taken to the cinema. But she was eager to learn about the latest developments in all the arts and asked her two guests many questions. Nothing they told her could ever shock her: she received everything quite coolly, indeed with friendly interest, and leaned across the table to hear better. These mealtime chats were so enjoyable for her that she lingered longer than she should have done over her coffee and only managed to tear herself away when, as often happened, a message came to her to say that one of the women in the servants' quarters had begun her labor, or there was a leper outside the kitchen waiting to be given a meal.

Gopi Moves In with Raymond

Gopi didn't care where he slept—on the sofa, on the floor, on two chairs pushed together. And he fell asleep very quickly; when there was nothing more to interest him, he dropped off at once. He looked childlike and innocent with his eyes shut and his long lashes delicately spread on his cheeks. Raymond sometimes tried to arrange him more comfortably, tucking in a pillow here or there, but really it was not necessary, for Gopi was absolutely comfortable already.

He was practically living in Raymond's flat. It had come about quite naturally: he didn't feel like going home, so he stayed on, from one meal to the next, from one day to the next. He liked being there. He liked being with Raymond and, just as much, he liked the flat, the bachelor's establishment. It was quite different from anything he knew at home. He had never missed privacy and comfort because he had never known them; now that he was making their acquaintance, he found they suited him. He moved around the place like its natural lord and master. He wore Raymond's dressing gown and silk scarves and whatever else fitted him. He took it for granted that everything that was there, everything that was Raymond's, was his.

This included Raymond's servant, Shyam. He had completely got over his shyness of Shyam and had no hesitation in ordering him around like his own servant. He found it easy to ignore Shyam's subsequent surliness, for he hardly noticed it; and it was only when Shyam refused outright to do some service for him that he reacted to him at all and then always by storming and shouting. It was up to Raymond to make what peace he could between them. When, in as delicate a manner as possible, Raymond suggested that Shyam had feelings that had to be respected, Gopi was at first astonished and then disapproving. He told Raymond that he was spoiling the servant. He was convinced he was right and set about proving it to Raymond with so much heat that Raymond realized it was useless to argue with him. In any case, he had already learned that Gopi was not amenable to argument. So he did his best to soothe Shyam and make it up to him as far as possible. Shyam kept threatening to leave and Raymond kept managing to persuade him not to, but he knew that the day might come when he would have to let Shyam go. He would be sorry when that happened, but there seemed to be no alternative.

Lee Meets Asha

Lee had brought several introductions from home, but she scorned to use them except when she felt in need of a really good meal. That was how she came to ring up Rao Sahib and to be invited by him to an evening party. There were many other guests and Rao Sahib did not have much time for her. He greeted her with the folded hands and obsequious smile of the gratified host but his eyes were roving above her head and, with the smile still warm on his lips, he darted away from her to greet some other newly arrived guests for whom his welcome was even more gratified and his eyes did not rove but were cast down in utter humility.

Rao Sahib was well-born. He came from a family who had assumed a royal title several centuries ago when a soldier ancestor had seized land and set up a principality of his own. The title was still theirs, so was some of the land, but nowadays of course, if one wanted to rule, one had to be democratically elected. Rao Sahib had already had himself elected to Parliament, and he had now set his sights higher—to become by and by a minister of state, a deputy minister, a minister. All that did not come by itself. One had to put oneself out, and Rao Sahib was ready to do so. One of his assets was the ability to entertain in style. Besides the palace in his native state, he also had a handsome house in New Delhi with large reception rooms, marble floors, pillared verandas, and a garden worked by three full-time gardeners. Another asset was his wife, Sunita, who also came from a royal family (though one even more minor than Rao Sahib's), knew how to control a houseful of servants, and was as modern in her ideas as her husband.

The evening party to which Lee had been invited was a very large one. All the glass doors had been flung open and the guests thronged in the drawing room, on the veranda, out into the garden which had been lit with fairy lights in the trees. It was not difficult to detect the guest of honor. He was a cabinet minister and looked quite different from the other people there. He was squat, bald, and ugly, and wore a muslin dhoti which showed off his short muscular legs to their worst advantage. Rao Sahib, hovering by his side, tried hard to look less tall and elegant. But this was not possible for him. However, his guest was not in the least put out by the imposing figure towering above him. He took his host's attentions entirely for granted and did not appear to be listening very carefully to his conversation. He was more interested in the trays being carried past by the servants and frequently stopped one and pointed at the carefully arranged canapés.

18

When Lee passed, in her bright yellow peasant skirt and gypsy earrings, he pointed at her in the same way. He looked her up and down keenly. When he spoke, it was with severity. "I have seen Western boys and girls behaving in an indecent manner in public places. It is not only kissing and hugging, other things also." His eyes weighed heavily on her; he seemed to know much and see far. "In the old days the blouse was worn with long sleeve, everything was covered up to here. Only the widows went without blouse and the upper part of their bodies exposed. Who cares about such old women? But in a young girl maidenly modesty is the first consideration. I speak to you as an elder brother to his sister."

No one else took any notice of Lee. It was easy for them to see that she was not an interesting personality so they did not waste their efforts in engaging her in conversation. She didn't mind. She was looking forward to the buffet supper that was to be served, and when it came she was not disappointed. Everything was laid out resplendently on the vast dining-room table: an endless succession of dishes piled with pilaos, curries, kebabs, salads, baked chickens, stuffed eggs, pickles, and curds. At one end of the table there were pyramids of Worcester plates and cut-work napkins and heavily decorated silver cutlery; Sunita, who had a real flair for table decoration, had arranged the flowers and crystal dishes with her own hands. Everything shone and glittered under the chandeliers. Lee began at once to move around the table, piling her plate with everything it would hold. The other ladies behaved with more circumspection and decorum, drawing back a little for each other, recommending one dish above another, exchanging the news of the day as they hovered with delicate forks over the serving dishes. Lee elbowed her way through without constraint. She had been living with Miss Charlotte for some time, and all those cheerful but meager mission meals had left her feeling very hungry.

She took her heaped plate and sat with it on the steps of the veranda. Here she could look into the reception rooms sparkling with ladies in silks and jewels. At the same time she could look out into the garden which was quite deserted now and lit only by the colored lights glimmering through the leaves of the trees; it was silent here, except for a fountain. Lee enjoyed being on her own. The food on her plate was excellent. It was the most refined example of Indian cooking she had yet tasted, full of delicate flavors and essences.

Now she became witness of a curious scene. A car appeared at the entrance gate but could not enter because of the throng of cars in the driveway. Some furious hooting followed. The watchman went running out, was greeted by an angry female voice, came running back again. Lee got up to see. It was a taxi with two women in it. One of them was leaning out of the window and shouting and snapping her fingers after the departing watchman. She ordered the driver to keep blowing his horn. She was becoming more and more angry. The watchman came running out again, followed by Rao Sahib and one or two servants. Rao Sahib was agitated. As soon as she caught sight of him, the woman in the taxi shouted, "Get them out! Out of the way!" She gesticulated her hand as if to sweep away all the cars blocking the drive.

Rao Sahib begged her to be reasonable. He asked how was it possible to remove all his guests' cars? She would have to get out and walk up to the door.

"With all this luggage?" There was indeed a great deal of it loaded inside and on top of the taxi. "And with Bulbul in that state—as usual she was sick on the plane. She is disgusting." Nevertheless she got out of the taxi. She seized Rao Sahib's face and kissed him several times.

He asked, "But why didn't you phone? Send a wire?"

"To come to my own brother's house? Anyway, there wasn't time. I decided quite suddenly. I couldn't stand it one second more. Bombay is hell. You will have to come out of there, Bulbul, and *walk*, nobody is going to drive you any further."

Bulbul crept slowly out of the other taxi door. She was groaning and looked very miserable, bowed and bundled up from head to foot in a huge silk sari discarded by her mistress. Asha bustled about and made the servants bustle about to unload her luggage. Lee was still watching. It was some time before Asha saw her and then she stepped up close to her and peered into her face.

"Please go in," Rao Sahib told Lee nervously. "Kindly help yourself to the sweet dish."

Asha was now peering at Lee's earrings. She gave them a swing. "Where did you get them? I like them. They're my style."

Leaving the servants to struggle with her luggage, she turned and walked through the gate to the house. Rao Sahib followed her. Lee also followed, and Bulbul crept in the rear. Asha was making straight for the reception rooms but Rao Sahib said, "You will want to take rest."

She laughed. "All right, all right, I know I look terrible. It's Bulbul's fault. She was sick all over me—she has absolutely no self-control. You can go now, darling," she told Rao Sahib. "You must get back to your guests."

She overrode his protests by kissing him again and then turning him round and giving him a push. She went up the stairs leading to the first-floor verandas. A bedroom was unlocked for her and she went in and gave orders as to the disposal of her luggage. Bulbul fell straight to the floor and lay there completely still.

Lee had also entered the bedroom and Asha seemed to take her presence for granted. She addressed all her remarks to Lee as to an old friend. Lee was still holding her plate of food, and after a while Asha said she was hungry too. So Lee went downstairs to refill her own plate and bring another for Asha. By the time she got back, Asha had opened some of the suitcases and partly pulled out their contents which now lay spilled over the bed and the floor. Her dressing case had also been opened and the dressing table was tumbled over with powder puffs, scent sprays, odd earrings, and bottles of pills. Asha was wearing a lace negligee. She had pulled off her clothes and left them in a heap on the floor: they lay there next to Bulbul, who was herself immobile and crumpled like a heap of discarded clothes.

Asha kicked off some of the things that had got scattered over the bed so that she and Lee could recline there and eat. At first Asha seemed perfectly happy. She ate with good appetite, but after a while her eating motions became slower and slower and finally stopped.

"You saw him," she said. "My own brother. And she hasn't even come up to greet me."

"They're very busy. It's a big party."

Asha pulled her mouth sideways in contempt.

"There's a cabinet minister," Lee urged.

"I don't know how he can bear to have such people in the house. Ever since he went into that Parliament, he has lost all self-respect. And it is she driving him on. You don't know how ambitious she is. It's no longer enough for her to be Rao Sahib's wife, now she has to be wife of an M.P. and from there on God knows where. And for this the sister is sacrificed. I suppose he thought I had been drinking. But I haven't had a thing—look." She breathed on Lee. "You see. But they're so ashamed of me. They are always terrified I shall do something to disgrace them." She felt compelled to add, "Sometimes I get into a mood and do things, but it is not always my fault."

Strains of music came up from the garden. Lee moved to the window to see. The guests had come out of the house and were scattered over the lawn. Some sat on chairs, other lay reclining on carpets that had been spread there. They all faced a small platform on which sat a young man playing a sitar. He wore an exquisite embroidered muslin shirt and rings shone on his fingers; his hair was long and curly. He bent over the sitar and caressed it as one making love.

Asha said from the bed, "Quite often I'm led astray by others.

Unfortunately I have a very romantic character. . . . How old are you?"

"Twenty."

"You look out. I can see you are also a romantic type of personality. I can feel it like vibrations."

"It's the music," Lee said.

"Isn't it fantastically beautiful?"

Raymond and Gopi Meet Lee

Raymond had visited all the famous monuments several times, both by himself and later with Gopi; now there were others that were not listed in the guidebooks but lay, scattered and half forgotten, throughout the surrounding countryside. Gopi didn't care much for ancient monuments, either historically or architecturally, and he had only the vaguest idea as to what they were; but he knew them well, for he had often come here with friends for picnics and to smoke and look at girls who had also come for picnics. Today he had brought Raymond to a disused mosque standing in a walled compound with some trees, a tomb, and several scattered graves. Raymond had hired a taxi, which they had to leave standing on the road, and then they picked their way through a narrow track and some tangled undergrowth out of which there suddenly grew a potter's shed with the potter sitting inside it. They also met a very old man walking behind a very old bullock. After that there was no one.

They climbed up a steep staircase inside the mosque. The steps and the passageways in which they ended were totally dark, slippery with moss, and smelling of bats, but finally led to a terrace: from here there was a wide-open view of sky and landscape. Gopi, tired of climbing, flung himself down on the paved terrace. Sheltering in the shadow cast by the great cracked stone dome above him, he lay with his arms folded behind his head. Raymond leaned over the parapet to peer down at the decorated walls of the mosque. He wondered about its date and guessed it to be around the fifteenth century. He leafed through his guidebook, hoping that perhaps he had over-looked an entry; but there was nothing.

Gopi said, "Why are you looking at that stupid book again?"

"It *is* stupid. I don't know how they came to leave this out. It's beautiful. Perhaps Lodi, I don't know—but the same time as those Mehrauli tombs. I think." He looked at Gopi, who had wearily shut his eyes. Raymond smiled and said, "It's very old."

This was a joke between them. Whenever Raymond specu-lated about a date, Gopi said, "It's very old." When Raymond asked, "Yes, but how very old?" he would say, "One hundred years," and if Raymond looked skeptical, he would emend it to five hundred years.

Gopi said in a lazy and tired voice, "If I weren't so lazy and tired—you know what I would do? I would take that book—and yes! I think I will!"

Suddenly he jumped up and tried to snatch Raymond's guide-book out of his hand. They struggled for it, laughing together. But it was too hot to struggle for long. Gopi let go—though before doing so he gave Raymond a push which was hard enough to send him sprawling against the parapet wall. Gopi laughed heartily; physical mishaps to others always amused him. Raymond also laughed, though, as a matter of fact, he had in falling somewhat grazed his arm.

Raymond continued to look out over the landscape. It had rained recently and there were sudden stretches of brilliant grass where one would have thought no grass had grown in centuries. Trees dripped with green, and hollows filled with rainwater glinted and danced with speckles of sun. Everywhere there were ruins in broken-off shapes—half a tower, a solitary gateway, steps leading to nowhere—and all of them set off against a water-blue sky that had small washed clouds frisking across it. And there was Gopi relaxed against the drum of the dome, grumbling he was hungry, why hadn't they brought something to eat, what was the use of coming to these places

unless you brought things to eat? He described a picnic he and
his friends had had in this same place, and all the food they had
eaten, and the games they had played. And he grumbled to
Raymond, "You see, this is the trouble—you don't play anything, you're not fun for me." But Raymond knew he didn't
mean it.

Raymond crossed over to the other side of the parapet and
now looked over the forecourt of the mosque with the little
tomb and the graves shady under trees. He checked himself
from wondering whose graves they might be. As he stood there
gazing out, brimful of satisfaction, he saw a girl come in through
a gap in the compound wall. She was an unexpected apparition
in that place: a Western girl in a yellow peasant skirt and gypsy
earrings. She wandered in and looked around and Raymond
watched her. Gopi, always sensitive to whatever Raymond was
doing, noticed a change in his attention and asked, "What are
you looking at?"

"Come and see," Raymond said.

Gopi stood beside him. He looked at the girl and began to say
bravado things, the sort he knew boys were expected to say
about girls. When Raymond didn't react, he thought perhaps he
wasn't going far enough so he went as far as he knew how. The
girl remained totally unaware of them. She shuffled off her
sandals and went into the mosque and then she came out again
and looked around the tomb and then she sat on a grave under
a tree.

Gopi said, "I'll go and talk to her." He said it like a challenge
and when Raymond didn't answer he added, "I'll pick her up."
It was a phrase he had learned fairly recently and he offered it
—half daring, half timid—as if he weren't quite sure about it.
But next he said, "You think I can't? You think I don't know
how? Just watch me!"

He turned and climbed down the steps leading from the
terrace. Raymond watched him emerge from the side entrance
of the mosque and make his way toward the girl. Raymond

enjoyed watching him—he was proud of him and the way he advanced like a purposeful conqueror, tossing the hair out of his eyes. Gopi had a boy's figure with very narrow hips on which his trousers sat jauntily. Ever since he had met Raymond, he had laid aside the somewhat gaudy shirts he used to wear in favor of the more elegant ones that Raymond bought for him. He had natural good taste and had learned very quickly.

Raymond saw the girl look up. He also saw a look of annoyance on her face. This deepened as Gopi went on talking to her. They were too far away for Raymond to hear what they were saying, but evidently Gopi was saying all he could think of and the girl was answering him very shortly. After a while she stopped answering altogether and looked away from him. Gopi too seemed to have run out of conversation. He continued to stand there, continued even to display his air of bravado, but evidently he did not know what to say or do next. Raymond realized he would have to go down to rescue him.

Although he pretended to be in command of the situation, Gopi was clearly relieved to see him. He said, "She is not a friendly person." There was a quite uncharacteristic leer on his face.

"Is he with you?" Lee asked Raymond. "Perhaps you could tell him it's bad manners to disturb people who want to be alone."

"Why does she want to be alone?" Gopi said. "Ah-ha—you see, she doesn't answer. There must be a very bad reason."

Lee looked at Raymond for help. Gopi too seemed to want help, to be relieved of the girl and the situation which were not turning out as expected.

"We'll go," Raymond offered.

But they didn't. They stood there rather awkwardly and in awkward silence till Lee asked Raymond, "Are you American?"

"English."

"Of course. . . . Are you with your embassy or something?"

"No. Oh, no."

The emphatic way in which he said this pleased Lee so that for the first time she smiled a little bit.

Now it was Gopi who wanted to go. His natural dignity had reasserted itself and he was anxious to leave a scene where it had suffered such a setback. Lee seemed to sense this for she suddenly turned to him. "I'm sorry if I was rude."

Gopi was no longer as impressed by apologies as he once had been. Living with Raymond, he realized that these people said sorry very quickly, perhaps even took some pleasure in it so that there was no need to forgive them every time. He ignored Lee and told Raymond, "Come on."

Lee explained, "I come to these places and I get terribly engrossed." She glanced rather nervously at Raymond: she was afraid he might be skeptical and put her down as just an intense girl. Of course she *was* intense, but that wasn't all, she liked to think.

"I love tombs of saints best," she said. "There was one in Madhya Pradesh—it was some saint who was also a poet, I've forgotten the name. It was a very out-of-the-way place, up a rock; terribly difficult to get to, it took me days. But it was worth it. The tomb wasn't much—the roof had fallen in—but there was such a holy atmosphere. I sat there for hours. Oh, I felt good. Not a soul came and it was completely silent except there was a stream somewhere near and of course lots and lots of birds. . . . Whose is that?" she asked, pointing at the small tomb facing them. It was decorated with a few broken blue tiles which glinted in the sun and the names of God were engraved into the stone. There was a wasp's nest hanging inside one arch.

"There's nothing at all in my book," Raymond said. "I find it frustrating but Gopi doesn't believe in guidebooks anyway."

"I think you're so right!" Lee said. "Who wants guidebooks? Either a place has good emanations or it doesn't. If you don't have feeling for that, then what's the use of knowing facts? They just blunt you. Don't you think so?" she said, turning round fully to Gopi.

27

Gopi responded. He liked her manner—her openness toward himself—and he liked what she was saying. She seemed a very different type of person from what he thought Westerners usually were; she certainly seemed very different from Raymond. He pointed at Raymond. "I've told him so often but he doesn't understand. I think he's too materialistic."

"Are you?" Lee asked Raymond earnestly.

"If Gopi says so." Raymond was glad to see Gopi relax and get over his hurt feelings; and he always found it amusing to be called materialistic by him.

Lee studied Raymond and said, "Really you look quite sensitive."

"He is not at all a sensitive person," Gopi assured her. "He doesn't believe anything except what he sees before his eyes. When I took him to Kutb and told him about the ghost of Adham Khan, he didn't believe."

"I never said that," Raymond protested. He had scrupulously refrained from making any comment, hoping to get by; but now he realized that he hadn't.

"You did not say but you thought. You thought it's all nonsense and Gopi is very stupid to believe in these things. But I think you're stupid." He said to Lee, "He doesn't believe in astrology."

"So many things come true."

"Everyone knows it. I can tell you from my own personal experience . . ."

He was now sitting next to Lee on the grave. He had very good feelings toward her. He felt he was making a new friend and he loved new friends. A sensation of peace and human affection came over him. He was very different from the boy who had come to pick her up just a short while ago.

Lee

I had a long talk with Miss Charlotte. She's been in India for thirty years and loved every moment of it. She hasn't always been in Delhi but has moved all around the country, in Calcutta and Kanpur and Hyderabad and up in Mussourie and some other hill stations. The mission used to have branches in all these places and she was moved from one to the other, wherever she was needed. I asked her which place she liked best but she said the work was the same in all of them. She looked very cheerful when she said that but my heart sank. I thought of the school room and the dispensary and all those people who come there. Especially I thought of their smell. Poor people in India all have it. It isn't that they don't wash but that they don't have the opportunity to wash well, or change their clothes very often; and they all live and sleep crowded together in airless places and this gives them a sort of dank herd-smell. And sick people have a worse smell. Once I asked Miss Charlotte to let me help in the dispensary, give out aspirins and things like that. But I couldn't bear it. All those people asking you to feel lumps in their bodies, and there was one old man with the toothache who opened his mouth wide and took my hand and guided it right inside to shake some blackened old molar that was hurting him.

Miss Charlotte is small and dumpy and wears terrible missionary clothes. Her face is completely round and it shines with happiness, it really shines. She goes to church only on Sundays and then she wears a hat (what a hat). She always says grace before meals but in a sort of businesslike way, the same way I hear her give orders in the kitchen; sort of brisk. I know she says her prayers at night because I've seen her. She was kneeling by the side of her bed in a white cotton nightdress; but it didn't take her long, and then she hopped up on the bed and pushed her nightie up her leg so as to rub ointment into her knee where she suffers from some rheumatic pain.

Well, I had this long talk with her but I couldn't get her really to *say* anything. Oh, she talked plenty but it was all about things I didn't much want to hear about though they were very interesting really: I mean, sort of anecdotes about incurables that had been cured, and cute little foundlings adopted by Swedish

29

parents, and Christmas Day in Kalimpong with a party for 450 orphans. She also spoke of some other missionary workers. There was one they all admired very much who spent fifty years in India doing marvelous work, though in the end she got very feeble and sick; she was nearly seventy by then. They all tried to get her to retire and go home to England but she kept putting it off, saying next year and then the year after. In the end she never went because she got chronic dysentery and died and was buried in the Christian cemetery at Gorakhpur. When she said that Miss Charlotte's face became absolutely radiant as if it were the most wonderful thing in the world to be buried in Gorakhpur, the fulfillment of every earthly desire anyone could possibly have. But when she spoke about some other workers who had not been able to stand the climate and had had to be sent home, then she spoke in a pitying way and was sorry for them. I asked were there many like that and she answered reluctantly, well quite a few, poor things. Some of them got sick with the heat and others got various diseases of which the most common were jaundice and amebic dysentery. I asked her had she ever had anything like that, and she said oh, yes, but she had always been very lucky and got over them quite quickly and afterward she was sound as a bell. Then she laughed and she *rang* like a bell, a very clear one, and obviously she considers herself a very very lucky person indeed.

So much goodness! Where does it come from? How do people get it?

I discussed this question with Margaret, the girl I share the room with. Margaret also wants to be good, but not in that way. In fact, she gets rather impatient with Miss Charlotte. She likes her all right but she can't sympathize with her *attitude*, which she says is old-fashioned and patronizing. She says people just don't come any more to India to do good, those days are over. What they come for now is—well, to do good to themselves, to learn, to *take* from India. That's what Margaret's here for. Above all she wants to be pure—to have a pure heart untainted by modern materialism. Margaret hates modern materialism. Of course, so do I; that's why we're both here. But I know that Margaret is more serious than I am in her search. Sometimes I don't know that I *am* searching for anything—sometimes I think maybe I'm just floating around, just not doing anything, just running away from things. But Margaret is always sure and doesn't lose sight of her purpose. She's been traveling about more or less the same way I have but not so aimlessly. She's spent a lot of time on trains and buses and she usually stays in rest houses or temples and all these sorts of public places. That way she says she's got to know a lot about the country and the people, but that's only secondary: it's herself she's in search of and wants to get to know—and not in any boring personal or psychological way, but she wants to find herself in her deepest essence where she's not only Margaret but what there is beyond and including Margaret. She has been staying in a few ashrams and met several gurus but has not yet found the right one. She has been to Pondicherry and saw the Holy Mother but she did not get any good answer there. She has also been to the place where Ramana Maharishi lived and died, and there she did feel the stirring of the right kind of response, but he is dead and what she wants is a live guru—someone to inspire her, she says —snatch her up and out of herself—simultaneously destroy and create her.

She's a very definite kind of girl. Even her coming here was a definite decision. She didn't just drift into it the way I did (because I'd heard about it and because other people had done it and because there wasn't anything else). Margaret came because she had to. It was an active step of revolt against her life at home and her family and what they and everyone else expected of her. None of this was good enough or true enough for Margaret. What really finally set her off was her sister's wedding. It was the usual kind of affair and we all know what they are. But for Margaret it was worse than just unpleasant, it was a catalytic experience which showed her the futility—no, not futility, what's the word she used?—anyway, this *nothingness* in which everyone lived and to which she too was expected to commit herself. But there she drew the line; that she could not have.

It might be all right for her sister Penny, but she and Penny had always been quite different. Penny liked clothes and dances and shopping and all the things their mother wanted them to like; she went out a lot and had different boy friends, and now she'd decided to marry this boy friend who was exactly like all the others only more so. Everyone was terrifically pleased and there was going to be *such* a wedding. Preparations for it went on for weeks and weeks. Penny and their mother were radiant, and of course no one noticed about Margaret, the way she was feeling. But she was glad about that, it gave her privacy and protection in which to work out her destiny. Finally there was this definite climax, which was when they went to buy her bridesmaid's dress. Naturally she was to be a bridesmaid, everyone expected it, she herself expected it really—she hadn't seriously questioned it but went along with the idea in the same negative way as with everything else. She was in the shop trying on this bridesmaid's dress, which was pale green with lace and rosebuds, and she could see it didn't suit her at all (no, those sort of clothes wouldn't suit her because she's got rather a stocky sort of figure and pale plump cheeks). But everyone was pretending she looked nice, and she could see her mother and Penny smiling approval behind her in the mirror, and the saleslady as well—all three of them standing there with this *lying* smile. At that moment Margaret knew she could not go on, that it was all a lie which she had to reject with her whole being. Terrific arguments followed, naturally, for days and days, but Margaret held out and she didn't stay for the wedding either, she was already in Bombay when it took place and so engrossed that she even forgot to send a telegram.

I admire Margaret. I like having discussions with her and I'm very glad I met her. What she says is always interesting, and her

32

purpose and everything she is. And I like staying here in our room in the mission, and our meals with Miss Charlotte, and Miss Charlotte herself. But all the same—I don't know—I do get bored sometimes. Especially at night. Everyone in the mission goes to sleep terribly early. They all get up very early too. But I can't fall asleep. There isn't a sound anywhere except for the fan creaking as it goes slowly round and round (it's a very ancient fan). The old servant lies out on the veranda on a string cot and sometimes he cries out in his sleep. I feel restless, I don't know what to do. I lean out of the window. The garden is wild and overgrown and full of exotic bushes with very strong scents. There's something sinful about these scents and also about the too bright moonlight that comes in through the window and falls on the whitewashed wall and the icon of Christ hanging there. It's so disturbing out there in the garden, so different from what it is in here. I keep thinking there must be tigers behind those bushes ready to spring, and surely there must be snakes in all that uncut grass.

At such moments I often think of Asha. Then I wish I were with her rather than here, and I even think should I get dressed and make my way across town to visit her. She'd be pleased to see me and not all that surprised either. She always stays up late. She doesn't usually have her dinner till nearly midnight.

Asha Opens Her Heart

Asha said, "I'm glad you've come, darling."

She was unhappy, she had been unhappy the whole day long. She had come to Delhi because she was tired of Bombay, but now Delhi was not working out any better. She had come with such an open heart but no one cared for her. All they cared about here was the changing structure of society and the future of the country within the framework of a socialistic pattern of development. Rao Sahib of course couldn't talk or think of anything except his Parliament and parliamentary affairs, and

33

Sunita was just as bad with all the women's meetings she had become involved with in order to further her husband's career.

There had been a meeting in the house that morning. Fifty absolutely horrible women had come. Rows of chairs were set out in the dining room and there had been speeches. God knows what it was all about: one moment they spoke about family planning and then it was adult literacy and then free medical aid for village women. Such long speeches they were too. Asha had done her best to sit through them patiently, but it had not been easy. And she had felt very much out of place. Most of the women there were housewives in cotton saris. Asha was in one of her silk trouser suits and she wore a matching pink turban because Bulbul had washed her hair that morning and it was still in curlers. She pretended she didn't notice the way everyone was staring at her and she sat with her legs stretched out and blowing smoke rings at the ceiling from her cigarette. At one point she got very thirsty and snapped her fingers at one of the bearers to bring her a drink. That created quite a stir. Asha noticed that Sunita, who was the chairman of the meeting and sat out in front, was beginning to get that tight, tense look Asha knew well. Asha liked Sunita, she knew she had her good points, but there were also things about her that Asha couldn't stand. She thought about these things as she sat there having her drink. When her glass was empty, she called the servant to refill it. All the women watched Asha out of the corner of their eyes. Sunita's face was now not only tense but anguished, and she kept pushing nervously at the puff of hair piled on top of her head. But Asha was feeling much more relaxed and cheerful.

Unfortunately the woman who was giving a speech wouldn't stop, she went on and on talking with excitement about the rights of women from the lower income groups to free legal advice and representation. She was an ugly woman with a mustache and huge arms swollen to a diseased size above the elbows. That wasn't her fault, Asha knew, but all the same who asked her to stand up there and lecture people and not know when to stop? She was spoiling Asha's mood. And there was Sunita up there, so fidgety and nervous and waiting for what Asha might do next. Asha almost felt as if she was expected to do something. She expected it of herself—she wasn't born to sit among a lot of housewives and listen to speeches about women's rights. She began to drum her feet on the floor, the way people sitting in the cheap seats in the cinema do when they are not satisfied with the entertainment. This amused her and she did it louder and also began to clap her hands in a rhythmic, regular beat. A sea of whispers, hushes and shushes, and subdued cries of "Shame!" began to surround her. Sunita half rose in her chair and rang a little bell for order and the speaker raised her voice to be heard above the noise. All this acted as a challenge to Asha —perhaps she even lost her head a little—she climbed up on her chair and now she was no longer the audience in a cinema but the audience at a wrestling match and like them she made fighting movements with her arms, flailing them around while shouting "Break his leg! Pull his arms out! Kill him!" and accompanied herself with cheers.

Naturally, Sunita had been very upset and she had stayed so all day. When Sunita was upset, her hair remained as sleek as ever and she cried with only one or two refined tears that rolled like pearls down her face and did it no damage at all. So Asha didn't feel bad—not till later when Rao Sahib came home and was told about what had happened. Rao Sahib spoke to Asha more in sorrow than in anger. There had been so many similar incidents in the past, his anger had all spent itself and there was only sadness left. When Rao Sahib was sad, Asha was too. She loved him very much—not for what he was now but for what he had been in the past when they were children together. He had been a very fat child and the doctor had forbidden all sweets and chocolates; but Asha had stolen them for him and they had both locked themselves in the bathroom so that he could eat. She could still see his fat cheeks bulging and chewing

—he had eaten very quickly in case he was caught and all these delicious things taken away from him before he could get his fill. He still had a very plump face, and although now he wore a mustache and quite a dignified expression as became an M.P. and there were big puffy rings under his eyes (cow's eyes like Asha's own), she remembered the little boy chewing chocolates and it melted her heart so that she wanted to cry. And it wasn't only the way Rao Sahib looked that affected her strongly, but what he was saying too. He was so right. He said what was to happen, what would become of her, how could she go on in this way: her escapades had been bad enough when she was a young girl but now! What were they to say to her now? What could anyone say to her? Asha had begged him not to go on, to spare her. Everything he said she said to herself a hundred times a day. If he was in despair with her, that was nothing compared to the despair she inspired in herself.

All this she told Lee with passionate contrition so that Lee became involved. There were just the two of them up; the rest of Rao Sahib's household was fast asleep. It was about two o'-clock in the morning. They were down in the drawing room because Asha couldn't bear it up in her own room—she couldn't bear the sight of her bed, which suggested nights of agonized thought. She had turned on all the chandeliers in the drawing room; she wanted as much light and life as possible. Everything sparkled and glowed—the cut-glass vases, the ormolu mirrors, the Persian rugs, the gold-brocade cushions, the seventeenth-century miniatures of doe-eyed girls engaged in spring rites framed on the walls: but the room remained desolate with just the two of them in it and profound silence all around. From time to time the watchman peered in at them through the open glass doors, and Sunita's two little Pomeranians had come down to snuggle on footstools, glad to have someone awake and keep them company, even if it was only Asha, who didn't care for them.

"I hate it," Asha said suddenly. "It's the worst thing that can happen to anyone. You don't know what it's like—to get old, I mean. I never thought about it when I was your age. I thought it would go on forever, I would always have a good time and be in love and have men in love with me. That's the best, by the way," she added and unexpectedly her face lit up.

Lee wasn't interested—she was really quite the wrong person to make this kind of confession to.

"To have someone really, really *mad* about you—so that he would do anything—and so anything you do, every time you care to smile at him, or just accept a present from him, it would just drive him crazy with joy. But it's nice the other way round too—when it is you who are crazy: only that way there is such a lot of pain. So much suffering." She saw Lee did not enter into her feelings and asked, "Haven't you ever been in love?"

"No," Lee said decisively; and added as decisively, "And I don't want to be either."

"Oh, Lee, Lee."

"Why should I?" Lee said. "It seems such a small thing—to get worked up like that just for one person."

"You don't know anything."

"I know I don't. That's why I've come to India—to try and learn." Lee was very serious; she sat bolt upright and frowned with concentrated thought. Her long earrings trembled a little against her neck.

"You have lovely eyes," Asha said. "What color are they? Gray? Or green? Lovely." She gazed at Lee with hunger: to have such skin! Untouched, unflawed.

But Lee was taken up with trying to express her thoughts: "If it's really like you say—like everyone says—then it's a waste. I mean, such feelings, they should go for something higher."

"There is nothing higher."

"I don't believe that."

"Listen to me. . . . Should I be telling you this? God knows. But I will because I love you. I truly truly love you, Lee, like a dear little sister." She put out her hand and snatched Lee's lying in the lap of her peasant skirt. She kissed it and then she squeezed it; she wore many rings which hurt Lee a bit.

"You've seen his picture on my dressing table? My husband. He was a rotter. I can't tell you. He was a rotter through and through. It wasn't only other women—but with boys too. . . . For him I was only an object—less, less than an object—for an object you can have some respect, you don't want to break it for nothing, it has some value. But for him I was only there to be ill-treated and crushed, the way he wouldn't do to a paid woman. But I was his wife and the only pleasure he took in me was to be able to humiliate me, to bring me lower than the dust under his feet. You don't like to hear all this, I can see from your face."

"Well, it's only that it's so painful, Asha."

"Yes, it was painful—terribly, terribly painful. But also you don't know what joy! What bliss and happiness I had in him! Not at the end—then everything went—*he* went—he was a sick man, he had cirrhosis of the liver, that's what he died of. But in our first years together, I can't describe to you—oh, my God, what can I say? Even to think of it is unbearable. . . . And what is also unbearable is to think that it has gone and there is nothing like it any more and won't be ever again. Now what is left for me? How should I spend my days? How go from one day to the other? *You* tell me."

"I can't tell you," Lee said.

"I know you can't. What should you know about it, my poor lamb? But don't go away. Stay with me. You have no idea how lovely it is for me to have you here. Shall I put on a record? Should we dance?" She rose impetuously but stumbled over Sunita's little white Pomeranian and gave it a kick that sent it flying from its footstool.

Lee watched impassively. She had never cared much for dogs, especially not pampered little lap dogs; and here in India they infuriated her.

Raymond Writes to His Mother

". . . Whereas a well-off middle-class Indian home will be stuffed with all the material possessions it can hold, the less affluent live in rather a bleak way. You remember I wrote to you about that rather nice boy I met, Gopi? Well he took me to tea with his family. His father is dead and his mother lives with his sisters and I think some more relatives in a couple of rooms in the upstairs part of a crooked little house in a very crowded locality. I don't know how many people are living in that house. I'm told only two families, Gopi's and the landlord's downstairs. But what families! That place was *bulging*. Most of Gopi's family had been banished into the second room and all that could be heard from them was whispers and suppressed giggles. Whenever the door opened they took the opportunity to peer in. Inside the room there was only Gopi, myself, his mother, and a couple of sisters who had been allowed in because they had to serve the tea. Conversation was very, very difficult. The two sisters didn't say anything and the mother couldn't say anything because she spoke no English. So she and I had to exchange a succession of smiles and she kept pushing plates at me and said, 'Eat, eat.' And I did eat—heaps of sweetmeats and other heaps of salty, spiced things. And the sisters kept coming in with more dishes and they kept refilling my plate and I kept at it manfully. I *had* to! It was the only thing to do, it was what I was there for; apart from feeding me they didn't know what to do with me.

"But they had taken such a lot of trouble. Not only frying all that food but cleaning up the room and making it as nice as they knew how. Only I'm sorry to say they didn't know how very well—esthetic living isn't something they ever pay much attention to, I think. There's hardly any furniture, just a sofa with worn-out springs and a couple of hard chairs which I think had been borrowed. The crockery too seemed to have been borrowed and none of it matched and some of it had cracks with dirt ingrained in them. Yes, I know, unforgivable of me to notice these things—but I promise I didn't make what you call my *fastidious* face, I really watched myself and did my best to be enthusiastic over everything. Perhaps I overdid it a bit—an awful lot of 'delicious' and 'divine' and 'most kind' and 'thank you so much'—but I dare say you would call that erring in the right direction. And I smiled, I think, continuously. So did Gopi's mother; it was all we could do. Sometimes a harassed expression would come over her face, and I saw she was perspiring with effort and every now and again she wiped her face with her veil. I too perspired, with effort *and* with heat.

"The only relief from the silence that engulfed our tea party came from the people downstairs, who seemed to be having a row. At one point they got very noisy indeed—and this rather animated our party and Gopi and his mother and sisters had a lot of uncomplimentary things to say about their neighbors. Evidently relations are strained. When the party was over and I was led away down the stairs, I was told to take no notice of them, which I didn't though they came pouring out to have a look at me; obediently I never glanced in their direction and neither did I turn my head when one of them called after me 'Good morning, sir,' which Gopi said was just a characteristic piece of impudence on their part. . . ."

Gopi Is Displeased with Raymond

Although Gopi had made no attempt at conversation during this tea party—he had sat there and scowled, disowning all of them—afterward it was not himself he blamed for its failure but his family and his guest. He was upset for days. When he was at home, he was sulky with his family, and when he was with Raymond, he kept picking quarrels with him. He found fault with Raymond's living arrangements and sneered at all his little decorations. He characterized him as a fussy, snobbish English sahib. The tea party was never mentioned between them, but Raymond knew it to be the cause of Gopi's displeasure. He had to admit that this displeasure was not entirely undeserved. It was true, he had tried hard—he had smiled, he had eaten to excess, and praised continuously—but he realized that Gopi was sensitive to the fact that inwardly he had remained withdrawn and critical.

Lee came to see them quite often now and Gopi enjoyed her company. He made it clear that he enjoyed it more than Raymond's. He would suggest some outing and then he would say to Raymond, "I think you don't want to come." Lee was surprised; she said "Oh, why not?" and Gopi would answer for him. He said, "He has been there before and he didn't like it at all."

Raymond did not contradict. He suffered but acquiesced. He stayed in the flat by himself and put on records of Indian music. He had grown very fond of Indian music. It had become for him like a distillation of everything he loved in Gopi and everything he loved in India. These two were now inextricable.

Lee and Gopi Eat Kebabs

Gopi had taken Lee to the place where the best kebabs in town were to be obtained. He always knew the best places: there was one shop called Lahore Milk House that sold the best buttermilk; another, Mithan Lal Halwai, had the best jelabis; a third, Your Fry-Up Please, the tastiest fried fish in town. This kebab place was in the Muslim area, just opposite the big mosque. They sat at a table inside the dark interior of the shop; the man rolling and frying the kebabs sat at the front, facing the bazaar, amid cauldrons and pans sizzling on open fires. The shop was a family affair and everyone smiled in a knowing way and looked sideways at Lee. Gopi was embarrassed but also proud. Even the little hunchbacked servant boy who came to wipe the table with a filthy cloth smiled in the same way. But Lee didn't notice anything, she was too busy eating the kebabs.

Gopi liked seeing her eat. She made swift, neat, dipping movements into chutney and other side dishes and chewed and licked her fingers and enjoyed just like an Indian. She could eat the hottest food, and bit into fierce green chilis with relish. Watching her, Gopi commented, "You're not like Raymond."

"No?" Lee said, too busy to be really listening.

"No. He couldn't eat this food. It would burn his mouth and how he would scream. And he couldn't eat with his fingers either—oh, no, he has to have his knife and spoon. Like this," Gopi said and gave an imitation of Raymond eating. He made very refined movements with imaginary cutlery. Lee, looking up briefly, laughed.

"But you're quite different," Gopi said with enthusiasm, leaning across the table toward her. "You know what I think? I think you were Indian in your last birth."

"Really," Lee said, too busy at present to realize that a very great compliment had been paid to her. "Hand me one of those, will you?"

"These?" He held out a chili to her but instead of taking it in her hand she darted forward and bit into it. "Hm, lovely," she said.

Gopi burned and blushed. He was aware that everyone, everyone in the shop had been watching them and had seen her bite into the chili which he held out for her; and for them, as for him, the gesture was as intimate as a kiss. There was a great silent gasp. Even the party of Sikhs at another table—huge burly men who had seemed totally absorbed in eating—even they had seen and their mighty jaws stopped chewing in wonder.

Someone came to serve them with a new plate of kebabs. He spoke to Gopi in an appreciative undertone. Gopi nodded and tried to smile. The man offered the kebabs to Lee, who said, "I couldn't." "Just one more, Memsahib," said the man, holding up one tempting forefinger. "Oh, all right," Lee said. The man winked at Gopi and moved off. The Sikhs made a joke to him as he passed and he answered with another joke. Everyone was having a grand time. To celebrate the occasion, someone put a record on the phonograph. It was a very old machine with a horn and the record too was very old. It was hardly audible, but "Ah!" everyone cried as they recognized the song. The woman's voice that emerged from the scratching and crackling was laden with passion.

"She is singing for her lover," Gopi told Lee. "She says, 'Love's madness has carried me away in its embrace.' It is a very old popular song. Everyone loves it. Ah!" He shut his eyes in ecstasy. "Now she is saying, 'Save me, bring me back, don't you see that I have been snatched away by this madness!' They are very beautiful words." He leaned again across the table toward Lee. "This place is a hotel also."

"I like it," Lee said. She looked around the little dark room: it was painted green and was dense with the smell of spicy cooking and incense. She liked the song too and the way everyone was enjoying it so much.

"The rooms upstairs are also very nice," Gopi said. When she didn't react, he swallowed once or twice and said with effort: "Would you like to see?"

"Not especially," Lee said. She had been inside a lot of homes by this time and was no longer as interested as she once had been in seeing how people really lived.

"There's a very good view," Gopi said temptingly. Lee showed more interest—as he had expected. How these people cared for views! Gopi had learned this lesson from Raymond. What it was they saw so much in a view God only knew.

"Would you like to see?" he asked again.

"All right."

Gopi felt victorious. He raised his hand and soundlessly snapped his fingers. The proprietor nodded and beamed. The hunchbacked boy was sent over to their table; he was carrying a bunch of keys as well as his filthy cloth.

Gopi jumped up. "Come on." But Lee took her time; she leaned back luxuriously in her chair and held her stomach. "I'm so full," she said happily. She saw everyone looking and smiling at her and smiled back. "Lovely food," she said. They nodded at her encouragingly. The record came to an end on a last note of passion and pain. "Again!" cried the Sikhs.

"Come on," Gopi repeated. The little servant boy also stood waiting. Lee stood up slowly. "I can hardly *move*," she said, holding her stomach again. Gopi followed her closely. He knew all eyes were upon him. He was a hero and he liked it, but he was also rather nervous. To hide this, he gave a jaunty hitch to his pants and walked in a careless, swaggering way.

They groped up the dark staircase, holding on to both side walls for support. They came to a landing with two doors and the boy opened one of them with his keys. He ushered them in and shut the door on them. The mosque was so close it seemed to be right there in the room with its huge domes and its flight of steps and the booths huddled at the foot of the steps. Lee gave a cry of pleasure and strode to the window. She stayed there looking out, so enraptured by what she saw that she quite forgot about Gopi.

He didn't know what to do next. For a while he stood behind her, also looking at the view; but he couldn't see what was so interesting about it—it was just the usual things. Then he turned back into the room and that wasn't interesting either. He sat by the side of the bed and eased himself out of his shoes; this was always a luxurious moment for him and he sat wriggling his toes and pulling and cracking them. Next he lay down on the bed. His eyes roved over the ceiling and down the walls; there was nothing to hold his attention except a framed sampler in cross-stitch hanging crooked from a nail. So he looked at Lee standing by the window. How slim and strong she was; her light brown hair trailed down her back. He desired her very much.

"What's that?" she asked. "What are they doing? Gopi, do come here."

He got up and joined her again by the window. He looked, but all he saw was the usual cotton-carders working the strings of their machines. Lee watched fascinated as the flakes of cotton rose and fell in fluffy clouds. Gopi put his arm round her and ran his hand down her hip. "Don't," she said and shook him off with an easy practiced movement.

What next? He felt utterly bewildered. He also felt that he was letting himself down—and not only himself but all the men downstairs whom he knew to be having exciting thoughts about what was going on up here.

Now Lee's attention traveled from the cotton-carders to the steps of the mosque. There were people going up or coming down from the mosque, stepping around others who sat there to rest or had stretched themselves out to sleep. Many of them were beggars and some importuned the passers-by while others held out their mutilated limbs in silence. There were some terrible sights down there, but Lee had already seen many like them in the course of her travels. She had begun to accept the fact that it was the fate of many to suffer hunger and disease. Just now the beggars seemed like essential props placed on the steps of the mosque to remind those who were going in to pray of how much there was to pray for.

Gopi again put his hand where it had been before; again she flicked him off with the same movement as of a practiced hand waving away flies. She really didn't notice or care; she was too engrossed in what was outside. Now her eyes had traveled up to the great domes hovering against a sky of a cerulean blue which she had before seen only in paintings depicting the birth or death of Christ. At that moment she had what she thought must be a mystic experience: at any rate, she felt a great desire to merge with everything that was happening out there—to become part of it and cease to be herself.

"Then why did you come!" Gopi suddenly shouted. She turned to him in amazement. She saw he was terribly upset.

"What happened?"

Her question, uttered in such innocence and her eyes also so clear and puzzled and innocent, increased his sense of humiliation. Why did she think she had been brought up here? What did she think of him? What opinion did she have of his manhood? Tears of rage stung his eyes. He could not put up with such insult. Suddenly he flung himself against her. He bit her neck like an angry animal.

"Hey!"

Lee fought back and she was quite strong. He was surprised by her strength and eased off a bit. He was still struggling with her but at the same time he also said in quite a begging voice, "Come and lie on the bed with me."

"No, why should I?"

"Please," Gopi said.

"Certainly not."

Then he let her go and lay down on the bed by himself. He lay there face downward and appeared in despair. She didn't know what to do about him. She wanted to get back to the window and look out and be filled by those wonderful sensations. But she couldn't just leave him lying there. Reluctantly she went and sat on the bed beside him. He didn't move. She couldn't see his face because it was buried in a pillow. "Turn around," she said. "Look at me."

"No, no. Please go away."

Although she would not at all have minded going away, it was not in her nature or upbringing to turn from distressful situations. She saw that they would have to have this out and prepared herself.

He raised his head to see what she was up to: then he flung himself round to face her. "Yes, go. I know you want to."

"No, I don't."

"Yes, you want to get away from me. Because you hate and despise me."

"Hate and despise?" she repeated. "Why are you talking like that to me?"

"It's the truth." He looked at her out of the corner of his eye and saw he had her attention. "You know it's the truth," he said. Perhaps they could have a quarrel. He wouldn't at all have minded that. Quarrels heated people, raised their emotions for one another; they could be exciting.

But Lee was not disposed to quarrel. She was busy criticizing herself. It was not true that she hated and despised Gopi but if he felt that way, obviously something had gone wrong, she had failed him somewhere. "Gopi, I *like* you," she said with sincerity.

"Then why did you push me away?"

"I didn't mean to. I was thinking of something else."

What to make of her? A girl who had been brought to a hotel room—had been led upstairs in full public view—and now she said she had been thinking of something else. And this was not an inexperienced, unknowing Indian girl like his sisters, but a Western girl who was traveling all round the world by herself. Everyone knew that Western girls were brought up on sex, lived on sex. She must have slept with many, many men, over and over again. This thought suddenly excited and infuriated him. Who was she to push him away?

"You're a bitch!" he cried.

"That's not fair, Gopi," she protested. "I didn't mean to hurt your feelings. I never thought of it, that's all."

"Never thought of it! As if you English or American girls ever think of anything else! Everyone knows it. Everyone knows what you are."

"Well, some of us," Lee admitted, trying her very best to be impartial and truthful. "But it's not true about everyone, you can't say that. It's not true about me."

Actually, he believed her. There was something disappointingly upright and cool about her as she sat there right next to him on the bed, prepared for serious discussion. But he didn't want to admit it to be true. He wanted to think about her as one thought about these girls, as the people downstairs thought about her.

"Then why did you come upstairs with me?" he taunted her. "Only for what? Only to sit here and talk and have conversation?"

"And see the view."

He wanted to laugh and he wanted to cry. Everything was going so wrong.

"It's a marvelous view. I'm glad I came, Gopi. And now I'm glad to be with you and that we're having this talk. It's good to have the chance to clear up any misunderstanding. I mean, regarding the way I feel about you."

"How do you feel about me?"

"I told you. I like you."

"Like! This is not what we have come upstairs for."

He was sitting up on the bed. They were very close together. She could see the tears that sparkled on his lashes. Although he already had a strong growth of beard, his complexion was as smooth as that of a child. His eyes were velvet and heavy. He looked very oriental. She wished they could be closer together in understanding, that she could explain herself better to him. But perhaps it was not possible by means of words.

"Okay," she said. She unbuttoned her blouse and took it off. She was wearing nothing underneath. He stared. He couldn't believe it for a moment. Then he wasted no more time. He was a strong boy, brimful of appetite though not very skilled. She suffered rather than enjoyed while he lay on top of her. But she was glad to be doing this for him and, at the final moment, thought to herself that perhaps this was part of the merging she had so ardently desired while looking out of the window.

By the Swimming Pool

When Lee took her to meet Raymond and Gopi, Asha was delighted. She always liked meeting young people. She also adored Raymond's flat and marveled at the way a man could make himself so comfortable and have all these nice ideas.

She took a special fancy to Raymond. She sat close beside him and asked him many questions and while he was answering them she touched his knee in an affectionate way. She heard about how he had come here to spend a year or two on his aunt's legacy, and she advised him about all the places he ought to see. She also invited him to come and stay in Rao Sahib's state of Maupur: "If you *really* want to see India," she said, sounding a little doubtful. Raymond said he did, very much, and he would love to come, thanks most awfully.

"It's very dull," she warned him. "Right in the desert—nothing to see, nothing to do," but then she looked round at the other two and added, "Of course if we all go, we could have fun. All four of us together." She became enthusiastic about this idea and seemed to wish that they could set off there and then. And failing that, why didn't she take them out for a nice drive, she said, she had Rao Sahib's car and chauffeur outside and they could go wherever they liked.

They drove to one of the big hotels which had a floodlit swimming pool. Although it was so late at night, the place was quite crowded. There was a band playing in white tuxedos and waiters hurried about with trays to serve the guests lying in deck chairs. Lee and Gopi hired costumes but Asha said she was too ashamed of her figure and would just sit and watch them. Raymond also didn't want to go in. Gopi asked him "Really? You don't want to? Really?" very solicitously; he had been solicitous and affectionate toward Raymond throughout these last few days, ever since he had gone off with Lee and left Raymond deliberately behind. Now it was as if he wanted to make up for that and also any other harshness he may have shown him.

Asha talked to Raymond. She still touched him as she talked, on his arm, his knee, but purely out of habit. While she had sat in the car beside him, she had squeezed herself against him but had felt no answering thrill. She understood; it did not make her like Raymond any less. Now she was telling him about the English governess she had had as a girl, a Miss Hart. Miss Hart had taught her to esteem everything English very highly. She had tried to curb Asha's appetite for Indian food in favor of a healthy diet of roast mutton and caramel custard. It was eating all that spicy food, Miss Hart had explained, that made Indian boys and girls grow up so quickly, for it heated the blood and caused premature lust. She had also insisted on a lot of exercise and had taught Asha to play netball and hockey. Although there was no one to play except herself and Asha, Miss Hart had played in earnest and cheered the two of them on as if they were a full team. "Oh, butterfingers!" she had shouted; or "Well played, Alice!" She had always called her Alice; she said she couldn't pronounce Asha.

"What's so difficult about Asha?" Raymond asked.

"I know. It was only an excuse. She hated Indian names, like she hated everything Indian."

"She sounds rather a horrible person."

"She wasn't so bad. Sometimes she was quite fun. I think she was just terribly homesick—especially at Christmas time. She hated spending her Christmas in India. But when there were English guests come to stay—like Mr. Timrose, the political agent, or there was a Colonel Freshwater with his wife, Mrs. Freshwater, and a daughter, I've forgotten her name, was it Rose? Or perhaps Violet. They always came for shooting. When there were people like that, Miss Hart was very happy. She came down for dinner in an evening gown that was held up with two straps and after dinner she played the piano for them, all English tunes like Gilbert and Sullivan and 'Tales from the Vienna Woods.' She spent a lot of time with them in the guest house, complaining about us. But when she left us and went back to England, she cried and cried and gave me her own penholder, which had a view of Brighton in it. . . . Hello, Gopi, I think that costume is too tight for you."

Gopi shook himself so that the water came dripping down on Raymond, who pretended to protest. Gopi did it again and said, "Why don't you come? It's so nice and cool."

"I prefer watching you."

"Oh, what's this?" He took the glass Raymond had ordered for himself and at once began to drink. He finished it all and then ran off, ostentatiously graceful, water trickling down his chest and back and making the hair look silky and matted. Both Asha and Raymond looked after him for some time in silence.

"Have you known him for a long time?" Asha at last asked and went on straightaway: "Do you like him?"

"Oh, yes," Raymond said coolly. "We're great friends."

Asha gave him a sideways look. She ran the tip of her tongue over her wide mouth, which always had too much lipstick on it. She drank her drink while listening to the band playing and watched Lee and Gopi throwing a plastic ball at each other in the pool. Raymond also watched. His hand tapped the side of the deck chair in enjoyment while the band played a very old Beatles song to rather a strange beat.

"My brother also had an English tutor," Asha said.

"And did he hate India?"

"Oh, no. He was quite different. Quite, quite different. You know, Raymond, shall I tell you—" She squeezed his hand. How strange it was to hold a man's hand this way and find it lifeless, unresponsive like a woman's or a friend's. She smiled to herself and squeezed it once more before giving it back to him. "Yes, it's true, he was a bit like you. He loved India—he loved being with us, and our food and all the festivals, and he was terribly happy when he was allowed to dress up in Indian clothes. He sat on the floor and listened to our music and ate betel and did everything that everyone else did. All the Indians were very fond of him. But the English people didn't like it at all, that he should behave like that. Mr. Timrose wanted my father to dismiss him, he didn't think he was suitable as a tutor. My father didn't like to disoblige Mr. Timrose but when he told Peter—that was his name, Peter Kingsley—and asked him to go back to England, Peter got terribly, terribly upset. He begged my father—he begged like an Indian person—with his hands folded —and do you know he even got down to touch Papa's feet? Everyone was quite shocked. But he didn't care what he did or what anyone thought of him, just so long as he was allowed to stay."

The huge plastic ball, thrown skillfully by Gopi, came bouncing on to Raymond. Gopi bobbed up and down in the pool, clapping his hands and shouting, "Come on, throw it back! We're waiting!" Raymond threw it back. Asha half lowered her heavy lids over her eyes and sucked Coca-Cola like a sphinx.

Raymond said, "If someone were to tell me now that I must leave, I think I'd do the same. Yes, I'd touch his feet to let me stay. I think I would," he said.

"You see, I told you Peter was like you." But then she sighed: "Poor, poor Peter. It was a tragedy. . . . You see, the reason why he wanted to stay so badly, he was involved with someone."

"I see."

"Not a girl."

Raymond was silent.

"I don't know what he saw in him. He was very ordinary— a clerk attached to the palace guest house—a quite uncultured person who couldn't appreciate Peter at all. I mean, Peter was intellectual—sensitive—like you, Raymond. . . . A tragedy," she said again, in a voice full of dark memories.

Shyam Gives Notice

Gopi was in a bad mood. He was often, indeed usually, in a bad mood early in the morning, especially when he had to go to classes. He was getting sick and tired of his college. At one time he had quite enjoyed going there—not to the classes, which had always bored him, but to meet his friends and sit around with them in the canteen; but now that he was with Raymond and was leading a different kind of life, these friends no longer seemed so interesting to him.

"Don't go, then," Raymond said, seeing how reluctant and cross Gopi was: and he looked tired—no wonder, since they had all been up to the early hours of the morning. Asha had come in her car, and she had brought some very sweet Russian champagne and carried them off for a midnight picnic in a ruined summer pavilion.

"Yes, it's nice for you to talk," Gopi said, looking malevolently at Raymond, who was still in his silk dressing gown and sipping his coffee at leisure. How easy life was for Raymond, how difficult for Gopi! Gopi felt harassed. There was nothing he wanted more than to cut his early-morning class but he had been doing it too often lately; if this went on, the college authorities would complain to his family and all sorts of unpleasant consequences would follow. Raymond could have no idea, he said, what it was like in a family such as his. Everyone bothered him all the time —not only his mother and his sisters but all his other relatives too. One uncle in particular was a constant torment to him. This uncle was an inspector in the public works department and in consequence considered himself a very important person whose achievement should be emulated. He wanted Gopi to enter government service and become a divisional officer like himself. "I don't want to be like him," Gopi said. "You should see him," he added gloomily. Then he said, "I think I will go away to Benares."

"Why?" Raymond asked, who hated it when Gopi said anything about going away.

"To stay with my other uncle. He is in business and I like it there very much. No one tells me do this, do that—go to college, pass your exams—" He held his head and groaned.

"Well, anyway, eat your breakfast," Raymond said soothingly.

"Where *is* my breakfast? Shyam! Hey, Shyam!"

After some more shouts, Shyam came in with something on a plate which he placed in front of Gopi. "Thank you, Shyam," Raymond said. Gopi stared at the plate, and when Shyam had already got to the door, he said in a voice of thunder, "I asked for puris."

Shyam stood at ease in the doorway. He said these were eggs, scrambled eggs, such as sahibs ate for breakfast. He was used to cooking for sahibs only and if this did not suit Gopi then there were other places he could go to—plenty of little shops in the bazaar where he could get the kind of Indian food he was used to.

Gopi wasted no time. He was across the room in an instant and struck the servant across the face. He called him some bad names and struck him again. Shyam cried out and put his arms up to protect himself, for Gopi looked as if he intended to continue hitting him. Perhaps he would have done so but Raymond held his arm. Raymond said, "Stop that, Gopi."

Gopi struggled but Raymond held on. After a while Gopi said, "All right, let me go, I won't hit him again." But Shyam cried, "Sahib, Sahib, hold him!"

Gopi saw that Raymond was seriously angry and began to defend himself. He said such insolence from a servant was not to be tolerated. When Raymond continued to look displeased, Gopi said it was all Raymond's fault—hadn't he warned him over and over again that Shyam was a bad servant and should be dismissed? Here Shyam chimed in and said that it was not possible for him to continue working for Raymond as long as Gopi was in the house, and Gopi cried yes, let him go, let him go today at once, now, now! And Shyam said he would go now.

Raymond turned away from both of them. He told Gopi in a weary voice that it was time for him to leave for his college. Gopi went in to get ready. He was very quiet. Shyam too was very quiet; he went into the kitchen and no sound was heard from there.

"I'm going now," Gopi said. But he lingered, glancing anxiously at Raymond's face. He said, "How could I let a servant insult me like that, how could I allow it? Please understand my feelings also."

"And *his* feelings?"

Gopi had a flash of pride: "Are you putting him on a level with me?" But when Raymond did not respond, he became soothing again: "But now it's all right, we won't quarrel about him any more. Because you won't let him stay, you'll dismiss him, isn't it?"

"It's not me dismissing him—he doesn't want to stay. You heard him." He added, "You'll be late for your classes."

54

Gopi went very slowly as if waiting for Raymond to call him back. But although Raymond knew that Gopi wanted this very much, he remained silent.

Usually, when there had been a scene between Shyam and Gopi and Shyam gave notice, Raymond would go to seek him out in the kitchen, to soothe him and persuade him to stay. Today he could not bring himself to do so. He felt the offense had been too great and that it would be an additional insult to ask him to stay. But he became aware that Shyam was waiting for him in the kitchen. Shyam moved about and coughed. Finally, when Raymond did not go to him, he came into the room. Raymond did not look up. Shyam began dusting. He moved slowly and dusted noisily. Then he began to sigh and make other pathetic noises. Raymond had to look up. He also sighed. Out of a full heart he said, "I'm very sorry, Shyam."

"Yes, sir," Shyam said. After a while he said, "How can I stay, Sahib? It's not possible for me to stay."

"I know, Shyam," Raymond said. "I do quite understand."

They remained in stricken silence.

"I'm very happy with your service," Shyam said in a broken voice. "My whole family is happy. We are all very happy." He cried out: "And now where are we to go? Where else can such a sahib like you be found? And such a fine quarter to live in."

Raymond winced. The fine quarter consisted of one airless room in a tenement facing a service lane. Shyam had once taken him there. He lived in a room on the first floor. It smelled of cooking oil and urine and was crammed with women and children and a sick old man lying on a mat in a corner. Everyone had smiled and smiled at Raymond. The sick old man had been raised to a sitting position to enable him to salaam. Even when they had pointed out certain deficiencies to Raymond—such as a burst drain and some dangerously exposed electric wiring— they had continued smiling as if their discomfort was of small consequence and they were only drawing his attention to it in case he might (without inconvenience to himself) be able to assist them.

"And now she is expecting again," Shyam confided. "In four–five months, yes, Sahib, there will be one more, what to do." But he beamed.

Raymond saw that it was his duty to beg Shyam to stay. They began their usual dialogue on the subject. Raymond said he understood Shyam's position perfectly and that in fact Shyam was quite right to want to leave, but that nevertheless as a personal favor to himself Raymond would be much obliged to him if he would stay. Shyam gave himself time to think this over, but finally shook his head and said how could he, it was impossible. So they carried on for a while. The outcome was a foregone conclusion. Raymond realized that, in view of other things, it was not as impossible to overlook the insult to Shyam's honor as had at first appeared.

Gopi Leaves

"No, don't, Gopi," Lee said.

Gopi was taking her to Raymond's flat and, as she walked before him up the stairs, he pinched her—not so much out of desire as out of bravado. He had gone to fetch her in the hope that Raymond would be glad to see her and they would all three of them have a good time together and then everything would be forgotten and Raymond would be happy with him again. He pushed open the door and shouted: "See whom I have brought!"

Raymond was glad to see her; and even more to see Gopi in such a good mood. He had been thinking of him all day. He remembered how Gopi had lingered before going out, hoping that Raymond would say something kind. Raymond had re-proached himself all day for saying nothing. How glad he was now to be able to make up for that! When he saw that he was forgiven, Gopi's spirits soared. He pinched Lee again and laughed uproariously when she slapped him away.

"I think she is a very cold-hearted girl," he told Raymond.
"She cares nothing for love, only for food."

"I *am* hungry," Lee admitted.

"You see!" Gopi flung himself with a great laugh on to a sofa and in his exuberance punched a cushion.

Raymond said, "I believe Shyam's baked a cake." After every reconciliation Shyam baked a cake. They were not very nice cakes—rather hard and tasting of baking powder—but of course it was the spirit in which they were offered that was important.

Lee exclaimed with pleasure and went straight out into the kitchen. But Gopi's face clouded. He said in rather a hard voice, "When is he leaving?"

Raymond blushed. He said, "No, he's not." And in answer to the look that Gopi hurled at him, he began to stammer: "How can he, Gopi, be reasonable."

Lee returned with Shyam behind her. He bore his cake aloft. It looked squat and a bit blackened but it sat proudly on Raymond's best hand-painted plate. Shyam placed it in the center of the table with a flourish. There was triumph in the way he did not glance in Gopi's direction.

Gopi got up and went into the bedroom, banging the door. Shyam solicitously helped Lee to cut the cake. He asked Raymond also to taste a piece but Raymond didn't hear him; he was looking at the closed bedroom door. After a while he went in there.

Gopi was opening drawers and pulling out his things. He kept quite a few of his clothes in the flat; now he was flinging them one by one on to the bed. "What are you doing?" Raymond asked with a beating heart.

Gopi did not answer but redoubled his activities. He kicked a pair of sandals that got in his way.

"Gopi, please. Listen to me."

"There is nothing to listen. Your servant insults me and you stand by and laugh. Very good. I understand." He pushed past Raymond, viciously pulling a pair of trousers off a hanger.

"How can I send Shyam away? Do you know how many

people he has to support? He just can't afford to lose his job—
I mean, his family would starve. Literally *starve*, Gopi."

"What do I care for his family!"

"You don't mean that."

Gopi cried, "Yes, you care for his family, but *my* family, you
laugh at and despise them."

"I don't know how you can talk like that."

"I saw with my own eyes that day. You didn't want to eat the
food my mother prepared for you and you didn't like our home,
it was not good enough for you. You made *this* face." He
showed which, with much exaggeration.

"I didn't, I didn't."

"No? Then perhaps I'm blind and stupid. And you despised
my mother also because she is only a simple lady and can't speak
English—"

"This is too bad of you, Gopi. You shouldn't say these things
to me." Raymond felt himself blushing again and again.

Gopi had now pulled out all his possessions and was roughly
bundling them together. "But it's all right. I'm going now and
you need never see me again. You can sit at home with your
Shyam and eat all your English dishes he will prepare for you."

He slung his bundle over his shoulder and was ready to leave.
Raymond got between him and the door.

"Aren't you my friend? Aren't we friends? Aren't we, Gopi?"

"No. You are not my friend. You care nothing for me. All
right, why should you care? I'm not such a very wonderful
person. Let me pass."

"How can you hurt me like that? Saying these things to me."

"You think I'm not hurt. You think I feel nothing."

He opened the door. He went out and Raymond went after
him, still pleading. He didn't care that Lee and Shyam were
there, listening; he cared only for Gopi and somehow to prevent
him from leaving. But Gopi didn't even look back at him; with
his bundle slung over his shoulder he walked straight out of the
flat. Raymond called hopelessly down the stairs: "At least take
a suitcase for your things. Please, Gopi!"

Gopi stood still for a moment on the stairs. He looked up at Raymond with dignity. "You may keep your suitcase. I want nothing from you."

Raymond Attends a Supper Party

The house was in the residential compound of the British High Commission. It was fully air-conditioned and tastefully furnished. The dining table was also set very tastefully. There were fourteen guests seated round it, some English, some Indian. Raymond was between a British Council wife and a stout, richly dressed Indian lady. The food was, like the guests, a judicious mixture of English and Indian and was served by bearers in white gloves. The party was going very well. The host, a counselor in the High Commission, had been in the diplomatic service since his university days and his wife with him, so both knew how to conduct a social occasion of this nature. Conversation was lively and general and ranged over many interesting topics.

"Say what you like," said the host, twinkling cordially at one of his Indian guests, "but you can't persuade me there's no special relationship."

"You're talking through your hat, Gerald," said this Indian guest, a joint secretary in the Ministry of External Affairs. He wore Indian clothes but spoke with a very English accent. "You're nothing more to us now than, say, the Dutch or the French or any other ex-colonial ex-power."

"Come now, Deepak, you can't deny that, in spite of everything, you still have a soft corner for us. It's like a family bond —don't we all sometimes want to shake off the family? But it can't be done. We just have too much in common."

"All right, Gerald, I challenge you! *What* do we have in common?"

"My dear Deepak—two hundred years of history to begin with."

Deepak waved this aside with excitable gestures at variance

with his cool English accent. "You foisted yourselves on us and it took all we had to throw you out again. If *that's* what you mean by special relationship—"

"But can you deny that in the process we did, like it or not, influence one another? That to some extent we did learn to speak one another's language?"

"Excuse me, Gerald, *we* had willy-nilly to learn yours; you didn't bother about ours."

"I don't only mean language, *per se*, Deepak. Look at the Americans—they speak English too, don't they—"

"If you like to call that English," shrugged another Indian guest speaking in the same Oxford accent as Deepak's. There was general laughter. For the moment English and Indians were united in a pleasant feeling of superior cultivation. Just then one bearer went round deftly substituting plates while another filled up glasses with the wine that was to accompany the new course.

"Do *you* feel there's a special relationship?" asked Raymond's neighbor, the British Council wife, a young woman in a cocktail frock that left her bony shoulders bare.

Raymond considered the question and had finally to say that he honestly didn't know.

"I don't know either," said his neighbor with the same honesty. "We certainly don't seem to have too many Indian friends."

"Oh, I have Indian friends all right," said Raymond.

"Real friends?"

"Very real," he said with feeling.

"You're lucky then. The only time we ever seem to meet any Indians is at dinners like today and cocktails and receptions and things. And they always seem to be the same people."

Both she and Raymond looked across at Deepak. He was sipping from his glass of wine and as he did so exclaimed with appreciation, "Oh, I *say*."

"Well, Deepak," said the host, flushed with food, wine, and

good humor, "you're in such a cantankerous mood with us today that I'm glad something pleases you at our table."

"My dear chap!" cried Deepak, holding up his slender brown hand in mock horror. "But it's all entirely impersonal, don't you see! On the personal level, my goodness don't you know what feelings I have for you and of course need I add"—and here he turned and raised his glass and made a courtly inclination—"for our most charming hostess." She raised her glass back at him and murmured warmly, "Dear Deepak," while making an almost invisible sign to one of the bearers, who was tardy in passing round the parsley sauce.

"I feel so odd," said Raymond's neighbor. "I mean, living the way we do, how can we, how do we have the *conscience?*"

Raymond looked back into her earnest eyes. She was intense and sincere and looked at him as if perhaps she expected an answer. But he only nodded, a little ashamed of not feeling as deeply as she did. As a matter of fact, his feelings were engaged elsewhere. He was thinking, as he thought all the time, where Gopi was now, with whom, what was he doing.

"When I first came," his English neighbor continued, "I tried to do something about it—I don't mean about things in general —how could I? how could anyone?—but just something to salve my own conscience. I joined all sorts of organizations and one of them sent me to distribute free milk to underprivileged children. . . . David told me I shouldn't. He *warned* me."

Just then his other neighbor claimed Raymond's attention. "Have you been to Kasauli? Oh, you must go. It is so quiet and peaceful, like an English village. All the cottages are in English style with honeysuckle. So pretty." A sweet, happy smile was on her face.

"Those children were underprivileged all right," said the British Council wife. "But that doesn't mean they got any of that milk." Raymond turned back to her. Her face was plain and gaunt, so unlike his other neighbor, who was plump and, though middle-aged, had a glowing brown skin and wore flowers in her

61

hair. "It was powdered milk in tins. Very convenient for selling on the black market. What can you do? Where do you start?"

The general conversation was getting more than animated. Several guests had raised their voices and were shouting across each other. One Indian gentleman kept striking the table with the palm of his hand and exclaiming "Hear, hear!" in approval.

"Within four years we shall be completely self-reliant in the production of screw valves!" Deepak shouted triumphantly at Gerald. "Another four years and our rolling mills will be supplying all our needs in small-scale hardware!"

"I know—a simply splendid job—but my point—"

"If you're going to say who built the roads, who gave you the railways, then my answer is indeed yes, but for whose benefit? Tell me that—*for whose benefit?*"

"What about Calcutta?" cried another guest, and at that there was such a hubbub that the hostess had to clap her hands for order: "You're all getting far, far too noisy!" she reprimanded. "You're supposed to be eating your pudding, not flying at each other's throats. I'm ashamed of the lot of you," she said in a severe voice, though accompanied by a merry wink.

"Do you know the Haffners?" said Raymond's Indian neighbor, helping herself with pleasure to the dessert held out to her by a bearer. "Such a nice young couple with UNESCO. Marilyn is expecting a baby soon. Last week they gave a lovely dinner —there was a marzipan dessert, it was colored green and in the shape of a fish. Oh, all right, just one more." She laughed indulgently at herself as she took another spoonful before allowing the bearer to pass on.

Raymond thought that Gopi might quite suddenly have decided to come back. Perhaps he had got tired of whatever he was doing—he did get tired of people and things quite quickly —or perhaps he wanted to come and make it up. It might well be that at this very moment he was in the flat. Perhaps he would wait for a while but then he would get bored with no one there and nothing to do and would go away again.

"David says it's no use feeling guilty," said the English neighbor. "He says that's simple self-indulgence. And pity of course is an insult. . . . What's the matter, am I being a bore?" she asked in surprise, for Raymond was suddenly on his feet.

"I'm so sorry," he said. "I am so sorry," he turned his apologies to the hostess. "If I could get to the telephone. So careless of me, I completely . . ."

Everyone was understanding and nice. He was taken out to the telephone. He dialed the flat. No, said Shyam, no one had come. No, there had been no telephone. No, no note had been left. At last Raymond asked, "Gopi?" "No, Sahib," Shyam said with satisfaction, "he has not called."

Raymond stayed for a while by the telephone, looking absently at a picture hanging there, an original abstract by a talented young Indian painter. Then he dialed again. He dialed Rao Sahib's house and asked for Asha. He was given the extension to her room but it was not she who answered. It was Bulbul. When they managed to understand one another, he gathered that Asha was not there, she had gone out. Where? Out. Suddenly Bulbul gave a scream of laughter in his ear and began to talk very fast. He could not understand what she said but it seemed to him that he heard the name "Gopi" in her stream of excited talk. He became excited too and shouted, "Gopi? She's gone with Gopi?" Bulbul went on and on, giggling and babbling, full of side-splitting tales. And Raymond could not understand a word!

A bearer passed, bearing coffee on a tray. Raymond appealed to him; he said if he could listen to the lady at the other end, if perhaps he would be kind enough to translate a little of what she was saying? The bearer put down his tray and took the receiver. He listened and Raymond saw the expression on his face change. He was first amazed, then outraged. He handed the receiver back to Raymond. "She is not speaking nice language," he told him and, taking up his tray, departed with dignity.

Red Roses

When Lee arrived at Rao Sahib's house, Asha was not there and Bulbul was just leaving in a taxi with a suitcase. She invited Lee to join her in the taxi. She was in high good humor. When Lee asked her whether she was taking her to Asha, she dissolved in laughter and poked Lee playfully as if there were a lovely secret. All the way she sat in a corner of the taxi with her sari pulled over her mouth soundlessly laughing into it. Lee didn't know what to make of this but thought she had better wait and see. After a while Bulbul poked her again and, opening the suitcase just a little way, invited Lee to peep inside. Lee saw a lot of lace underwear and several transparent negligees before Bulbul shut the suitcase again, very quickly as if afraid her precious secret would fly out there and then.

They drove to the hotel with the swimming pool. Bulbul seemed to know her way around there very well. She went straight up in the lift to the top floor and beckoned Lee to follow her. They went in. Asha lay on a huge bed of gilded wrought iron, amid an expanse of pale lilac sheets and puffed-up pillows. Her limbs were disposed languorously and her eyes were half shut. When she saw Lee, she gave an exclamation of pleasure and, opening her arms wide, invited Lee into them. Lee could not refuse to enter this embrace. After a while she discovered that Asha was silently laughing to herself in the same way as Bulbul had done.

At last she let Lee go but only to seize her hands and press them hard between her rings, saying, "Oh, my darling, my Lee, *what* shall I tell you."

"What?" Lee asked.

At that Bulbul collapsed again. Asha's eyes danced as she looked at Lee: "Well, sweetheart," she said. "It's happened again."

"What's happened again?"

"I'm in love."

Lee suppressed a groan of exasperation. She disengaged her hands from Asha's and got up. She pressed a few buttons and concealed lighting sprang up here and there and taped music began to play. "Nice place you've got here," she said.

Asha laughed. "Don't pretend to be so cold. I know how you really are."

"How?"

"Don't pretend. I know."

"What do you know?"

"He told me."

"Who's he?"

From among the clothes piled on an armchair Bulbul extracted a pair of man's shorts and held them up for all to see. Asha scolded her but she didn't mean it; really she was as amused as Bulbul. Lee tried to ignore them both and stuck her nose into a great bunch of red roses that stood on a table. There was a little card in an envelope next to the vase.

"Read it!" Asha called from the bed.

Lee drew out the card. It said, "For Asha and Gopi from Asha." She had used her lipstick to write this and also drawn a heart stuck through with an arrow. Lee put the card back.

"Now do you know who told me?"

"Yes, but I don't know what there was to tell."

Asha made a playful exclamation, but the next moment she was quite serious and said, "Come here, darling." Reluctantly Lee went back to the bed. Asha remained serious and it was in an almost solemn voice that she said, "You mustn't be ashamed of it."

"Oh, Lord, Asha."

"It's a very beautiful act of nature." As she said this, Asha's voice was not only solemn but also lowered in respect so that Lee couldn't help laughing.

"What *did* he tell you?" she asked.

Gopi and Asha

As a matter of fact, in recounting it to Asha, Gopi had rather exaggerated his afternoon of love with Lee. He wished to impress Asha. She impressed him so much that he wanted to give her something in return. He succeeded in intriguing her and she kept asking him more and more questions so that, bit by bit, almost in spite of himself, he had transformed that unsatisfactory encounter into something far more resonant.

That was during one of their first days in the hotel suite Asha had engaged for them. Gopi was deeply thrilled to be there. He kept turning on the taped music and the concealed lighting. He also studied the room-service menu and it enchanted him to order dishes he had never heard of and have them brought up to the room at all hours of the day or night. He moved from one pastel-covered telephone to the other; he ordered and countermanded his orders. Sometimes when Asha slept—and she slept quite a lot, overcome with love and all those drinks Gopi kept ordering—he went down to the swimming pool and swam rapidly up and down as if wanting to exhaust his own inexhaustible energy; or he went into the smart men's shop in the hotel lobby and ordered clothes on credit and ran up quickly to the room to try them on while Asha watched him.

But when she called him, he willingly left the mirror to go to where she lay on the bed. At such moments he became like a child with her. He laid his head on her bosom while she stroked his hair and murmured to him. He shut his eyes and she tenderly kissed the closed lids. Then she began to question him in a soft voice. She wanted to know every detail of his experience with Lee. "I always thought she was a cold girl," she said and then looked at him so expectantly that what could he do but laugh ironically and say "Cold?" like a person who knew more than he would say. And she was delighted and kissed him again and again. At other times she would ask him about other girls, and then too he felt compelled to hint at ineffable experiences.

But in fact his adventures in that field had never been all that satisfactory. He and his friends had several times visited the prostitute district but no one had bothered to take much trouble for them. They were just boys, young and undemanding and very easily satisfied. Once even they had been bundled out quite unceremoniously when a party of older men with more money to spend had unexpectedly arrived.

Everything that he had been disappointed in on those previous occasions he now found in Asha. Of course he was also thrilled by the luxurious surroundings in which their relationship unfolded—how different from those slum tenements in which the prostitutes lived!—but more than that, much much more, was Asha herself. It was true, she was not young, indeed she was old, her body was soft and sagging but, as he pressed himself against it and inhaled the odor of her flesh (pampered for a lifetime with oils and French perfumes), a rich new world opened to his mind as well as to his senses. His love for her was also his love for her past and everything she had been and done in it. There were her rich and famous friends; there were her lovers. There was her husband, who had treated her so cruelly and yet whom she had loved so gloriously. He had been a spendthrift and perhaps in many ways a worthless fellow but he had been a poet. All these years after his death, Asha was still suffused by the poetry he had taught her and she often quoted Urdu couplets to Gopi that ravished his soul away. Poetry for him, as for her, was a reflection of—a straining after—all that was finest and best in human life and as she spoke these verses —"O nightingale, forgive me your death, it was my tears that drowned you"—their feelings rose to a pitch.

Lee

Margaret has heard of a new swami. He's supposed to be wonderful. He speaks English and lives in Benares. She wants me to go with her. I might.

Today the mission had its expulsion order from the government of India. It wasn't quite unexpected but all the same it was sad. After all these years here Miss Charlotte will have to leave. She didn't say much—in fact, she didn't really say anything—but was busy all day as usual. In the evening Raymond came. I had asked him to come and meet Miss Charlotte and I'm glad I did, it was certainly a success. I can see now that Raymond has lived mostly with middle-aged ladies and probably he misses their company here, for he was so pleased with Miss Charlotte. She asked him all those questions she's always asking Margaret and me, only he was much better at answering them. It turned out his mother has the same literary tastes as Miss Charlotte—terribly fond of George Eliot and Hardy—though his aunt (the one who died and left him a legacy) had more of a preference for the Brontës and the metaphysical poets. He said they often read to each other at home, he and his mother and his aunt when she was still with them; and Miss Charlotte said that they had had readings at home too when she was a girl, she remembered them so well, they had read all of Dickens and Thackeray and other classics. She thought nothing helped a child form good literary tastes so much as such readings aloud in the family circle, and Raymond agreed. They agreed about everything. They really took to each other.

All the same, I could see he was quite pleased when she went to bed and he was left alone with me. I knew he wanted to ask me something and also that he didn't know how to start. He went on talking to me about things that didn't matter a damn to him (or to me), just so as to keep polite conversation going and not make it look as if there was anything he wanted except only the pleasure of my company. So at last I interrupted him to say I knew where Gopi was. To which he said, "Oh, yes," and his voice shook only the tiniest bit and he seemed about to continue his boring conversation. But I cut him short again and told him about Gopi and Asha. I felt someone had to do this, though I wish it didn't have to be me. He is very pale anyway but now his face was quite chalky. He quickly lowered his eyes with the ginger lashes, I suppose so that I wouldn't be able to see the expression in them. But he still went on trying to make indifferent conversation.

I said, "Raymond, you don't have to be so *controlled*, not all the time."

He said, "Then what do you expect me to do?"—quite dry and sharp.

Suddenly I began telling him about the new guru Margaret has heard about. I said she and I were thinking of going there. He pretended to be interested in what I was saying, though when I was finished there was a pause and I could see he was thinking of something quite different. I said, "Why don't you come too?"

"And do what?"

I said, "Raymond, please don't pretend to be more stupid than you are."

Perhaps I sounded a bit hurt—anyway he made an effort to concentrate more of his attention on me. He said, quite gently and patiently, that he was sorry but surely I knew that he didn't care for these things. It might be that he was wrong, he said, but he simply wasn't interested. I said it *was* wrong—what was the use of coming to India if all you did here was to be a tourist? Tourists don't live, I told him, they only look—and looking is nothing, it doesn't change you, it doesn't help you really and truly find yourself. He pretended to be listening but he wasn't at all, I could see that very well. His thoughts were quite different and how they made him suffer. That made me mad—that he should suffer like that and be so entangled in these feelings and making no effort to free himself. And I decided there and then that *yes*, I would go with Margaret. I was fed up with everything here, with all these small things that engulfed people. I didn't want anything like that to happen to me.

Raymond Writes to His Mother

"... I meet Miss Charlotte quite often now and like her very much. So would you. She would fit in very well at Hazelhurst, and I can quite clearly see her and you going for long walks together—she *strides* in the same way you do—and having animated discussions on life and literature, both of you shrieking in high, girlish voices. I can't get over the way she's so *English,* considering the years she's been out here and the sort of work she's been doing. Of course I'm very sorry about the extradition orders and am in fact trying to help her get them revoked (*not* hopeful), but in a way I rather like the idea of her being back in England. You know, the gardens here are full of English flowers like larkspur and phlox and pansies and sweet peas. Whenever I see them, I get a strange feeling and wonder what are they doing here, how did they grow, and how are they managing to survive. I get the same feeling with Miss Charlotte.

"I'm off tomorrow at 4 A.M. (grisly hour). My itinerary is as follows: Jaipur, Udaipur, Ahmedabad, Bombay, and then on my way back I'll just stop by at Agra for another look at the Taj Mahal and of course the great and glorious Fatehpur Sikri. Shyam is still hankering to come with me but I'm afraid I'm not quite grand enough to be able to travel around with my own personal body-servant. Besides, those air fares are rather prohibitive. Everyone is telling me all I'm missing by not going by car or train, and I dare say I am, but I want to be a tourist —I *am* a tourist—and get quickly from one place to another without having to take in great drafts of India on the way. Now, darling, please make a careful note of these addresses to which you must write and don't get them mixed up because you know how disappointed and anxious I'll be if I don't find your letters waiting for me. . . ."

Lee Writes to Asha

". . . I think of you quite often and then I think you would be happy here too. I know it. Sometimes when you speak to me about those things you're always speaking about I feel that really that's not what you want at all, really it's something else you're looking for and this something else is the same I'm looking for and Margaret and so many others and perhaps even everyone in the world if they only knew it. Margaret keeps saying that her eyes have been opened and that's true but only if you remember that this means the *inner* eyes and those of course are not only vision but all other faculties as well, including the very highest faculties we have. If only we wake up to the fact that we *do* have them—or are woken up to that fact, because most of us are too corrupted to find them for ourselves. Swamiji has asked me to tell him about all the people I know. It's important for me to do this, to reveal everything to him so that I can become the new person he wants to make me and I want so much to be. When I told him about you he was very interested and he agreed that you too are a person looking for the right way. And he wants to help you and I want it too that you should come to him. If only I could give you some idea of him but that's not possible, I don't have the words. There are all sorts of people here and they all have different problems but now every one of us is learning to see how trivial these things which we thought important really are. So far our group is still quite small but more and more people will come to him not only from here but from all over the world and he is in fact planning to make it a world movement and will be leaving for a foreign tour as soon as it can be arranged. I'm sending you some literature—Swamiji says you should see this—I'm afraid it's locally printed so not very good but it will give you some idea. Swamiji would like you to show it to Rao Sahib too and other political people and if you want more to distribute please write and we will send . . ."

Asha Feels Old

Gopi threw his brand-new silk robe round himself and tied the belt with an easy, practiced movement. Asha watched and admired him. She sighed and said, "He loves you so much."

"Who?"

"Raymond."

Gopi was used to Asha's disconnected thoughts. He said, "I'm also very fond of him."

At that she burst out laughing. She looked into his face and stroked his cheeks, laughing at him.

"We're great friends," Gopi urged, puzzled by her laughter.

"Oh, you're so sweet, and how I love you, how I love you!"

Gopi held the hand with which she was stroking his cheek and, opening it, gently kissed the palm. Then her laughter changed to sorrow. She felt so terribly unworthy of him—of his youth and his innocence. She had discovered long ago that he had no idea of his true relationship with Raymond. He really genuinely thought they were just great friends. Asha had made no attempt to enlighten him. She felt it was right he shouldn't know about these things but should remain fresh and sprightly, a devotee only of natural love. But here her own guilt stabbed her like a dagger: she knew there was nothing natural about her own relationship with him.

She gazed into his face. Her lips trembled. "I'm so old," she said.

He couldn't bear to hear her say that. And yet there was no getting away from the fact. He was relieved when the hotel bearer entered with the drinks that had been ordered. Gopi gave Asha hers and then leaned against the pillows by her side and sipped his. Now all bad thoughts disappeared and he was contented and satisfied again.

She told him, "I had a letter from Lee," but in so sighing a voice that he asked, "Is she sick?"

"Oh, no. She is very, very well. Give me my purse."

He fetched it for her and she gave him the letter to read. He frowned a bit over it in an effort to understand; he always read slowly and with his lips moving to form the words. He also looked at the pamphlets but here he was on surer ground; he didn't have to read them carefully because he knew what was written in them. His eyes passed swiftly over the blurred print and he swayed his head in unquestioning appreciation. These were holy, good, and true things.

"She wants me to come there," Asha said.

"Yes, why not? We can both go for two–three days."

Asha sighed again and said nothing.

"It will be quite nice," Gopi said, getting enthusiastic. "When I was small, my mother took me sometimes to visit her guru's ashram. They have quite a jolly time there and the food is not bad. Of course it's all vegetarian but nicely cooked in ghee and there are a lot of sweets that people bring. Now what's the matter?"

"No, no, nothing," she said with tears streaming from her eyes. She tried to wipe them away. She hated herself for disturbing him. But she could not help herself. She began to talk rather quickly, as if to explain herself and take away the puzzled expression from his face. "I know a holy person. She is called Banubai. She has a house in Benares and once I went to live there with her. Oh, she gave me such peace. If only I could have stayed with her. But when I went back to Bombay—" Those had been terrible days. She had meant to lead such a good life, of restraint and devotion, but when temptation came her way she had flung herself into it head over heels. And yet the temptations had been by no means irresistible—just the usual pleasures that she was really quite sick and tired of. She had had an affair with a film producer whom she didn't care for all that much; he had even disgusted her but she didn't have the strength to give him up and in the end it was he who had thrown her over in favor of a fat little starlet.

"We'll go," Gopi said, trying to cheer her up. "You see what

Lee has written—where is it?—'and I think you will be happy here too—' "

Asha snatched the letter from his hand and tore it up. "Why does she write to me like that? She's mad—a mad girl, I always knew it."

In the Ashram

The ashram was not actually in Benares but about ten miles outside it. This was deliberate policy on Swamiji's part: he did not wish to batten on the holiness of the past but to inspire new souls with a new spirit. It was also convenient that land was going cheap in that area. It had at one time been earmarked for new industrial development but, apart from a brick kiln and a few foundations that now remained as holes in the ground where snakes lived, no development had taken place. Here Swamiji had acquired an acre of land and had put up some hutments for himself and his followers. Of course the hutments were only temporary and great schemes already existed in blueprint for the future development of the ashram.

The surrounding landscape was flat, bleak, and dusty. The hutments were strictly utilitarian, with tin roofs stuck on brick walls that heated up like ovens in the sun. Swamiji put his faith in the trees that had been planted all around, but of course it would take time for them to grow and meanwhile they were not doing too well on account of lack of water and also some blight that tended to attack vegetation in the region. There were many flies and mosquitoes, the kitchen arrangements were inadequate, and the sanitary ones primitive. But all these physical discomforts could be and were interpreted as blessings, for what surer test could there be of a disciple's sincerity than the ability to overcome discomforts? There were many who fell short and one by one they went away, and Swamiji saw them do so with a smiling, loving acquiescence. It only made him draw those that remained closer to himself.

They were a mixed lot of Westerners and Indians, but he encouraged them to think of themselves as one family and quite often they managed to do so. It was easiest when they were all grouped around Swamiji and he was giving them one of his beautiful discourses or leading them in singing devotional songs. One of the hutments had been fitted up as a communal prayer hall and here they gathered morning and evening for their devotions. Although this hutment was as utilitarian and cheaply furnished as all the others, it had been decorated by loving hands and a beautiful atmosphere prevailed. The room was dominated by a large, colored picture of Swamiji's own guru, a very holy man who wore no clothes and sat on a deer skin. Underneath this there was a big velvet armchair with an antimacassar embroidered by one of the disciples and here Swamiji sat with two devotees waving a peacock fan over him. They all faced the picture of the holy guru and Swamiji sitting beneath it, and then how they sang! With what inspiration! Of course it was he who inspired them to call after him—"Rama!" he sang, "Gopala! Hari! Krishna!" in his melodious, smiling voice, and then who could resist following him and also calling out those sweet names and being filled with the savor of them. But however loudly, however devotedly they sang, it was never enough for Swamiji—always he begged for more, always he led them higher and higher, to sing out louder and louder—"Rama! Gopala! Hari! Krishna!"—he incited them to break out again and again in those names, to fetch them forth out of hearts that must be coaxed to overflow with the love of them. Then the human voice alone was no longer enough, there must be cymbals too and conch shells to proclaim that joy: but still above all that holy din and all those voices rose *his* voice, forever ahead of them, almost mocking them to come up there with him, to soar as high as he did. And they tried and tried, they tried their very best, and he led them on to such a pitch of excitement and frenzy that it became almost unbearable for them, the joy of it exhausted them, and who knows what would have happened

75

every morning and evening if he hadn't known the exact point at which to stop them? Then they all fell silent and smiled and felt happy and light as if simultaneously they had been relieved of and had achieved something.

When Lee and Margaret first came to the ashram, they did not find it easy to sing with the same abandon as the others. They were stiff and shy, locked up within themselves. But slowly, as the days passed, cunningly, he enticed them out of themselves. To each of them it appeared and became clear beyond doubt with each successive meeting that he was concentrating only on her. At first Lee thought she must be imagining it—after all, there were all these others, all intent only on him and drawing their inspiration only from him—what was so special about her that he should single her out from among them? To cure herself of her misapprehension, she would lower her eyes away from him but she could never do so for long because he seemed to be drawing her back, beckoning to her, telling her come, look up, look at me. And when she did, sure enough, there he was smiling at her—yes! at her alone!—so that she had to smile back and sing the way he wanted her to and cry out "Rama! Gopala! Hari! Krishna!" with as much abandon as she could manage. And afterward, when he distributed the bits of rock sugar that served as holy offering, then too at her turn, as he put it into her mouth, there was this special message for her, this speaking without words that went right through her and reached, it seemed to her, into regions which no one had hitherto penetrated. So was it any wonder that, whenever she left his presence, she felt dazed and wanted to go away by herself and not speak to anyone? And she began to notice that Margaret behaved in the same way—she too would be quite silent and sunk in her own thoughts and for hours together they would lie like that side by side on their string cots in the hutment they shared. And when they did speak, it was in a gentle distant way as if their thoughts were distant, and each imperceptibly smiled to herself at something beautiful within.

76

An Old English Lady

The first person Raymond looked up on his return was Miss Charlotte. She was very pleased to see him back again and eager to hear all about his trip. She was, however, on the point of going out to pay a visit and she invited Raymond to accompany her. They took a short cut through the old British cemetery. It was quite shady here with many old trees growing over the old granite graves. Miss Charlotte allowed Raymond to relieve her of the large and heavy gunny-cloth bag she was carrying. From time to time she pointed out some interesting grave to him. Although most of these dated from the nineteenth century, there were a few more recent ones, and indeed some belonged to people whom Miss Charlotte had known when she first came. She showed him the resting place of the Reverend Mellow, who had been in charge of the mission at that time and had died of cholera contracted during an epidemic. He had been in India for twenty years and had been so attached to his work here that he had never once bothered to go on home leave. How sad he would be today, Miss Charlotte said, if he knew that his dearly beloved mission was to be closed down.

"You haven't managed to get an extension?" Raymond asked.

"I'm afraid not." She got down to pluck a few weeds from Reverend Mellow's grave. The stone was plain and inexpensive and rather a contrast to the much grander and older graves surrounding it.

They reached their destination, which was a modest brick structure adjoining the church. Miss Charlotte explained that it was a home kept up by the church for English people in India who had nowhere else to go and no money to live on. "They're all very old people now," she said. Certainly, the first person they went to see was a very old lady indeed. Raymond had never seen anyone with skin so shriveled, discolored, and hanging in rags from the bones. But she still thought it worthwhile to dress correctly in shoes and a brown polka-dot frock, and

77

what was left of her hair was kept tidily under a net. When they went in, she shouted, "Who is it! What do you want?" but was reassured at once when Miss Charlotte identified herself.

"And I've brought a nice young man to see you," said Miss Charlotte.

The old eyes searched in Raymond's direction. They were a strange, rinsed blue and seemed to look from a long way away; one of them was blotted by a cataract. But she did not bother about Raymond for long; just now the gunny bag seemed to be of more interest to her, and to relieve her anxiety Miss Charlotte began to unpack it at once: "Your ketchup—and this is something new—sandwich spread—I thought you'd like to try it for your tea."

She placed her purchases on a little cane table, which was one of the few pieces of furniture in the room. Everything was very clean—spotless—though somewhat bleak. The walls were plainly whitewashed, and the cement floor scrubbed to the bone.

"Bless you, my dear," said the old lady when all these goodies had been unpacked. Now truly she could give her attention to Raymond, and again the old eyes searched in his direction; he guessed that she was unable to make him out in detail but was only attempting to delineate him in space.

"English?" she asked.

"Yes, indeed," said Miss Charlotte. "He's only here on a visit."

"I'm very pleased to meet you," said the old lady. "Very pleased indeed. It's a pity I can't get up to greet you but it's on account of my legs, you see." They were indeed badly swollen and so were other parts of her. "When you get to my age, you have to expect these things. I'm eighty-six, you know." She waited as if expecting some comment on this fact. Raymond said, "Incredible," which appeared to satisfy. "Yes, eighty-six on the twenty-first of April. That's my birthday, the twenty-first of April, the same day as the Queen, so it's easy to remember. I'm so sorry, my dear, I can't offer you a cup of tea but you see what

78

it's like here. Hardly the place to receive guests, I'm afraid. It would have been different in my own home."

"This *is* your own home," said Miss Charlotte brightly, but for this the old eyes floated in her direction with a scornful look before floating back again to Raymond.

"Can you smell it?" she asked him.

He hesitated to answer—the room had a smell of carbolic soap emanating from the washed floor and one of old age emanating from her; but it seemed she meant the smell of cooking that came seeping in from outside.

"Mutton stew—when they know perfectly well I can't stand it. I've told them over and over again I want my rice and curry; at least that has some taste to it. But it's because of him upstairs. I think he bribes them in the kitchen. Those people would do anything for a bribe."

"Don't they cook your curry on alternate days?" Miss Charlotte said. "And look at the chutney I brought you—that'll make everything taste nice."

"He pretends he doesn't like Indian food. He says it's too hot for him, burns his tongue, he says. Of course that's just his lies and hypocrisy to show everyone how English he is. English, is he? Well, I have a story to tell about that if anyone cares to ask and I should care to answer." She swayed and smirked but the next moment remembered something unpleasant that made her stop. "He knows very well I know what I'm not supposed to know—that's why he's telling all those lies about me. To pull the wool over people's eyes. Have you heard the latest? He's been telling Ayah and all the servants that my father—*my father*—kept a shop in Amritsar. Really, I ought to laugh and I would if it weren't such a hateful, detestable, wicked lie. Hand me that," she told Raymond, pointing to a metal plaque propped up in the center of the mantelpiece.

She took the plaque between both her hands, and when she had gazed at it long enough, she gave it to Raymond and told him to read it. "Out loud," she said. He read that this plaque had been presented to Lieutenant F. J. Peck of the 13th Bengal Infantry to commemorate his participation in the relief of Lucknow, December 1857.

"My father," she said impressively, and indeed Raymond held the plaque with wonder and looked from it to her as she sat there swollen and discolored in her polka-dot frock.

"Put it back," she ordered. "Now you know what to say next time you hear him tell that lie. The things he's been telling people, someone ought to do something about it. Not that anyone believes him of course, because everyone knows he's a liar through and through. He's just rotten with lies. Rotten and stinking!" she shouted, croaking, apoplectic, but with surprising energy.

"Shall we say our prayers now?" suggested Miss Charlotte.

"All right, dear," the old lady said at once and meekly.

Miss Charlotte slipped from her chair down to the floor in a practiced, agile movement. The other two remained where they were but lowered their heads respectfully. Raymond thought how hard the floor must be under Miss Charlotte's knees, but he knew she didn't feel it. Surreptitiously he looked over at the old lady. Her head was still lowered but she was looking at him out of the corner of one of her blotted eyes. She closed it at him in a wink that made him look away again quickly. Miss Charlotte prayed out loudly and in a voice full of faith and joy.

Raymond Writes to His Mother

". . . I always feel strange walking into the High Commission compound. It's so tremendously clean—you can't help thinking that no place in India has the right to be that clean. And all that smart new suburban architecture and the Mums sitting gossiping by the swimming pool and calling in loud voices to their children splashing about inside. When a stranger like me comes in, they glance round for a moment and look at you with those cold eyes, you know, the sort that say since they don't know you obviously you're not worth knowing. The tennis courts are usually occupied by girls with stout red legs playing men also with stout red legs and they call to each other across the net in those same loud voices in which the Mums call to the children. It's funny, everyone here seems to have this same *commanding* sort of voice, even the children. (Or is it the way English people always speak and I've forgotten?)

"Mr. Taylor couldn't have been more cordial, was very pleased to see me, insisted I have a drink. He's a counselor and so gets a special bungalow, fully air-conditioned of course and with fitted carpets. When I talked about Miss Charlotte, he made a face—in a nice way, showing how he was not hiding his feelings from me—he said yes, he knew about those people, and one did feel sorry for them and no one could deny that they *had* been doing good work—but unfortunately the Indian government was rather sensitive about them and High Commission could hardly afford to stick its neck out for them because alas there were so *many* things the Indian government was sensitive about. . . . Here he sighed, and I could see that he had plenty of troubles of his own. I think he was about to tell me about them when Mrs. Taylor came in and said she hoped he wasn't forgetting the Wodehouses at eight and he hadn't even changed yet, darling. So of course I jumped to my feet, and he got up too and put his hand on my arm and said he hoped I understood his problem and I said I did. And actually I did— things are like that nowadays—it's all right to use those loud voices inside the compound but outside they have to be rather circumspect. . . ."

A Secular State

Rao Sahib's office was done up in wood paneling and had an enormous teak desk with a silver inkstand on it. Rao Sahib sat behind this desk in a carved chair that reared above him like a throne; on the wall behind him hung a colored portrait of the

President of India. Rao Sahib was leaning back in his chair and explaining himself to Raymond.

"You may take note that I am speaking as a secular state and hence these restrictions would apply to all denominations. Our policies are framed regardless of any particular creed but only on the basis of the widest application of principle. . . ."

He was talking himself into a trance, and Raymond, sitting opposite him, felt in danger of sinking with him. He made an effort to rouse himself. He proffered the opinion that Miss Charlotte's activities were of an entirely philanthropic nature and that her concern was solely with material and not at all with spiritual conditions. Rao Sahib was traveling too smoothly on his own track of ideas to make it easy for him to switch to another, but when Raymond had respectfully tendered this point, he made a sincere effort to accommodate him and succeeded so well that he was soon launched on another flow of words.

"While not denying the value of the philanthropic work that has been done by many of these missions in the past, we must stress the fact that philanthropy is a form of charity that the government of India, indeed I may say the people of India, can no longer allow themselves to accept. The giant task ahead of us is one that must be solved not through the individual efforts of foreigners whose presence in our midst is an anachronism but through our own machinery of parliamentary democracy and nationalized socialism. . . ."

Raymond was sad. Rao Sahib's words were so big and Miss Charlotte's efforts so small. He thought of her little school for sweepers' children and the cluster of sick people on her back veranda to whom pills and bandages were dispensed. In the face of those giant problems and that giant machinery Rao Sahib spoke of, what did any of it amount to? But there was Miss Charlotte herself, and for her sake Raymond again ventured to interrupt Rao Sahib, who again obligingly shifted his discourse and admitted that yes, it was not to be denied that there were cases of individual hardship which the government of India would indeed do its best to take note of; but was it not true to say—Rao Sahib appealed to Raymond—that in the upheavals of history there was bound to be individual suffering that no power on earth was able to prevent? It struck Raymond how kind Rao Sahib was being in giving him so much of his time and in taking the trouble of explaining the standpoint of his government to him at such length. So courteous was Rao Sahib that he gave the impression of having no other work but to sit here and talk to Raymond; and he seemed ready to extend the interview indefinitely when they were interrupted by the entrance of his private secretary, a deferential young man in suede shoes on which he tiptoed up to Rao Sahib's desk to remind him of his next engagement.

"Oh, dear dear dear," said Rao Sahib. "You see what comes of having such interesting chats." He stared down at the papers the young man had glided before him. "Your speech, sir," the young man murmured.

"Ah," said Rao Sahib. He looked down at it and read fleeting phrases which seemed to please him. His chest swelled over his desk, his face shone with interior smiles; he cleared his throat and patted it. He appeared impatient to launch forth on his speech and to anticipate pleasure from its delivery.

"At six-thirty," said the secretary, looking at his watch as if apologizing for its impertinence.

Rao Sahib got up and said "Do forgive me" to Raymond, who also got up. He held his hand out across the desk and shook Raymond's warmly. Midway he stopped short and looked inquiringly at Raymond's necktie.

"Pembroke," Raymond said.

"My dear chap," said Rao Sahib, shaking Raymond's hand all over again and with redoubled warmth.

Lee Writes to Raymond

". . . This girl Evie is getting to be a sort of ideal for me. She's been with him for three years and it's all she wants and all she *is* really. He's writing this book on the 'Essence of the Upanishads' and he's dictating it to her bit by bit, just as the thoughts come to him. It's going to be a very revolutionary work, because it's the first really serious attempt to fit Indian thought into the framework of Western apprehension in such a way that it's not only with the mind that we shall be able to understand it but with our whole being which is really the only way to really know anything. Evie is also taking down whatever thoughts he throws out during the course of the day, and need I say that this keeps her very busy because he's so *phenomenal,* I mean it's so fantastic the way his mind is always alert. He himself is always tremendously alert—I can't imagine him ever feeling tired, and as far as I can see he doesn't, he's always awake long after the rest of us have gone to sleep and he's always the first up, so that sometimes I wonder whether he ever goes to sleep at all. And because he keeps these fantastic hours Evie has to too. She doesn't ever like to leave him in case he says one of his things while she's not there and then it would be lost forever and she'd never forgive herself. She also spends a lot of time writing up her notes, so she's always working hard and as she's not very strong it's really a miracle how she keeps it up.

"Margaret is funny nowadays. I don't know what's the matter with her. Of course she's studying very hard because she's taking the Way of Knowledge but that's no reason why she should get so snappy. She spends a lot of time meditating on her mantra (we all have a different mantra to meditate on that he gave us when he formally adopted us as his disciples). But it's not making her one bit serene the way it should. She and I and Evie are in the same hutment, and she's always picking on us for nothing. I try to ignore it as much as possible because I don't want to be disturbed in my mind. The other day she went for poor Evie—she accused her of using her towel, which Evie hadn't done, but even if she had what did it matter? And Evie never said a word to defend herself, she just looked down and smiled that pale smile she has. But that made Margaret madder than ever. Afterward she kept muttering horrid things about her, how she didn't trust her one inch, that Evie was smarmy and deceitful and that it was sad to see Swamiji so taken in by her and unable to see her in her true colors.

"But it's stupid of me to write you these things and I'm giving you entirely the wrong impression of our life here. I wish I could tell you about it, describe it to you as it is. If only you would come and see for yourself! I know if you did you wouldn't want to go away again ever. Swamiji is also convinced of it and often says, 'I wish Raymond would come.' Yes, he calls you Raymond and knows all about you, he has this power of knowing people before he's actually physically met them. And he knows like I do, Raymond, that you're *wasting* India, which has such supreme things, such *gifts* to give those of us ready to take them. . . ."

Friendship Renewed and Transformed

Gopi asked, "Aren't you pleased to see me?"

"It's been a long time," Raymond said. He was staggered by Gopi's unexpected appearance in the flat. He had come bounding up the stairs and was suddenly in the room—radiant and smiling as if nothing whatsoever had come in between.

"I know," Gopi said. "But I've been thinking of you so much."

This was not true. Gopi had hardly thought about Raymond at all—he had been too preoccupied to do so. But once the idea of visiting Raymond occurred to him, he wasted no time at all but rushed to see him. And now that he had come, he was very glad: all the pleasant hours he had spent here came back to him and the memory made him feel so good that he threw his arms round Raymond and hugged him with true affection.

85

But Raymond was shocked by this embrace and moved away from him. Then Gopi was shocked too and cried, "What's the matter! Are you angry with me?"

Raymond was trembling and could not answer. Weeks had passed, and now Gopi came and asked what was the matter.

"Don't you want to speak to me?" Gopi asked sadly. "Should I go away?"

Raymond knew that if he said yes, Gopi would obey, he would slowly walk down the stairs feeling very, very sorry that Raymond was angry with him.

Raymond shrugged and said, attempting indifference, "Now you've come—"

"Are you ill?" Gopi asked, looking searchingly into Raymond's face. "You look pulled down. Have you been to see a doctor?"

"Don't be silly."

"Is there bad news from home? Is Mother well?"

Raymond felt that Gopi had no right to ask him these intimate questions as if everything was as it had been before. Yet he saw that Gopi was absolutely sincere in his concern. There was so much tenderness in his eyes and his voice that Raymond's determination to harden his feelings began, in spite of himself, to weaken.

"Asha and I speak of you so often. Always she asks, I wonder how Raymond is, what he is doing now. . . ." As he spoke, Gopi looked slyly sideways at Raymond as if he were asking him whether he knew about himself and Asha. And Raymond blushed, so that Gopi saw that he did know, and that made Gopi burst out laughing in a mixture of embarrassment and pleasure. He said, "She likes you very much," and laughed again—and then he wanted to talk about Asha and share his happiness with Raymond and also draw him into it because he was so fond of Raymond and wanted him to be happy too.

He flung himself on Raymond's sofa in his old position—half lying, half sitting, utterly at ease. He cried out how good it was to be back again and Raymond could not help himself but had silently to agree that it was good—very, very good—to see him there again in the flat which had been so bleak without him. And when Gopi indicated with a smiling glance the space left empty on the sofa, Raymond went and sat there and both looked at each other and were glad—yes, Raymond could no longer and wanted no longer to hide the fact that he was.

"Do you remember," said Gopi, beaming now that Raymond seemed to be pleased with him again, "that evening when she came? And we all went swimming—Lee too—have you heard from Lee?"

"Yes." Raymond added ruefully, "Poor Lee."

"Why? No—she's very happy—and it is a very good place. We want to go and visit her there, Asha and I. . . ." Again he looked sideways at Raymond, again he laughed. He longed to talk to Raymond about Asha but at the same time he felt shy.

Raymond went on talking about Lee. "I suppose it was to be expected sooner or later—obviously she's the type."

"What type?"

"To fall for one of these people."

"Oh, no," Gopi said, rather shocked, "he must be a very holy person."

"Perhaps."

"Asha thinks so too." Now he could no longer restrain himself but blurted out, "Do you like Asha?" He went on in a rush—"Because she likes you very much, how often she speaks about you, we both speak about you and I say yes, he and I are great, great friends. . . ."

"Such great friends," Raymond suddenly said, "that you haven't bothered to see me or ring me or give any sign of life to me for nine weeks and four days."

Gopi was silent in astonishment. It did not seem to him that any time had passed at all—the minutes had flown so lightly for him—and even if it had, he couldn't understand why Raymond should be bitter about it. It did happen sometimes that friends were prevented from meeting, but that did not make any difference to their feelings for each other. His feelings for Raymond had certainly not changed at all. He murmured, "I wanted to come very often," but with downcast eyes and all the joy gone out of him.

Then Raymond felt sorry and thought, wasn't it enough that Gopi was here now, wasn't that happiness enough that he must hark back to what was past and of no importance to anyone but himself? So he said, "I know you were busy," meaning it as an apology for the way he had spoken.

Gopi swiftly raised his eyes and tried to search out from Raymond's features what there might be in his heart. Their glance met for an instant and Raymond had to look away: he could not bear the beauty of Gopi's eyes nor the surge of emotion that they evoked in him.

"She's very kind to me," Gopi said, misinterpreting Raymond's expression. "Look at this shirt—just feel it"—he stuck out his sleeve at Raymond and waited till he did feel it—"you see, what silk it is."

"Yes, it's very good."

"She gave it to me." He added, "And so many other things." And when Raymond said nothing, he thought he had to say more. "Whatever I want, she buys for me. She's very rich."

Raymond said quickly, "I know she's very generous. I like her."

Gopi's face lit up. "Really? You really like her?"

"Very much."

"You don't know how she speaks of you—she thinks you are wonderful and she is always wanting us to be together with you, she keeps saying, where's Raymond? Why don't we call Raymond?"

He looked at Raymond with love. He sparkled and shone. And Raymond felt, whatever happened, he couldn't let him go again.

The weeks of privation had schooled Raymond in patience,

88

and he was content to be able to see Gopi in between Gopi's other commitments—to his college, his home, and to Asha. This undemanding attitude pleased Gopi and made him feel more affectionate toward Raymond than anything else could have done. He came to look on Raymond's flat as a place of refuge and visited at any hour of the day or night it suited him. He lounged around there wearing nothing but a lungi tied around his waist and spent a lot of time fast asleep in whatever place —a sofa, the floor, Raymond's bed—he happened to drop down. Then Raymond moved around on tiptoe and slipped pillows under Gopi's head to make him more comfortable. Once, while he was doing this, Gopi suddenly opened his eyes and looked at him and smiled so sweetly that Raymond's heart turned right over.

There was a change in Gopi. Even Shyam noticed it, and it made him ready to serve Gopi with better grace. It was not exactly that Gopi had become more considerate toward him, but he now behaved more as if he were used to servants like Shyam and no longer felt it necessary to assert his own superiority. Gopi's attitude toward Raymond himself had changed too. He had always had his moments of tenderness, but they had been fleeting. Now they were there almost all the time and he was so kind and considerate that Raymond didn't know what to do to show his gratitude.

Raymond was quite prepared to accommodate himself to Asha. If it was not possible to see Gopi alone, then he was ready to join him and Asha in any outing to which they cared to invite him. And they did invite him quite often—at least Gopi did, he thought it was nice for all three of them to be together. Sometimes, for reasons he didn't analyze, it was even a relief to him to have Raymond there and not have to be alone with Asha. So it was that the three of them went for long drives together in Asha's car, or booked seats for the matinee show at the cinema. Or sometimes Asha went on one of her marathon shopping expeditions, with both Raymond and Gopi walking behind her to carry her parcels. She went from shop to shop, buying insatiably till she was exhausted and then they all three went back to the hotel and she flopped down on the sofa with her feet resting in Gopi's lap; and he would massage them to soothe her so that she sighed with gratitude while Raymond sat apart from them in an armchair and looked down into his drink.

A Quarrel

Sometimes, when Asha did not feel like going to the hotel, she would summon Gopi to Rao Sahib's house. The family and the servants were used to rather odd people coming to visit her so Gopi was by no means a surprise: on the contrary, compared with some of the others, he stood out in an agreeable way.

He himself was not always pleased with Asha's other guests. Once he found her sitting on the veranda entertaining a group of men friends; these included a musician, a dancer, and a big burly wrestler. When Gopi came, she made everyone shift their chairs so that he could sit beside her. She cupped his face between her hands and kissed him tenderly. He felt terrible with all these people looking on and suppressing their smiles at what they saw. But Asha noticed nothing or, if she did, she didn't care. She was taken up with talking to her guests and reminiscing with them over happenings in the past. These were all amusing, and Asha was laughing and slapping her own and other people's knees.

Afterward, when they had gone, Gopi reproached her. "What sort of friends are these for you to have?"

She shrugged: "Anyway, they're good fun."

"Tcha," Gopi said in deep disgust. "And such dirty talk you made with them."

"It's all just talk," she soothed him. "That wrestler, what a big strong fellow he is, but he can't do anything with a woman, I have it on best authority. And the other one, the dancer—you saw how he was looking at you—" She burst out laughing.

90

Gopi didn't want to hear. He snatched up a magazine and engrossed himself in its pages. He frowned and scowled. Asha stopped laughing. Her mood changed completely. After a while Gopi heard her sigh and give out other signs of a disturbed mind.

When he went on reading, she said, "I had another letter from Lee. She wants me to come there." She added, "I want to go."

Gopi turned the pages of the magazine.

"Lee says we shouldn't go running after material enjoyments, that there is never any true satisfaction to be found there. Yes, she is right. For a short time you loved me but now you don't care anything for me. You care only for Raymond."

Gopi looked in amazement over the top of the magazine.

"It's true," she said.

"You're mad."

"But of course I'm mad! Who wouldn't be mad! My God, when I think of my life I wonder at myself that I'm still here and not locked away in some lunatic asylum or dead from suicide."

"But you said you *like* Raymond."

"Yes, I like him."

"You said you want him to be with us."

"Poor boy, what should he do? Nature is to be blamed, no one else." She fetched another great sigh from the center of her being and then she said, "Where were you last night?"

"I was with Raymond."

"In his flat?" She looked at him narrowly but he had his magazine up again. "You shouldn't stay with him at night, it gives a bad impression. And I was thinking so much of you yesterday, I thought if only he would come to me now. But of course you were with Raymond, so how could you come to me. Put that away!" she cried, and snatching the magazine out of his hands, flung it far out into the garden.

Gopi jumped up in a rage. His eyes fell on the empty whisky glasses left behind by her friends. He raised his hand and swept it across the table. The glasses broke on the stone floor of the veranda and splintered into many pieces. There was a smell of whisky dregs. Asha had also jumped up. She looked at the broken glass, she looked at Gopi standing there enraged. A sort of exultation rose in her. She stepped up close to him and raising her face challengingly to his said, "Why don't you hit me! Go on, hit me!"

Gopi's fury subsided. He stepped back from her but she came up close again. "Why don't you?" she urged. Her eyes flashed with desire and seemed to be devouring him so that suddenly he felt afraid of her.

Transience

Lee walked away from the evening devotions, feeling exalted and purified. She always felt that way after singing hymns with Swamiji. Over the hutments, over the snake holes, over the flat, barren landscape stretched the evening sky—an opalescent texture tinted in the most delicate and unexpected shades of pink, orange, even pale green. It seemed to Lee that it shone with the same glory with which the singing of hymns had filled her heart. She had intended to do some long-delayed sewing on her neglected underclothes, but now she felt she could not do this, it was not possible for her to sit there like a quiet, rational creature. Instead she went to the hut in which Swamiji lived. The door was always kept open so that the devotees could go in to him whenever they felt in need of him. Today, as Lee went in, there were as usual quite a few people with him, but the moment he saw her he said, "Ah, yes, I was expecting you."

Of course, she might have guessed: he always knew what she was going to do before she herself knew it; or perhaps it was he who guided her or compelled her in the direction he meant her to go.

"Come here," he said. "No, nearer. Here." He tapped the floor beside himself and she happily sat there. Evie was on the other side of him, with her pen and the notebook in which she took down his thoughts. She was so pale and weak and blonde that she was almost invisible. Swamiji with his dark, weathered skin and his orange robe glowed beside her. But he glowed anyway—anywhere—beside him anyone would become invisible.

"Evie and I are having one of our violent quarrels," he told Lee. "Now you've come you can decide between us. Evie is a very, very obstinate person."

"Swamiji," Evie deprecated mildly in her mild voice.

"She insists that 'transience' is spelled with an 'e' and not an 'a.' What am I to do? Everyone knows what fine English she speaks whereas your poor Swamiji, how can I open my mouth before her when the whole world knows that I'm only a very ordinary babu." He laughed and made them all laugh with him. He often referred to the fact that, while still in worldly life, he had held a position as clerk in the income tax office. "Now I'm very happy that you have come, Lee, because I hope you will please come out in my favor with regard to the matter of transience."

"Well—" hesitated Lee.

"You see! You see!"

"I can't help it," laughed Lee in apology.

"You can help it," teased Swamiji. "If you really love me as you pretend to do then how small a thing would be an 'a' or an 'e' to you." He was still smiling, but everyone realized that what he was saying now was on a different level. They strained forward, and Evie's ballpoint was poised ready. "In real love the things that are thought to be impossible turn out to be not only possible but so easy that it is little children who can do them the best. In the world of love two and two do not have to make four —transience does not have to be spelled with an 'e'—" Someone gave a little cry of admiration and Evie bent over her copy book and scribbled joyfully.

"Okay," said Lee. "With an 'a.' "

"Ah, no, you're cheating. You are pretending to believe but if you really believed you wouldn't have to pretend, it really would be an 'a.' . . . Where are your friends? Why aren't they here yet?" He looked at her with his half smile and his forehead pushed into quizzical wrinkles so that his cap rode up on his scalp. He always wore this cotton cap to cover his head, which was almost bald.

"You haven't written to them," he accused her.

"I did write—I showed you—"

"You forgot to post the letters." His narrow eyes were fixed on her, through her, shrewdly. She knew he could see right into her and it both thrilled and frightened her.

"Truly not, Swamiji."

"You are telling me lies," he said without relaxing his gaze.

"As if I *could* tell you lies," Lee said quite indignantly. She dared to look back at him but could only do so for a little while.

"Lee, Lee, you know I'm teasing." Now he was infinite gentleness. How he *knew* her, knew how to deal with her, handle her, make her his: and that not in private just between the two of them but before a whole room full of people.

Music at Rao Sahib's

There was another big party at Rao Sahib's to which Asha invited both Raymond and Gopi. It was like all Rao Sahib's big parties with a lot of rich people in beautiful clothes interspersed with one or two politicians in plain white homespun. Rao Sahib was pleased to see Raymond again and introduced him to the guest of honor who, this time, was a lady minister of state, a big woman in a thick cotton sari and huge, fat, naked arms. She was holding forth on the beauties of the simple life of which she herself was a strong adherent. Rao Sahib explained to Raymond that, before reaching her present eminence, she had been in charge of a communal center known as Shantinivas. It had been run entirely on Gandhian principles. Everyone spun their own clothes and drank goat's milk and pure water drawn from the well.

She looked at Raymond in a kindly manner and asked him at once whether he spoke Hindi.

"We had a Norwegian girl at Shantinivas, she learned to speak our language so beautifully. How she took to our ways! She always wore our sari and ate our vegetables cooked in our Indian way. Of course no tea or coffee—no one at Shantinivas takes tea or coffee. I would like you to visit Shantinivas," she told Raymond. "But please don't expect any of your Western luxuries—if you want those, then please don't come to Shantinivas, you may stay here at Intercontinental Hotel." She laughed, so did others. "Everyone gets up at five and after our ablutions and bathroom we sing our hymns. Beautiful! Then our simple breakfast. Everything at Shantinivas is simple and healthy. We have the old type of privies, and it has now been proved by German doctors that these are the best type for health, especially for women who are carrying."

Asha came and rather unceremoniously took Raymond away. "There is some trouble," she said. She took him out into the garden, where there were carpets spread on the lawn with cushions and bolsters for the recital of Indian music that was to follow. The musicians had already arrived. The accompanists were seated on the rug arranged for them, tuning their instruments, but the soloist was arguing with Sunita. He looked respectful but distressed. She cut him short, she said, "Of course your fee will be paid in full," and swept away. Asha stopped her just as she was entering the house to rejoin her party. "What can I do?" Sunita defended herself. "We must respect her wishes."

"What wishes?"

"She doesn't want the musicians. She wants us all to sing hymns, like at Shantinivas."

"To sing hymns? All that lot in there? Oh, my God!" Asha gave a shout of laughter.

Sunita said haughtily, "Rao Sahib and I think it is a very fine idea."

"You must be mad. Completely dotty." Sunita tried to get away but Asha wouldn't let her. "What about the musicians?"

"They will be paid."

"Paid! And their feelings?"

Sunita managed to get past Asha without making any comment about their feelings. Asha was indignant. She went straight up to the musicians, who were indeed very much upset. The accompanists were packing up their instruments with a sad, resigned air while the soloist paced up and down waving his arms so that the sleeves of his delicate white kurta flapped like angry wings.

"This is the way artistes are treated in this country today!" he shouted at Asha. "I will show you my press cuttings from foreign tours, then you will see what appreciation is shown abroad. Pack up!" he yelled at his accompanists. "Why are you waiting? Go home! There is no place for you in India today."

"Wait," Asha said. She picked up some cushions and began to stagger away with them. She shouted for servants to come and help her. She ordered them to roll up the carpets and pick up the bolsters and carry them to another part of the garden. They were reluctant but did not dare disobey her, especially as she herself was working with such vigor. Raymond tried to restrain her but she wouldn't hear him. Loaded down with cushions, she said that those who wanted to listen to music could listen to music and those who wanted to sing hymns could sing hymns. When he asked where the hymn singers were going to sit now that she was carrying all the arrangements away, she laughed crazily and said they could sit on the grass, what else, what did he think, that there were carpets and cushions at Shantinivas?

"We're starting now," she said. "Go in and tell them."

Raymond hesitated, but when she said, "All right, I'll go myself," he went to prevent worse from happening. He didn't know whom he should appeal to. Sunita and Rao Sahib were inviting people to come outside so that the hymn singing could start. No one seemed very eager, and they tended to linger over their drinks and wherever they could to help themselves to new ones from the trays that the bearers were still carrying around. Raymond made his way through the crowd, skirting the circle that surrounded the lady minister. He found Gopi in a quiet corner at the back of the room; he was sitting on a small brocade sofa with an extremely attractive girl in gold tissue whom he appeared to be entertaining very well. It seemed a pity to disturb them.

"Asha's calling you," Raymond said.

"This is Promila," Gopi said. "She is called Pam for short and she is studying psychology at Miranda House. She has promised to psychoanalyze me."

"Oh, no," said the girl. "I wouldn't like to hear your dreams."

"They are beautiful dreams," Gopi said, looking into her eyes. She giggled and shifted a bit farther away from him, setting up myriad little tinkling noises from her earrings, her bracelets, her anklets, her toe-rings, and tiny bells inserted into her hair.

"Asha's calling you."

"I think I would be a very interesting subject for you," Gopi told the girl.

"Yes, I can see very well what sort of a subconscious you have. Oh, bearer, bearer!" she cried to a passing figure with a tray. "I'm dying for another lovely apple juice." The man stopped and she stretched out her hand for it. But she withdrew it again, for just then Sunita came up and announced that the hymn singing was about to start.

Strains of music sounded from the garden. Raymond saw Sunita's hostess smile fade and give way to a look of amazement and premonition. She hurried out and Raymond followed her. They found the sitar player at the expository stage of his recital. His accompanists sat behind him, swaying their heads to the music and nodding significantly at each other whenever he plucked a particularly exquisite note. Asha, the sole audience, had disposed herself regally in the middle of a carpet; she leaned against a bolster and with an extra cushion propped under her elbow for comfort. When she saw Sunita, she at once shut her eyes and was too absorbed in the music to see or hear anything.

The guests came streaming out of the house. Their party clothes glittered under the illuminations from the trees. The lady minister clapped her hands and they all sat in a circle on the grass. Sunita, with a last despairing look at Asha and the musicians, hurried to join them. But Raymond stayed behind; there was nothing he could do, so he thought he might as well enjoy the music.

It was very enjoyable. Liquid notes melted out of the sitar and trembled on the night air. There were no illuminations in this part of the garden, only moonlight; the fine white clothes of the musicians glimmered and so did the white flowers that bloomed like jewels on surrounding bushes. The raga had now reached the stage where the maestro was showing his skill at ornamentation. He strung and restrung his notes like pearls and each pearl had been rounded by generations of artistry. Such music demanded a quality of the ear as refined and a sensibility as delicate as the music itself. Raymond desired to give these but could not help being distracted by what was happening in the lit-up part of the garden.

Led by the lady minister, they had begun to sing hymns. They started off with Gandhiji's favorite hymn—a rousing tune and heartening words about the Oneness of God whether worshipped as Ishwar or as Allah. Unfortunately most of the guests did not know these words and they trailed behind the leader, who sang in a loud, manly voice, sometimes clapping her hands to rally the others along. They kept tripping up and some of them giggled at their own ineptitude, which made others sing louder in order to cover up. They sounded terrible.

Asha saw Gopi sitting in the circle on the grass. He was singing vigorously and sometimes he turned his head to smile at the girl in gold tissue beside him. "Go and get him," Asha whispered to Raymond, though at the same time she continued to sway her head to the music to make it appear that there was no slackening of attention on her part. Raymond also went on swaying his head, pretending he hadn't heard her, but she nudged him so that he had reluctantly to get up.

As he approached the other circle, the lady minister waved him into it. She rounded her mouth to sing the words more clearly and nodded at him to try and repeat them after her. *"Ishwar Allah Tere Nam,"* she sang, and the others sang—Rao Sahib and Sunita both trying to look as if they were enjoying themselves, singing wholeheartedly though like everyone else stumbling over the words. Gopi, however, seemed quite familiar with them and was able to sing out lustily; he was also one of the few people there to whom it came naturally to sit cross-legged on the grass. The girl next to him kept shifting uncomfortably, arranging her voluminous gold skirt this way and that; and although Gopi tried to teach her the words as they went along, she kept getting them wrong and that made her dissolve in giggles. Gopi too was amused. He seemed really to be enjoying himself, and not at all pleased when Raymond whispered Asha's message to him.

"Sabko Sanmati De Bhagvan!" the lady minister ended with a flourish. She turned to Raymond and translated the line for him: "Give us all good sense, O Lord!" she said, adding humorously, "Yes, and I think we need it—we Indians are not very famous for our good sense." That was a good joke spiced with truth and everyone appreciated it; and amid the general laughter she cried, "Come now, once again!" and in exhilarated mood began to lead them from the beginning: *"Raghupati Raghav Raja Ram*—louder!" she cried. "With all your heart and soul! Let Gandhiji himself hear us from up there!" Then they all raised their voices with hers, drowning the delicate strains that came softly sobbing from the other part of the garden, where Asha reclined alone against her silken bolster.

When Raymond came back without Gopi, she looked at him inquiringly. In reply Raymond shrugged. "He won't come."

"He *won't* come?"

"Sh."

The tabla player had now begun to accompany the maestro, and they were working themselves up to a contest where each tried to outwit the other with superior skill. The sitar flung a phrase of unmatchable beauty toward the tabla, which responded by not only matching but even surpassing it, so that the sitar was forced to try again: and so they continued to cap triumph with triumph, challenging one another to soar higher and higher and up to heaven if possible. Each of them secretly smiled to himself, and sometimes they also exchanged smiles in a mischievous way, for each knew what pride there was in the other's heart. They were too engrossed to be conscious of their audience, and by this time they had also reached a crescendo of noise under cover of which it was easy for Asha to question Raymond.

"What's he doing there?"

"Singing."

"Who's that girl? . . . Don't shrug like that! You look stupid. What did he say?"

"Nothing. How could he? He's singing."

Asha said a bad English word. After a moment she said, "Tell him I want him to come at once."

Raymond didn't answer. He smiled at and with the musicians, wishing he could be allowed to listen in peace and let his excitement mount with theirs.

"If you don't go, I shall go myself."

"Don't be a fool, Asha." He laid his hand on her knee to soothe her. "Why don't you just sit here and listen. It's so marvelous."

She pushed his hand away and got up and walked away. Once she looked back at him as if defying him to stop her. But he made no attempt to do so, and only looked after her in despairing resignation. He saw her step over several people in the circle and make her way toward Gopi. He saw those people stop singing to look up and gape at her. Rao Sahib started to his feet and tried to reach her but too late, for she had already got to Gopi and was standing over him. She appeared to be tugging at his hair; Gopi put up his hands to defend himself—she tugged harder—was she trying to pull him up by his hair? Whatever it was, it was sufficiently disturbing to stop the singing and the lady minister, who had been clapping in time with the hymn, remained frozen with her big arms held apart in mid-air.

Now the sitar and the tabla had reached their highest crescendo—higher than this it was not possible for human beings to go. Then there was nothing left but to cry "Enough!" in surrender and bend across playfully, gloatingly, triumphantly to slap each other's instruments and laugh. And Raymond cried "Bravo!" and they turned toward him, those two courtly artistes, and acknowledged his applause with humility and grace.

part II

THE HOLY CITY

Asha Packing

"Don't let her go!" Bulbul cried.

She flung herself flat on the floor and grasped Rao Sahib's feet in supplication. Rao Sahib tried—in vain—to shake her off, and at the same time looked helplessly at Asha, who was throwing things into a suitcase with grim abandon.

"Why are you doing this?" Rao Sahib appealed to her. But she didn't stop. "There is no need," Rao Sahib appealed again.

Asha turned on him for a moment. "You yourself should be telling me go away, get out of my house!"

Rao Sahib suppressed a sigh. How many scenes of this nature he had gone through with his sister! As always on these occasions, he was affected with mixed but strong feelings; to relieve them somewhat, he turned on Bulbul and kicked his feet in a renewed attempt to free them. Asha also turned on Bulbul, cursing her for a mischievous, wicked old woman, but in fact Bulbul rather enjoyed being the center of their attention. She released Rao Sahib and raised herself from her horizontal position on the floor to a more vertical one on her knees. She stretched her hands folded in prayer into the air and turned now this way to Rao Sahib, now that way to Asha, to implore them both. To Rao Sahib she said, "Don't let her go." To Asha she said, "Take me with you, don't leave your old Bulbul behind." She moaned in distress but all the same there was a glint in her eyes which looked not unlike enjoyment.

Rao Sahib and Asha knew it was not possible to stop her, so they ignored her instead. Rao Sahib sat down on the bed and said, "Why do you want to go?"

"I have to go," Asha said. She left off packing and became quite calm and sat next to him. "Not only because of what happened—oh, God!" she cried, remembering.

"It doesn't matter," Rao Sahib said. Actually, it did matter— the lady minister had been much offended—but for the moment, seeing his sister suffer so, Rao Sahib was prepared to forget.

"I want to go away," Asha said. "I want to leave everything behind. Give it all up."

Rao Sahib had heard her talk like that before. So had Bulbul. It threw the latter into a new paroxysm of distress and, pointing at the small suitcase Asha had been packing, she cried, "This is what she is taking!"

Asha had packed only her plainest, simplest saris, and just a few of them. Everything else was left behind. She said, "It is all I need from now on."

Rao Sahib asked, "Are you going to Banubai again?" He argued, "What use is that? You know what happened last time."

"Last time I wasn't ready yet."

"And now?"

Asha cried out loud, "What *else* is there!"

Rao Sahib wanted to help her only he didn't know how. He had never known how. Asha was so different from him, from Sunita, from everyone he knew: nevertheless he loved her. He said, "Why don't you learn Russian? It's good to learn different languages," he urged in reply to her look of surprise. "It needn't be Russian. Any language will do: for instance, Persian or Arabic would also be very good. Or Turkish. Don't cry, Ashi. I'm saying this only for your own good."

"I know," she said, crying more.

"You should have something to occupy your mind. And learning a new language is a very fine discipline."

She kissed his nose, making it wet with her tears, and said, "Let me go to Banubai. At least let me try with her."

Rao Sahib sighed in resignation. "Should I book your plane ticket to Benares?"

"No, no plane. I shall go by third-class train."

"Aie!" cried Bulbul in shock and horror.

"I don't care at all," Asha told Rao Sahib. "What does it matter if I travel third-class or first-class air-conditioned? That's nothing. Really, I'm so tired of it all. Of all this," she said, plunging her hand among the silks billowing all over the bed and the floor where she had tossed them in her frenzy of packing. Now she tugged at the first one that came to her hand—a rich orange sari with a gold border—and threw it toward Bulbul. Bulbul caught it skillfully. Asha pulled out another one and was about to throw that as well when Rao Sahib put his hand on her arm to restrain her. He said soothingly, "You can do this later. Tell me about the ticket first."

"Tomorrow. Tonight. As soon as possible."

"Will you take Bulbul?"

"No. I don't want her. You keep her. Let her stay here in the quarters."

"If you want her, you can write."

Bulbul took no interest in this exchange, though it concerned her so intimately. She was busy folding the orange sari that had come her way. She turned it this way and that, stroking it lovingly, and also scratched her finger along the border to test the pure gold thread.

Gopi the Gay and Gallant Bridegroom

One of Gopi's uncles had come with a momentous proposal, which threw the family into a turmoil of excitement. Only Gopi refused to be excited; in fact, he refused to discuss the matter at all. This necessarily dampened everyone's spirits, for without Gopi's cooperation nothing could proceed.

The proposal the uncle had brought was for one of the sisters —aged nineteen, and certainly high time for her to be married —and it was from a prosperous family in Benares, the owners of a sugar mill. The boy was eminently suitable, twenty-two years old and after studying for a B.A. had already entered the family business; a tall boy, a little dark in complexion perhaps but otherwise handsome, healthy, and sober. The uncle had brought a photograph, which was scrutinized by all the family, and the sister in question managed to get a peep too, after which she became very quiet and introspective. The boy also had a younger sister whom her family desired to settle at the same time; and what could be more desirable than a double wedding, for as everyone knew such double ties within a family strengthened the bonds of mutual interest and affection. The uncle had also brought a photograph of the girl and everyone looked at it eagerly except Gopi, who refused to look at all.

His uncle urged him: "With such a family your whole future is assured." But Gopi said nothing. He was aware of the desperate looks all the women were throwing at him and the way they hovered round him. The uncle's tone became a mixture of cajolery and testiness: "At your age I was married, settled, one child, another on the way." Gopi looked with heavy dreamy eyes into the distance, attempting to hear, see, think nothing. The uncle's testy note increased. "Yes, in those days we were not asked—when the family said we were to be married then we were married, finished, no talk." Gopi's expression did not alter, only his eyes blinked once as he continued to stare into fathomless space. "And that was the right way!" suddenly shouted the uncle and banged his fist so that the teacups rattled on the tin tray.

Gopi's mother came hurrying up, making soothing shushing sounds. The uncle was trembling, and it was evident that there

108

were many harsh things on his tongue; but he controlled himself, thus bowing to the spirit of the times. Nowadays young men could no longer be commanded by their elders as of old, but some show had to be made—God knows why—of consulting their opinions. As if anyone that age could have any opinions! Anger swept over him again; he poured tea into his saucer and sucked it up, trembling with emotion. Gopi's mother looked at Gopi imploringly; at the same time she slowly passed her hand over his back round and round in a massaging movement as she had done when he was a baby suffering from indigestion. This affectionate hand passing soothingly over Gopi's back burned him with red-hot irons of reproach. He knew exactly what it was saying—please, for my sake, you're my good son, and what about your sister? Round and round it went, tirelessly as only a mother can be tireless.

Gopi got up so abruptly that his mother started back and his uncle had a shock and spilled tea out of his saucer. Gopi dashed out of the room. One of his sisters was hanging up clothes on a line strung across the veranda. He brushed past her and went into their second room, in which he found some more sisters and their friends. They were all sitting on the floor with their knitting and when he came in they looked up at him and burst out laughing as if they had just been talking or at least thinking about him in a special way. Seeing all these round young faces laughing up at him, he felt better, and when they shifted to make room for him in their circle he was glad to sit down there. He had always enjoyed the company of these girls and had grown up playing games and having jokes with them.

Now they were playing an old favorite called the alphabet game. They went through the alphabet and round the circle, each having to say a particular thing beginning with a particular letter. They had been through films, countries, names of people they knew, and had got on to animals. Gopi joined in with zest. A—for ass, for antelope, for ant, for anteater—as they went round, the girls in the latter part of the circle were having difficulty thinking up new ones and Gopi rushed in to help them with cheeky suggestions. "Alephant!" he shouted and was slapped for it, "Alpana!" he said, mentioning the name of one of the girls, and promptly two of them gagged him by holding their hands over his mouth. Then they got on to B—buffalo, bison, and bird—but the fourth girl looked mischievously at Gopi and, sticking out the tip of her tongue, said, "Bridegroom!" That was a lot of fun for all of them—yes, then the tables were turned on him and how they giggled and mocked at him and called him "Gopi the Gay and Gallant Groom." He took it in good part, he loved being teased by them. Then the next girl carried the joke further—"Bride!" she said—so that they all looked at Gopi's sister, for whom the proposal had come, and it was her turn to be teased. Overcome with shyness and pleasure, she hid her face behind her veil but managed for a second to peep at Gopi over the top of it. He interpreted this glance in a way that was not agreeable to him, and it threatened to spoil his enjoyment. Only he wouldn't let it, so firmly he cried, "Bear!"—to which they protested it wasn't his turn, but he outshouted them with "Boar!"—"Bee!"—and "Bull!" and finally called the name of one of the girls—"Bina!"—and then "Beautiful Bina!"—and for this they all turned on him and beat him with their slippers till he hid his head in his arms and laughingly begged for mercy.

With Banubai

Asha's life with Banubai was simple but not dull. Banubai lived in a house by the river; it was an old house with many unexpected little rooms and verandas in which unexpected activities went on. One room held the offices of the University of Universal Synthesis and also served as the living quarters of its founder-president; an exponent of the Kathak school of dance held his classes on a veranda; in another room a scholar of the Purva-Mimamsa philosophy was editing his papers. Many people came

110

and went, and most of them were visitors for Banubai. She liked to help people and give them spiritual comfort, so they came to her and she talked to them. She wasn't in the least surprised to see Asha turn up; in fact, she said she had been expecting her. Asha shared Banubai's simple meals and at night she rolled out a mat on the floor of Banubai's room and lay down to sleep on it. She had left all her jewelry behind and wore only white cotton saris. She was at peace.

This may have been partly due to the atmosphere of the city, which was an ancient and holy one, but mostly it was the effect of Banubai's personality. Banubai was an extraordinary woman. She came from a rich Parsi family and had had a pampered upbringing and the best education possible at convent schools in India and finishing schools abroad. But she had always been an unusual person with unusual gifts. She could look deep into other people's personalities, and it enabled her to have so immediate an intuition of what activated them that it was often possible for her to tell them something about their past and make a guess at their future. She gained quite a reputation that way, and people began to come to her for guidance. At that time she was still living with her parents in Bombay in a large rococo Edwardian house. It was a strange experience for her parents to have all these people coming to visit their daughter, and it was only because they realized that Banubai was too special a person to be kept only to themselves that they managed to tolerate these visitors who brought their Hindu smells of asafetida and sweat among the Persian carpets, French furniture, and English silver.

Her reputation was not only established among poor people —always the first to recognize a saint—but extended to the educated classes. She even had a number of sophisticated, highly Westernized visitors, and if most of them came in the first place to see her as a curiosity, some of them were truly impressed by her powers. That was how Asha had first come to her—many years ago when Asha was still young and beautiful and Banubai in early middle age. Asha had come with a party of friends; it had been a sort of outing for them, in between some other social events. Banubai didn't take much notice of any of the friends but she was at once interested in Asha. It was as if she saw something in her that others couldn't see. She told her that she had a spiritual nature, and although the friends tittered, Asha suddenly became very serious. When it was time to leave, she told her friends to go ahead and she herself stayed behind and had a long talk with Banubai. That was the beginning of their association, and although many years passed during which Asha felt no need of her, in her moments of deepest crisis she often turned to Banubai.

Banubai's parents were dead now, the Bombay house was sold, and Banubai lived in Benares in a few rooms rented in the crowded old house on the river. But really it was only outwardly that there was any change. Banubai was old now but only in her body; her spirit remained as it had been. She had lost all her teeth and had never bothered to have a new set fitted, but her smile was as radiant and childlike as before. She was tiny and skinny and her face had puckered itself around the cavern of her toothless mouth; for many years now she had always worn the same rather bizarre costume that she had devised for herself—a pair of men's wide cotton pajamas, a loose shirt over them, a mass of bead necklaces, and a turban wound around her head. She perched on the edge of a bed, bright as a bird, with bright eyes and a bright, bright voice.

"Oh, you'll never change!" cried Asha, overcome with admiration of her friend's ever youthful spirits.

"And you too will never change," said Banubai.

At that Asha groaned, for she felt it like a stone sitting on her —all the change that had come over her since she and Banubai had first met.

But Banubai insisted, "You are still the same, always the same." She sucked in her cheeks as if to suppress a smile. "I'm sure you have been having another love affair?"

112

Asha admitted as much by flinging her hands before her face in shame.

"You see. Always the same. . . . And with a very handsome young man?"

"Oh, Banubai, Banubai!" Asha was in pain but she was also half laughing. How good it was to be known and understood so deeply! She said, "Banubai, what shall I do?"

"What have you come here to do?"

"Just to be with you."

"That's enough, then."

And, for the time being, Asha also found it to be enough. Banubai had a little girl servant to cook her meals but her cooking was not good enough for Asha, who pushed her aside and took over from her. Asha was a marvelous cook and she enjoyed it too. She squatted over the bucket of coal, which constituted Banubai's kitchen arrangements, and she stirred and stirred in little pots, and sang as she stirred, and took a pinch of this and a little bit more of that, and flung it in and stirred again, and superb smells unfolded throughout the house. Banubai adored these dishes that Asha prepared for her, and she licked everything up and then she licked all her fingers one by one. They also sent food down to the founder-president of the University of Universal Synthesis, or sometimes they had him up to eat with them, which he enjoyed very much, for he was a lonely and frequently hungry old man. When she wasn't cooking or doing some other little household tasks, Asha listened to Banubai talking to all the people who came to see her with their problems. Sometimes tears came to Asha's eyes when she heard the terrible troubles that oppressed people; but Banubai was never downcast—she said it was good for people to suffer that way, it helped them to realize more quickly just what sort of stuff this world was made of and consequently to turn away from it into another, better path.

And Asha felt that yes, Banubai was right. What were all her troubles finally—what was the world, what was Gopi or her own

113

advancing years and frequent despair: it was all really nothing. This feeling came over her particularly in the evenings when she sat in the window of Banubai's house and looked out over the river, where boats went up and down and people dipped and prayed and the setting sun made the river pink and silver: then it was as if that expanse of holy water washed all heavy things away and left her calm and light.

Lee

We're in the middle of one of our domestic crises because the latest cook has run off again. They're always running off for some reason or other (usually they say they're not being paid enough). Swamiji discussed this crisis with Evie and Margaret and me—well, actually he didn't discuss it so much as dispose of it. Evie said she would do the cooking but Swamiji said no, he needed her, and then he told Margaret that under special decree she was appointed cook for the day. He was twinkling at her ever so humorously. She cried, "Oh, but Swamiji, I can't!" which was quite true, she can't. He said why not try and he would be very interested to taste the result of her experiment; he turned to Evie and me and asked wouldn't we be interested too. Margaret kept on protesting for a while but it didn't do her any good, in the end she had to go. Swamiji continued to joke with her, but she became quite still and serious and just before she went she did a funny thing: she bent down and touched his feet, sort of prostrating herself as she did this in utter humility. She seemed to like doing it. I was surprised but no one else seemed to be. I also somehow felt uneasy—as if something unpleasant had occurred.

Of course as always (how does he do this?) he knew what I was thinking. He said, "You've never done that to me." When I didn't answer, he kept on saying, "Have you?"—challenging me —till I had to say no. Then he smiled and looked at me sideways and wrinkled his forehead so that his cap rode up: "I think you're too proud to do it?"

I didn't know what to say. I couldn't admit I was too proud —I never felt proud with him, never—but it was true that I wouldn't do what I'd just seen Margaret doing.

"Lee is a very proud girl," he said to Evie. "Proud and obstinate," he added and turned again from Evie to me, and there was something different in his eyes now: it was as if he were measuring me, testing me for strength.

I said, "It's not true, I'm not."

"No? Then why don't you do it?"

He waited. But he knew I couldn't and seemed to be mocking me for this disability. At last he said to Evie: "You do it."

She got up without one moment's hesitation and bent down to touch his feet. She did it so beautifully. He patted her head which was bent before him but he wasn't looking at her, he was looking at me over the top of her and even triumphantly, as if he had proved a point against me. And I felt ashamed, I felt he was right and that he had proved a point against me—I *was* proud, I *was* obstinate—but I couldn't help myself, I still couldn't do what he wanted me to.

I left him so quickly that it was like running away. At that moment I wanted to run fast and far. But in fact I only got as far as the kitchen. The kitchen is at the outskirts of the ashram and it isn't a new hutment like the other buildings but an old brick shed that had been left standing on the land when Swamiji took it over. As I passed, I heard a groan from inside, so I knew Margaret was in trouble.

She was sitting on the floor with her knees hunched up and her head resting on them. She was making retching sounds. I told her to go outside and she ran and I heard her throwing up. I began to feel sick myself. The kitchen didn't have any windows, only a hole just under the roof; the walls had heated up like an oven, and there were a lot of flies buzzing about. I looked around for what could be done about cooking. There were three rusty bins, which I opened, and found lentils in one, rice in another; the third was empty except for a cockroach enjoying some bits of dried flour stuck in a corner. The only vegetables

115

were some onions in a basket. Out of these materials a meal had somehow to be cooked for the whole ashram.

I went out and started lighting the fire in the cooking range, which consisted of some bricks placed on the ground against the outside wall. I vigorously waved a bit of bamboo fan to get the sparks alight; it was terribly hot, with the sun and the fire. Perspiration ran into my eyes so that I had to keep wiping it away.

Just then Evie came up and said, "He's calling you."

I got irritated; I said, "Well, I can't come now, can I?"

"Where's Margaret?"

"Can't you hear her?"

Evie clicked her tongue in that gentle, pitying way she has. She stood there, watching me, so I told her to help me. She hesitated—I could see she was thinking how Swamiji would be cross if we didn't come, so I said, "He's going to be a lot more cross if there's no lunch." Then she pitched in. I must say, she was quick and efficient. We got the fire going, we cleaned the lentils and washed the rice and cut up the onions. After a while Margaret joined us, looking like death. I gave her some cauldrons to take to the pump to see what she could do about getting the dirt out of them. She came back after a time, looking rather hopeless, and with the cauldrons wet but no cleaner. Evie said, "Never mind," and snatched them from her and poured oil into them out of an old tin she had found. We slid the onions in and the oil splashed up high and a drop of it fell on Margaret's hand so that she cried out in pain. She put her hand to her mouth and sucked the sore spot but she said, "Okay, thanks, I'll carry on now."

We ignored her.

"He told *me* I had to cook today." She said it as if we were taking a privilege away from her and she wasn't going to let us. She tried to take the ladle with which I was stirring out of my hand but I said, "Watch it, you'll get burned again." She quickly jumped back. She stood watching us, not knowing what to do,

116

and then she went round to the other side of the shed and started throwing up again.

I said to Evie, "You know, I think there's something wrong with her. . . . I often hear her at night being sick like this."

"It's the heat," Evie said.

I didn't think it was only the heat but there was no time to argue. We kept on working till we got things going. Then we slacked off a bit and looked at each other. We both laughed—she looked terrible and I must have looked the same with my face red and wet and blackened with soot. We could still hear Margaret.

I said, "Why did he tell her that? He knows she can't cook."

Evie turned away from me as if she thought I'd said something that shouldn't have been said. I knew how sensitive she was about any word of criticism uttered against Swamiji; usually I'm sensitive in the same way but now I felt different. I said, "She should have said no."

Evie pretended to be very busy stirring. I could see her wince, as if really I had hurt her, physically hurt her. But I kept on. "Why didn't she say no? She should have. Why not?"

Evie blushed painfully and bent her face over the cooking. She stirred and stirred. At last she said, "The least we can do is obey."

"Why?" I cried. As if I didn't know the answer—usually I would have known it, I would have said myself, "in return for everything he gives us"—but now I was in a rebellious mood. And the strange thing was, it wasn't him so much I felt rebellious against but against myself, my own feelings.

Asha Writes Two Letters

Asha and Banubai often gossiped about old times. Together they recalled many incidents of Asha's past and they laughed a lot—especially Banubai, who was always bubbling over with laughter even at things that were not funny at all but sad.

117

"Why are you sad?" she asked one day when she and Asha had been recalling incidents from Asha's married life. "Those were happy, happy days. No? They were not good? Then you should be glad they are over. But to be sad—for what?"

"It was my fault. I was to blame. Everyone warned me—Rao Sahib pleaded with me on his knees—"

"Rao Sahib is a fool," Banubai said. She had been the only person to encourage Asha to get married. She had liked Asha's husband very much and said that, in spite of his faults, he had a pure and beautiful soul. Later, when the troubles had started, she had always taken his side against Asha.

"You only liked him because he was handsome," Asha accused her.

That made Banubai laugh a lot. It was true, she was fond of handsome men and liked to make a fuss of them. "What about the new one?" she asked. "Is he nice-looking?"

Asha shut her eyes, as if unable to encompass Gopi's beauty in thought or words.

"Tall?"

Asha shook her head.

"Slim?"

Asha nodded, trying to suppress her smiles.

"Big eyes?"

Asha showed how big. Banubai drummed her knee and opened her mouth wide with pleasure. Then Asha took a sweetmeat and popped it into Banubai's laughing mouth to silence her. Banubai chewed gaily. She loved sweets as much as nicelooking boys, and Asha often bought her soft crumbly milksweets, which she could easily mash between her gums.

Although Banubai lived on a spiritual plane, she had retained a lively interest in the world and all its passing show. "Leila," she called it, or "God's play." She said that we owed it to Him to be fascinated by Him in all His divine moods and aspects. So she wanted to hear every detail of Asha's life—about her apartment in Bombay, and the parties she went to, and all her friends. She was particularly interested in Lee, and often urged Asha to ask Lee to come and visit them. She didn't like it that Lee was staying with Swamiji.

"Is he a dangerous person?" Asha asked.

Banubai wouldn't commit herself, though she made it clear that, if she had a mind to, there was much she could tell about him, and all to his disadvantage. Asha became worried. She knew how much harm these sorts of people could do once they got a hold over someone. She decided to write to Lee and went up on the roof where she could sit undisturbed. Even when she had finished writing, she did not go down again. It was evening time and the steps leading down to the river were getting crowded. Boats went up and down and the people sitting in them chanted to the setting sun, and some of them floated little paper boats loaded with candles and flowers. On the steps just below Banubai's house there was the usual concourse of widows. They all looked alike, for they had all shaved their heads and were so thin and old that not much was left of their bodies; they wore white cotton saris with nothing underneath, so that their emaciated arms and shriveled, hanging breasts were visible. They had come to the holy city to purify themselves of all the desires of the senses, and now they lived only to pray and die.

They were splashing about in the water, and their voices came faintly floating up to Asha. They were cackling and singing. They were happy. To want nothing except to pray—that was indeed happiness! Asha herself felt heavy with bad thoughts and desires. The lively festive scene moving up and down on the river and the bright orange sun setting into it and flushing the sky with colors that were reflected back from the water— all this did not lead her to anything higher but increased her worldly longings. It was Banubai's fault. Banubai should not have asked her all those questions about Gopi. Now Asha could not stop thinking of him—and to think of him was to desire him unbearably. The pad of writing paper on which she had written to Lee was still balanced on her knees, the pen still in her hand. It trembled in her hand. But she knew she had no right to write to him. The only thing she still had a right to in life was to be like those widows splashing in the holy water below. She shut her eyes and begged for help to overcome her temptations. But that day her prayer was not granted, and when later she went down to the post office, she was carrying two letters to post.

Lee and Swamiji

Swamiji smiled and said, "You're angry with me, I can see."

He had sent everyone away. They were alone together under the tree. There was only one full-grown tree inside the ashram, a huge banyan with ancient gray roots spreading in all directions. It was shady here and quite cool; there was even a little breeze rustling about among the leaves. He had never done this before—sent everyone away so that they could be alone together. In fact, they had never been alone together.

"Tell me why," he said, "so that I can try and improve."

Lee hardened herself against him. She said, "You know Margaret can't cook."

He laughed: "Is that all?"

"You made her do it. You *bullied* her."

"Bullied . . . bullied . . . I like that word. Do I do it to you also? Tell me."

He leaned forward; his eyes were screwed up and the tip of his tongue protruded mischievously from between his teeth. Lee didn't like the way he looked at that moment—there was something in his expression that made her turn her face away from him.

"Look at me," he said lightly. When she remained with her face averted, he said it again, in the same light tone, but when still she did not turn, he put out his hand and grasped her chin and turned her face toward himself. She cried out at the touch of his hand.

He compelled her to look into his eyes. She was aware of nothing but his eyes. They were quite different from usual—no longer narrow and shrewd, they appeared enormous and glowed and burned with a supernatural power. Looking into them was more than she could bear, but he would not let her look away. He raised one forefinger and slowly, slowly he brought it forward and while she watched it, in fear and fascination, he finally brought the tip of it to rest between her eyes. Again she cried out. There was something like an explosion in her mind and circles of light sparked and revolved within its pitch-black night; all the time she remained aware of his eyes. "Lee, Lee!" a voice called as if from far away, but it was his voice.

He took his forefinger away again. "Why are you crying?" he asked.

She said, "I'm not." But when she put her hand to her eyes she found she was. She felt amazed and ashamed; she hadn't cried in years.

"Now you will say that I'm bullying you also." He smiled gently. "But you like it when I bully you. Isn't it?"

He laid his hand on her small breast. He did this quite casually and as if it didn't mean anything to him. But what a lot it meant to her! She trembled and shuddered as she had never done before for anyone. He said, "How small you are. Like a child, a tiny girl." But he took his hand away again and said, in quite a different voice, "I have a letter for you."

He took it out of his orange robe and held it before her eyes. "Who is it from?"

She shook her head. She didn't know, and she didn't care. At that moment she couldn't care for anything.

"It's from Asha," he said. He drew it from its envelope, which had already been opened, and showed it to her. She put out her hand to take it but he drew it back again. "She is quite near to us," he informed her. "She is staying with a lady called Banubai. Quite a famous lady," he said, smiling in a way that suggested he knew more about Banubai than she might like him to know. "Now I think you're angry that I opened your letter."

"What's it matter?" Lee said.

"Really? You're not angry? You don't mind it?"

She put up her hand in a gesture that begged him not to tease, not to play with her in this way.

"You're glad I opened it? . . . Say that. Say you're glad I take all things away from you and do what I like and how I like with you."

After a longish silence Lee said yes.

He gave her a smile that was full of triumph for both of them. He ran his eyes over the letter again and said, "She wants you to visit her."

"When?"

Again he smiled in the same way. "When *I* say," he said, and then he tore up the letter and threw the pieces to the ground.

Raymond Writes to His Mother

". . . From your air of quiet reasonableness I deduce that you're cross and Uncle Paul is cross too. Am I really as valuable to the firm as you both make out? I wish I could believe it. Yes, I know I said one year but that was before I came, before I ever knew what I was going in for. It's impossible to explain to you, darling, or to anyone who hasn't actually been here—but this is not a place that one can pick up and put down again as if nothing had happened. In a way it's not so much a country as an experience, and whether it turns out to be a good or a bad one depends I suppose on oneself. Well, no more of this what you call abstract talk—which in any case is for you alone. For Uncle Paul I would add that I'm working on this study of shrines about which I wrote to you both and which I feel might be an interesting idea for the firm sometime in the future. A slim volume of specialized interest. . . . No don't tell him that, he will have a fit. But seriously, it is a good subject and is involving me in some fascinating research. . . ."

Raymond's Fascinating Research

Gopi and Raymond were spending a lot of time together. They went around old monuments the way they used to and reclined under trees in beautifully laid-out old gardens. They often wore Indian clothes, exquisitely starched and embroidered kurtas over wide muslin pajamas. There were other young men similarly dressed reclining under other trees, and Raymond felt as if all of them, including himself and Gopi, had been arranged there very carefully amid the grass and flowerbeds and channeled waterways. Sometimes he and Gopi went away for weekend trips to nearby places, but it didn't really matter where they were. The setting and atmosphere seemed always the same, and Raymond was happy wherever they were. He thought Gopi was happy too. Gopi did not speak much, but Raymond liked these silences between them which seemed intimate and beautiful to him. He did not suspect that Gopi's thoughts were often far away.

Some time after Gopi had received Asha's letter from Benares, he and Raymond went on a weekend trip to visit one of Raymond's favorite Moghul tombs. To get there meant driving through the congested streets of an unattractive north Indian town and then crossing a bridge over the river and getting stuck in a noisy traffic jam of cycle rickshaws and bullock carts. But once the tomb was reached, there were the usual quiet green gardens and the old trees to sit under and no noise except birds singing. Inside the tomb it was cool and dark. A brass lamp cast a dim light over the catafalque from which there also smoldered rose-scented joss sticks.

Raymond peered lovingly at the paintings set in the dark niches of the outer chambers. There was a fish on a plate, fruits on a tree: somehow it was everything that was sensuous, beautiful, and desirable in the world. He called to Gopi to come near and share his enjoyment. Gopi wasn't interested, but he obligingly stepped closer. Raymond turned from the paintings to explain something to him and now, as he looked into Gopi's

123

sweet young face, he realized that it filled him with the same
sensations as the paintings so that he felt himself brimming over
like a glass into which too much wine has been poured.

At that moment Gopi said, "My family want me to get married."

Raymond's mood was so calm and esthetic that this information merely served to arouse a pleasing vision: he saw Gopi
dressed up in turban and garlands riding on a white horse to the
house of his bride. Bandsmen surrounded him, piping a rousing
tune, and young men danced.

"They have found a bride for me," Gopi said.

Raymond saw this bride—fully veiled, tinkling with orna-
ments; she stepped forward to receive Gopi as he crossed the
threshold of her home. She garlanded him.

"Do you want to get married?"

"No . . ." Gopi said but in an unsure way so that Raymond
laughed.

Raymond walked round the rest of the tomb, and when he
had seen enough, he went out into the gardens. Here there
were those real trees and real birds that he had seen distilled
on the walls inside, and how much more they sparkled now that
he had seen them in their essence. And Gopi was still with him,
walking by his side. Together they went and sat on the outer
wall, which overlooked the river.

"Just now it's so difficult for me at home," Gopi said. He
explained about his sister and the way she looked at him and
they all looked at him so that he felt guilty and terrible. When
he found Raymond sympathetic, he added, "I want to go away
for a while. I think I will go and stay with my uncle in Benares."
He glanced from under his lashes to see how Raymond was
taking this news.

Raymond took it well; he said, "I'll come too."

Gopi swung his legs and drummed his heels against the wall.
He was silent. Raymond said, more stubbornly, "I want to
come."

"It's so dull there. You wouldn't like it at all."

"Then why are you going?"

"I told you. . . . It's not good for me at home now—with all that—you know. . . ."

Raymond knew that Gopi was concealing something. Raymond's pleasure in the day went, and with it his good mood. He looked out over the river, which was sluggish with bits of refuse on it and a few broken-down barges. When he looked back into Gopi's face, he saw that it had become guarded and shrewd.

Gopi said, "There are some family affairs to be settled. I have to be there."

He sounded anxious to please and nervous of being asked too many questions. Raymond wanted to ask them but he knew that, if he did so, he would compel Gopi to lie to him.

Banubai Gives Counsel

A family in deep trouble had come to see Banubai. There were several women, several men, one or two children. All sat on the floor of Banubai's little room and looked up at her where she squatted cross-legged on her bed. The expression on their faces was one that Asha had frequently remarked in Banubai's visitors: a deep, ingrained despair lightened, as they gazed at her, by flickers of hope.

They had come with a bizarre story—but then, so many people who came to Banubai had such stories. Again and again Asha was amazed at the manifold byways of human affliction. This family had lost one of their members a few months ago. He had lain down to sleep as usual at night and next morning he was gone: simply gone. They searched and inquired everywhere but no trace of him could be found. He had taken nothing with him—he was in the nightclothes in which he had gone to sleep —all his money, all his possessions were left intact at home. Where was he? Had he lost his memory, got up in the night and walked away, and no longer knew where he was or who he was?

125

There was no question of his having run away—all had been normal that night—he had had a good supper of spinach and maize bread and then as usual he had drunk two glasses of water and lain down to sleep. He had talked about buying tickets for a weekend show at the circus which had recently come to town. Had he been murdered? But then how could anyone come into his house, into his bedroom, drag him away—and not a single member of that large family to hear a sound, not even the wife who slept by his side?

"Ah, you poor people!" cried out Banubai.

Silently they joined their hands and raised them to her in supplication.

"What do you want me to do?" she replied. "What can I do? I'm just an ordinary person like everyone else." She spread out her arms so that they could look at her and judge for themselves how ordinary she was: though she did not look so at all, with her strange clothing and the bright glow on her face.

They hung their heads. They were weary—it was so difficult to keep on hoping. They had been to many places already; for weeks they had been doing nothing but wander round to astrologers, fakirs, and others with reputed powers.

"Come here," Banubai said to the woman who was his wife. She grasped her hand, she opened and shut it, turned it over this way and that in great concentration. Everyone watched with renewed hope: perhaps there would be a revelation after all. But when Banubai had done this for some time, she pushed the hand away and motioned the woman to go and sit again on the floor among the others.

"I can't see anything. I can't tell you anything. Only this I know: that you are suffering. Day and night you are on thorns. You think this way, you think that way, and there is no relief in anything. You think of him wandering no one knows where, perhaps in some jungle, perhaps in a strange city, you think of him solitary and alone with no money and no clothes and perhaps not even knowing his own name."

126

A great sigh rose from them. It was as if they were begging Banubai to desist from tormenting them in this way. But she went on without mercy, and Asha knew that her cruelty was part of the cure she was offering them.

"Perhaps he is dead," said Banubai. "Then he is a corpse, but you don't even know in what condition: whether he is buried or unburied, burned or unburned, perhaps wild animals are eating him—no, you must listen! Because this is what you are listening to all the time, not from me, but from within yourselves. These are the thoughts and visions that trouble you without cease whether you are waking or sleeping. If you want to have peace of mind, then you must cleanse yourselves of these thoughts as of a sickness or evil. You must join your hands not to me and not to the astrologers and the policemen and the swamis and the babas and the matajis and God knows who else you are running to and perhaps paying out money to, not to them but to the One who has willed that it should happen so. If He wills it, He will bring him back; if not, then not—whichever way it turns out, you must submit within your hearts and know it is for the best. Now go," she ended, for suddenly she was utterly exhausted.

They got up and touched her feet and went out. Asha noticed that they looked somewhat lightened, that perhaps she had penetrated them with her words and done them good. It did not always happen—some people went away as unhappy as they had come—but Banubai did not care one way or the other. She gave what she could and was indifferent as to the outcome of her efforts. Now she lay on her bed, spent for the moment, a shriveled little old woman.

Asha bent over her soothingly. She massaged her feet and ankles. She said, "You give too much."

Banubai made a gesture of resignation that said what else was she there for but to give.

"People should spare you," Asha said.

Then Banubai opened her eyes. She said, *"You* should spare

me. . . . Don't stop, I like it," for Asha had left off massaging in shock. She started again and Banubai shut her eyes and relaxed. When she continued to speak, it was with her eyes shut and in a gentle voice. "Your restless thoughts are like pinpricks to me."

"I'm not restless, Banubai."

"Who are you thinking of at this very moment?"

Asha groaned. Then she said, "It's true."

"Does he know where you are? Have you written to him?" When Asha could not speak for shame, she said, "You see, I knew it. How can you try and hide yourself from me?"

"I wrote to him, 'I have gone away—I shall never see you again in this life—good-bye.' "

"And now all the time you are waiting for him to come."

Gopi in the Holy City

Gopi always liked staying with his uncle in Benares. This uncle was far more prosperous than the rest of the family. He was in business and had done well and built himself a brand-new house to a modern design. Here he lived with his family in great comfort. The main preoccupation of the family was food, and as soon as Gopi's aunt got up in the morning, her first thought was always what to cook. Besides the day's meals, provision had also to be made for snacks in between, and all the glass jars in the cupboards kept stuffed with homemade delicacies. Then there was a lot of cleaning to be done, for they were all very proud of the new house and every door handle had to shine and every colored stone in the terrazzo flooring to gleam like a freshly washed pebble.

Besides Gopi's uncle, there were also a son-in-law, an elder son, and a younger son, all of whom were employed in the family electrical business. However, it did not take up too much of their time and they were left free to spend many hours at home reclining in the most comfortable room in the house. They were frequently joined by other male relatives and friends and neighbors who came to share in the unending stream of refreshments that were carried in by the women. There was much laughter and jokes and nice songs from the radio. Although some of the jokes were hearty and male, everything was kept very respectable, for they were a decent Hindu middle-class family with no drinking or smoking or other bad habits. Sometimes there were family outings—picnics to a nearby beauty spot, or a visit to the cinema if some new picture had come to town.

Gopi joined in all these activities with pleasure. He was very friendly with his cousin Babloo, a boy just a year or two younger than himself and with the same interests. Babloo looked up to Gopi and was sincerely anxious to learn from him. Babloo and his friends had the reputation of being the most advanced group in town. They spent a good deal of their time in a new discotheque, which had been opened on the former site of a disreputable hotel. They were very proud of this place, which played not only the latest Hindi film songs but also well-known Western hits. Gopi joined them there and pretended to be impressed by the music, the bright colors, and the groovy slogans on the walls. He also pretended interest in Babloo's friends and their outdated conversation. They admired him for his Delhi sophistication and his superior knowledge of girls, clothes, restaurants, films, and film people. Often their mouths dropped open in wonder as they listened to him and he leaned back in the chair and talked in a casual, throw-away manner while flicking ash off a cigarette.

The main topic of interest was always girls, and here Gopi had a lot to say with which to astonish them. Babloo nudged his friends on either side of him with his elbows and said, "Did you hear that?" He also threw out tantalizing hints that at night, in the privacy of the bedroom they shared, his cousin let him into many more secrets and told him things that, if his friends could but get an inkling of them, would make each hair on their bodies stand up in wonder. But actually Gopi was in this respect a disappointment to his cousin. In the past, as soon as they had turned off the light, Babloo would say "Now tell" and Gopi would begin to tell—all in the greatest detail and getting more and more extravagant as the hours wore on. But this time it was not like that. Gopi fell asleep as soon as the light went off, and though Babloo called his name several times, he continued sleeping. Then Babloo turned over in disappointment and went to sleep himself, taking solace in whatever dreams came to him.

But Gopi was not really asleep. He lay in the dark, thinking. He thought mostly about Asha. It was for her sake that he had come to Benares, but he had not yet been to see her. Every night he said "tomorrow," but when morning came there was always something else to do, and he was partly sad and partly relieved not to have to see her that day either. He could not account for this behavior in himself. He also could not account for his reluctance to reveal even her name to his cousin. When he had had nothing to tell, he had made such a lot of it. Now that he really had something—and what a tale! if Babloo could but guess at some small part of it!—now he kept quiet and pretended to be asleep. He could not understand himself. However, as he was not much used to self-analysis, he turned over on his side and was soon really asleep.

Plans for Departure

The mission was closed. There was a lot to do—the house to be sold off and all their affairs wound up—and Miss Charlotte was so busy that she had no time to indulge in regrets. But she was worried about the servants—Solomon the cook, Joseph the bearer, a couple of ancient ayahs called Rosie and Salome—who had all been with the mission for many years. They lived at the back of the house in a row of brick quarters and had multiplied and proliferated with children and grandchildren. Now they would need new jobs and new homes. Miss Charlotte spoke to Raymond about this problem. She especially tried to engage his interest on behalf of Solomon the cook who, she said, made excellent roast potatoes. She wondered whether there might not be a job for him in the High Commission. She looked at Raymond hopefully. Of course, she said, the meals in the mission had always been rather simple but still . . . "Once you're a good cook, you're a good cook, don't you think so?"

"Quite," Raymond said.

He did not feel he could do anything for Solomon or the others. He was often being asked to help people to get jobs. There seemed to be so many people, but not all that many jobs. That same morning Shyam had come to him accompanied by a person whom he introduced as his cousin-brother. An affidavit was needed from Raymond to state that this cousin-brother had worked as his driver for the past two years. Raymond protested. "But I haven't been here two years. And I don't have a car."

Shyam said soothingly, "Only they want like that. For nothing. Just your name, Sahib." He had pressed a form on Raymond and a pen obligingly opened. But when Raymond had refused to sign, he had not been offended. He had said something to his relative in a reassuring undertone, and they had both gone away cheerfully. Raymond knew it was not the end of the matter but that Shyam would continue to work on him day after day. He would say, truthfully, "If you don't help, who else is there for us?"

Besides finding jobs for her servants, Miss Charlotte had many other problems. One of these was all the old English people whom the mission had been caring for. Now she was trying to make arrangements to put all of them together in a home in Madras where they could be looked after by the church. But it was a very difficult task to persuade these old people to move out of their present homes. In a week or two, as soon as she had got the sale of the house on the way to a settlement, she was going to start off and travel around to the various places where they were scattered. Most of them were in the hills—in Simla, Mussourie, Ooty, Mount Abu. It would certainly be a nice trip for her—quite a little holiday—but in the meantime who was going to visit her friends in the home near the mission who were so used to her twice-weekly appearances? She really didn't know whom she could ask to go in her place. There was a fractional pause, and then Raymond said, "I may be going away myself in a day or two."

"How lovely for you. Another tour?"

"Well, no, actually, I'll be going with a friend. He's visiting his uncle in Benares."

"Benares is such a fascinating place."

"Yes," Raymond said. "I'm looking forward to it."

Raymond Arrives in the Ashram

Raymond had difficulties in finding the ashram. He had hired a taxi at the airport and they drove around for a long time before discovering that the ashram was not actually in the holy city but several miles outside it. By this time it was the driver's mealtime and he said he could not go any farther, so Raymond had to get out with his suitcase. They were now in the middle of the holy city in one of a network of closely packed streets where tumble-down houses were perched above ramshackle booths. Raymond stood in the sun waiting for a taxi but the only transport available were cycle rickshaws. He had always looked with embarrassment on the passengers sitting at the back of these frail vehicles while the emaciated driver pulled and panted. However, when no taxi came and the sun got hotter and drew all sorts of fetid smells out of rotting vegetables and other refuse, he could hold out no longer. The rickshaw took him to a bus depot and, after a journey in a bus, he was deposited in the middle of what seemed to be an endless stretch of barren plains. Carrying his suitcase, he began to walk. The day ended, the sun began to set, the heat abated. Raymond did not notice. Sometimes he sat down to rest. He never thought he would find the ashram—he never thought he would find anything, or arrive anywhere—but suddenly, right there in that desert, there was a huge board which said in huge lettering: *Universal Society For Spiritual Regeneration In The Modern World.*

Swamiji took it for granted that Raymond had come to stay in the ashram. He was glad. He assigned a place to him in one of the hutments, and Raymond lay down on a string cot and was at once asleep. When he woke up, it was morning and Lee was standing over him saying, "He wants to see you as soon as you're up."

Raymond looked at her closely. At first sight she looked the same—unlike the other disciples, she did not wear a sari or an orange robe—but there was something in her face, her expression, that was different.

"I wrote you such a lot of letters," she said. "You never answered. And he kept asking for you."

"Has Gopi been here?" When she was silent, he continued. "Have you heard from him? Do you know where he is?"

"Why, where should he be?"

"He's here in Benares. Staying with his uncle."

"So that's why you've come," Lee said.

For a while they were silent. Then Lee said, "I thought you'd come because of what I wrote."

To this Raymond said nothing.

"*He* thinks that's why you've come." She sounded both reproachful and unhappy. Raymond was sorry she should feel like that, but did not think himself to blame. He had not pretended that he had come on any business other than his own.

He asked, "You haven't seen him at all?"

"Who?"

"Gopi."

His face was strained, and Lee said, "My God, Raymond, are you still on that?"

"He just went away. He'd been talking about it and I said all right I'll come with you but he didn't seem to care for that and

133

one day he simply went off. Without a word to me," Raymond said, swallowing as if he were swallowing something hurtful and bitter, aggrieved like a woman.

"I hate to see you this way," Lee said.

"He sneaked away from me. Why did he have to do that? Does he hate me so much? I've tried hard to be nice to him— to make him like me and like being with me, and I thought he did, he *said* he did. But it seems I don't mean a thing to him. Not a thing. After all this time."

"Asha's here too."

After a pause Raymond said, "I didn't know that."

"She wrote to me," Lee said, stubbing her toe against the rough floor, embarrassed, not knowing whether she should have told him or not.

"No, I'm glad you told me," he said, guessing this. "He could have told me himself instead of all those lies. When did I ever try and stop him from seeing her? Did I ever say a word? On the contrary, I encouraged him—I even went along with him —the *hours* I've spent with those two. I never asked them to consider my feelings, and I'll say this for them, they didn't. But that's all right, I'm not complaining, I asked for it myself. . . . I shouldn't be saying all this to you."

"You shouldn't be saying it at all! You shouldn't *be* like this! No one should."

Both couldn't speak for a while. Raymond felt shaken but also relieved to have been able to talk to someone. Lee was upset too—to see him in this state which she knew to be deeply wrong.

"I'm glad you came," she said at last with feeling. "Even if it was for the wrong reason. After you stay here for a while, listening to him, or just being near him, it'll all change for you. You'll see. It'll just drop off and be nothing. All you're feeling now and everything that seems so important to you: you'll laugh at yourself. But I know it's no use my telling you—you'll have to learn for yourself, through him. . . . Are you all right in here?"

she asked, looking round the hut. "Which is your bed? This one? One string is broken. We'll get it fixed."

"I'm not staying here, you know, Lee."

She looked at him.

"I'm leaving this morning. Isn't there a hotel in town?"

"Yes, for American tourists," she said with scorn.

"That will suit me then."

"But I thought—and *he* thought—"

"I never said so."

She sat very straight on a bed, staring in front of her.

"You know I can't stay here," he said. "It isn't the sort of place I would ever stay at. You know that. I came to see you."

He noticed that she looked stricken and even afraid. She had always seemed invulnerable to him, but now he saw she was so no longer.

"What will he say?" she asked. She lowered her eyes. "He'll be angry." She really *was* afraid, he could see.

Swamiji Eats Lunch

But in fact Swamiji didn't mind at all. He even encouraged Raymond to go and stay in the hotel. He said that Raymond would be more comfortable there. He thanked him very sweetly for staying in the ashram for that one night and apologized for its shortcomings. Later he several times visited Raymond in the hotel. He seemed to like going there. The hotel was, as Lee had said, intended mainly for foreign tourists and had been made as comfortable as possible. It was fully air-conditioned and licensed to serve liquor, and there was a bar and a dining room with a buffet table at which cold cuts of meat were served. Swamiji always accepted the drink that Raymond offered, and usually had more than one; once or twice he stayed for a meal in the dining room and ate his way heartily through the full course, including the meat dishes. Sometimes he came alone, sometimes accompanied by Evie. Evie didn't have any drink, or any meat dish either. She sat with her hands folded in the lap of her white cotton sari, waiting for Swamiji to say it was time to go. Then she got up at once and they went home together on the bus.

Swamiji unfolded his plans to Raymond. He was trying to organize a lecture tour in the United States and, wherever he spoke, he would gather new disciples and found a new center for his movement so that a network would be established from one end of America to the other. On the way back he would also lecture in Europe and found other centers there. With the funds collected from these foreign tours, he would build a big comfortable air-conditioned ashram here in the holy city, on the very site where his present ashram stood. This ashram in India would remain the main focus of the movement, and Swamiji himself would spend some time every year in residence there. But mostly of course he would be traveling—going from one center to the other, lecturing, gathering new disciples, establishing new centers in new countries until he had covered the entire globe and his movement had become a worldwide religion uniting men of all creeds and all colors into one family and so bringing peace and harmony into the world.

It was, he explained to Raymond, essentially a movement of Today, of Now. In the old days men of high spiritual development had had only limited resources at their disposal with which to radiate outward; hence their influence had also been limited in scope. But nowadays, thanks to the developments of the modern world, everything could work jet-swift, enabling Swamiji's beams to penetrate into the farthest corner of the remotest country on the map. That was progress indeed! Nor would Swamiji stand in its way but on the contrary he intended fully to avail himself of all its manifold devices. He would travel everywhere by airplane and helicopter, and also multiply his presence by means of television appearances. The printed word would not be neglected, and besides syndicated articles about himself and his work in all leading newspapers of the world, there would be feature articles with illustrations in photo magazines. The more subtle points of his doctrine would be expounded in published book form—and here Raymond's advice would be particularly valuable to him, for he had heard from Lee, and heard with interest, that Raymond was in the publishing business. He nodded to Evie, who was nursing a cloth parcel in her lap. Evie unfolded the cloth, which was snow-white and tenderly embroidered by hand, to reveal a bulky manuscript within. This, said Swamiji, handing it to Raymond, was something of a first fruit of his literary labors—his and Evie's—a collection of his discourses and significant sayings up to the present time. Of course the work would grow and swell into many volumes, for there would be many more discourses and Evie had the habit of taking down his sayings every day. Meanwhile, however, he would be glad to make a first offer of the present manuscript to Raymond's firm.

Raymond liked him. He found him to be cheerful and amusing company, a relaxed person though giving an impression of tremendous energy. Raymond liked it best when he came without Evie—he found it difficult to ignore her silent presence and felt compelled to keep offering her things: "You're sure you wouldn't care for a drink? Just a tomato juice? a Coke? a glass of water?" In reply, she put up one frail hand as if to say please don't bother about me, I'm not here, or if I am, I am as nothing. But—unlike Swamiji, who did so without effort—Raymond could not regard her as nothing, and consequently it was a relief to him when she was left behind. He did wish, though, that in her place Swamiji would sometimes bring Lee and once he even asked him to do so. But Swamiji said no. He said Lee wasn't ready yet to come out of the ashram and mix freely in the world.

"But if Evie can come—" Raymond ventured.

Swamiji vigorously waved his hand to and fro in a negative movement. He couldn't speak, as his mouth was full of fish. They were in the hotel dining room, where Swamiji was Raymond's guest for lunch.

"Evie is quite a different case," Swamiji said when he could. "It doesn't matter where she goes, what she does, nothing can shake her." He gestured to a bearer to bring the tray round again, and the man came hurrying over. Raymond had noticed that everyone was very eager to serve Swamiji. His air of authority pervaded the dining room. He was also an object of curiosity to the other diners who were mostly elderly Americans. It was not every day that they could see a holy man in an orange robe sitting right there having lunch among them. Swamiji remained quite undisturbed by the attention he was getting and went on enjoying his food.

"Evie is firm," he said. "I have made her firm. But Lee—" he laughed. "There is still a lot of work to be done with Lee."

"What sort of work?"

"Ah, Raymond, that is a very long story." He pointed his finger into his empty beer glass and the steward himself came quickly to refill it. "Thank you, my son," said Swamiji, and drank heartily. "You see, Lee is now in my hands. She is my responsibility to mold and to make. But before I can mold and make, I have to break. The old Lee must be broken before the new Lee can be formed, and we are now only at the first stage of our task."

Raymond blushed bright pink. He could not speak for a while, afraid that if he did he might speak more rudely than he would wish. Swamiji asked, "Is this the butter knife?"

"That one," Raymond said, pointing to it.

"Ah," said Swamiji gratefully and proceeded to use it. He was always asking about these little points of etiquette. He was preparing himself for his foreign tours and did not wish to do small things incorrectly. He learned very fast—perhaps because he was so unembarrassed about it—and ever since his first visit to the hotel dining room had made giant strides forward in his table manners.

"But who decides that?" Raymond managed at last to ask in a steady voice.

138

"Decides what?"

"When someone has to be"—Raymond swallowed, trying to speak without distaste—"broken and remade."

"The guru decides it." Suddenly Swamiji laughed at the expression on Raymond's face. "But that is another very long story and why should I spoil your lunch?"

"No, I want you to tell me." When Swamiji continued to laugh and shake his head, he said, "Why not? You think I wouldn't understand?"

"With your mind perhaps yes, but there where it really matters—this fish is quite delicious, I think I shall have one more little piece, what about you?"

"And Lee—does she understand where it really matters?" He squirmed on the last phrase.

"She wants to. She desires to. She longs to with all her being." He put down his fork and looked sideways at Raymond with his shrewd, narrow, laughing eyes: "But you don't want to, you don't even begin to want to."

"That's true."

"So we can be excellent friends, and I think we are excellent friends, you and I, isn't it, but I can never be your guru."

Raymond laughed. "Perhaps that's just as well."

"But of course! Of course! It is a great relief to me. Do you think it is easy," he said, smiling but serious, "to be someone's guru? To take over this responsibility so that the other person need do nothing but have trust and faith? Only to say: now I am yours, take me, do what you like with me; and so this person is in the guru's hands and the guru carries this person over stick and stone."

As he spoke, his eyes darted here and there and he was aware as always of everything that went on around him. He was aware, for instance, that one of the American ladies at the next table had been trying to catch his eye; so he allowed it to be caught and even answered with a smile which made the lady blush like a girl, and drop her eyes, and pat the pearls around her elderly neck.

"Yes, Raymond, I think you are a little bit angry with me about Lee, isn't it? Perhaps you are thinking—look at him, the old rascal, he comes here, he eats and drinks and enjoys to his heart's content, while my poor friend is asked to give up everything. But please understand—it is only when you have given up all enjoyment so that it is no longer enjoyment, it is only then that you can have these things back again. How far Lee is still away from this goal! I have to help her and guide her every step so that she will know that everything is nothing and also that she herself is nothing. Only then can she belong to me as the disciple must belong to the guru."

The bearer came with the next course but Swamiji ignored him, for he was taken up with what he was saying: he leaned toward Raymond and his eyes did not look shrewd or laughing now but they glittered in a strange, passionate way. "I want her to be mine. She must be mine completely in heart and soul and —yes, Raymond," he said, easily able to read his companion's thoughts, "in body also, if I think it necessary. That is quite by the way only. Ah," he said, turning at last to the bearer who had been patiently, even reverently, waiting, and helping himself from the tray, "I think this is called roly-poly pudding, isn't it? A great favorite with me."

And he smiled—first at the pudding, and then, his eyes beginning to rove and dart again, at the American lady at the next table who had been greedily awaiting this smile; and then his eyes roved farther, all round the dining room, at all the foreign guests eating their lunch, and he regarded them in a sort of easy, speculative manner as if one day perhaps, if he wanted to, if he cared to, they would all be his.

Gopi's Life Takes on Complexity

In the mornings Asha was quite domestic. She had all the rooms swept out and afterward she went shopping for her own and

Banubai's meals. She looked like any middle-class, middle-aged housewife in her plain cotton sari and a plastic shopping bag on her arm. That was perhaps why Gopi did not recognize her at first, not even when he came up quite close to her. But she had recognized him from a long way off—perhaps because he was already there in her thoughts, he was there all the time really even when she was thinking and doing something quite different.

When at last he saw her, he was so overcome by her changed appearance that he quickly averted his eyes, not wanting her to see the expression in them.

But she had seen. She said, "Yes, everything is changed now." She passed her hand ruefully down her face, which was innocent of all makeup. "And I'm glad it's changed," she went on. She didn't sound glad but she wanted to be. She also wanted to be glad that he had come upon her so suddenly before she could be tempted to improve her appearance. Now he could see her as she was, as she *wanted* to be. It was good—she was glad—and yet also how that look of his stabbed her!

Still looking away from her, he muttered, "I got your letter."

"I'm very happy with Banubai. She and I talk of so many things. All spiritual things," she said with a sigh. Then in a different tone—"When did you get my letter?"

"Two–three days ago." He was still muttering.

"I sent it four weeks ago."

"The post nowadays is terrible." But he saw himself that this wouldn't do and continued quickly, "I'm staying with my uncle. There is some family business, I have been very busy, every day I said today I will go but every day my uncle—and there is my aunt also—"

"You have been here all the time?"

"—and many cousins—"

"And only today you come to me? And here I sit waiting and waiting!"

He looked up at her. Her eyes were flashing, and now truly she looked like Asha again, and her voice too was like Asha's. He kept quiet, letting her scold him and not really listening—and indeed, she herself no longer quite knew or cared what she was saying, so that after a time the words died away and they both were silent. They were almost alone on the steps. It was late in the morning and there were just two shaven-headed old widows, one of whom stood in the river washing her length of cloth while the other was spreading hers out to dry. Smoke rose from a little stone hut in which a hermit lived and was cooking his midday meal. There was such peace and calm, it was like a presence and one that recalled Asha to herself.

She said, "I only wanted to see you to tell you that I'm a different person now." Except that having him there beside her again, she realized how far she still was from her goal. She shut her eyes. She said, "You had better go away."

"All right." He got up at once. He wanted to obey her and cause her no further pain. But he too was sad. He walked away from her sadly with his head down. He walked down the steps, toward the river, not thinking much but vaguely hoping that a boat would come quickly and take him away. He stood waiting on the same step as the old widow drying her cloth.

Asha called him back. She told him "Come tomorrow." She saw the surprise flitting over his face and it irritated her. She said, "Banubai wants to see you. . . . I want her to see you. It will be very good for you to meet with such a person." She spoke rather severely.

When Banubai first saw Gopi, she clasped her hands together in delight and gazed her fill at him; then she beckoned him close to her and pinched his cheek and finally—a very special treat reserved only for very special favorites—she opened the tin in which she kept her best sweetmeats and popped one into his mouth. "What about me?" asked Asha jokingly. "Don't I get a nice sweetie?" "Certainly not," Banubai joked back. "You're not a pretty little son like he is." And she ruffled his hair with a loving hand, and both she and Asha smiled and smiled at him while he, embarrassed but pleased, lowered his eyes so that his long lashes tickled his blushing cheeks.

Banubai encouraged him to come again and again. If he missed a day, she reproached him and told him how her heart had been restless for him. She said, "Now that I have found you again, I can't bear to be without you."

It appeared that Gopi had been her son not only in one but in many previous incarnations. They had been born under all sorts of different circumstances—once as queen and prince, another time merely as potter's wife and son—but always, throughout the ages, as mother and son: so was it any wonder that the moment she saw him she knew him again and that she felt for him the way she did. Gopi was greatly impressed by this information and gladly agreed to call her Ma and to treat her in every way like a mother—of course not like his own mother with whom he tended to be brusque and irritable but with all the reverence that a son traditionally owes to his mother whose blessing he craves more than food.

He went to visit her whenever he could and she rejoiced at the sight of him and often refused to see her other visitors when he was there, even those that had come with very grave problems. Asha of course was always there with them. It seemed to her that, under Banubai's influence, her own relationship with Gopi was also changing and that her feelings for him were beginning to be transformed into purely maternal ones. She enjoyed cooking tasty dishes for him and she loved touching him the way Banubai did—ruffling his hair or patting his cheek or holding his hand in hers; and it seemed to her that she was quite satisfied with that and wanted nothing more.

Gopi enjoyed their company and would have liked to spend a great deal of time with them. But it was not always easy for him to get away from his uncle's house, and especially not from his cousin Babloo. Babloo wanted to be with him all the time and accompany him everywhere. Whenever Gopi wanted to go off to see Banubai, he had to invent lies and excuses for Babloo or sneak away as best he could. Babloo soon guessed that Gopi was hiding something from him, and at once assumed that it was something to do with girls. This idea excited him unbearably so that day and night he nagged and teased in order to discover the delightful secret. He did not succeed, but he remained convinced that there was one. He especially enjoyed hinting at it when there were others present and indulged in nudges and winks which Gopi found both embarrassing and dangerous.

The situation was further complicated by the fact that there was now a lot of talk in the uncle's family about the proposal that had come for Gopi and his sister. All agreed in thinking it a very fine one and did their best to overcome Gopi's resistance. They were more subtle than Gopi's mother and Delhi uncle had been and, refraining from getting angry or cajoling, confined themselves to throwing out remarks of a more general nature. For instance, when Gopi sat relaxed with the other men in the sitting room, enjoying a game of cards and the delicious refreshments brought in by the women, then someone would begin to talk about the advantages of a happy, settled domestic life. All agreed that it was the only state of true contentment known to man. Examples were cited of the miseries of those who, perhaps through their own fault or, more often, due to an unpropitious fate, had to drag themselves through life unmarried and uncared for. Gopi did not take part in the conversation, neither was he expected to. But everyone was very nice to him. When he played a card, it was greeted with exclamations at his cunning and skill. Only Babloo kept winking at him and throwing out cryptic remarks. No one knew what he was talking about, and Gopi tried not to hear him—in fact, he tried not to hear any of them but concentrated with all his might on the cards he was holding, which he arranged and rearranged to their best advantage.

At first Gopi didn't know whether he was glad to see Raymond or not, but quite soon he decided that he was. It was good to have someone to whom he could talk almost quite freely. He went to visit him in his hotel, and the two of them were together as before with Gopi half lying across a sofa and Raymond intent on making him comfortable and stirring the ice around in Gopi's Coke to make it really cold.

Gopi told him all about the marriage proposal. He very seriously propounded the many advantages that were attached to it. In the end he said, "They are quite rich."

Raymond was appreciative.

"They want me to go into their business. Sugar mills," he added in a tone of respect.

"What about your college?"

Gopi did not look happy. He never did look happy when his college was mentioned. He said, "Yes."

"Aren't you going back there?"

He made a helpless gesture with his hand.

"Your finals are coming up, aren't they?" When Gopi made the same gesture, Raymond asked, "You don't think you'll pass?"

Gopi shrugged indifferently. He said, "And what if I pass? Yes, all right perhaps I can get a government job like my uncle in Delhi, four hundred and fifty rupees a month with increment every five years." Suddenly he became passionate: "You don't know what it's like—not to have enough money—you have never had to live like that. At the end of every month before her allowance comes my mother has to send to the neighbors. Usually she asks only for rice and flour, but sometimes she has to ask for money also. When I was small, she sent me to ask. I didn't like the face people made when they gave. Naturally, they don't like to give, no one likes to give when you're in need."

Raymond said gently, "Yes, I think it'll be nice for you to get married." He added, "And I'm looking forward to the wedding of course."

"It will be very big and costly. I'm glad you will be able to see a real Indian wedding."

"*Your* real Indian wedding," Raymond said. After a while he added, "When it's over I'll go home."

"Oh, no! You must come with us to Kashmir. How can you leave India without first seeing Kashmir? Never. I wouldn't permit it."

"You're going to Kashmir?"

"For my honeymoon. Why are you laughing?"

Raymond's laughter was full of affection. He was content. He felt everything was working out well. Gopi would get married, and after that picturesque event, Raymond would go home. It would be a fine note on which to leave. Of course there would be the sorrow of parting but even that would have its own sweetness.

Then Gopi said, "Asha is here."

"Have you seen her?"

"Of course. I often visit her."

Although Raymond did not ask any questions or make any comment, Gopi suddenly said with great energy: "Everything is quite changed now. Asha is staying with a very saintly lady and under her influence Asha also. . . . She is like a mother to me."

"Who?"

"The saintly lady. . . . And Asha too." Suddenly he got angry and shouted, "You understand nothing! Nothing! I don't want to talk to you." He struggled up from the sofa.

Raymond said, "What did I do? Please sit down and tell me what I did."

Gopi said, "No, I'm going," but nevertheless sat down again, looking indignant. "I can see from your face you don't understand! You don't know anything. You have no idea of our culture. In your culture there is nothing—only sex, sex, sex—so how can you understand what it means to be mother and son, what a beautiful relationship it is for us."

Raymond made no comment but asked instead, "What's the date of your wedding?"

Gopi shrugged in ill humor.

"I'd like to know so that I can arrange about going home. Buy my ticket and all that."

But Gopi had no interest in Raymond's plans.

An Unsuccessful Meeting

The day Gopi took Raymond to Banubai she was in a very tender mood. There were some people with her, seeking her guidance, but as soon as Gopi entered she broke off her conversation with them and, raising both her hands, cried, "Here he is! My own little son!" She made him sit beside her on the bed. She asked him if he had slept well and what he had eaten for his breakfast; while he answered, she smoothed his hair and caressed his face. She was completely engrossed in him as a mother in her favorite child. She had no time to spare for anyone else. When Gopi introduced Raymond to her, she hardly acknowledged him beyond throwing a swift glance in his direction. This glance reminded Raymond of Swamiji, who looked at people in the same way.

Asha came in with some food she had cooked for Banubai. She too did not have much time to spare for Raymond but greeted him quite casually and as if they had met just yesterday and under similar circumstances. Banubai began to eat, but before every bite she took she first put a morsel into Gopi's mouth. He allowed himself to be fed, opening his mouth with the innocent, helpless air of a child. All the people in the room looked on with admiration. They said that Banubai had made Gopi her son the way the Lord Krishna was the son of his mother Yashoda: that indeed she saw and worshipped the Lord Krishna in Gopi and that all her playing with him was really an act of devotion. They felt privileged to be allowed to witness this act. Only Raymond did not feel privileged—in fact, he was embarrassed and did not like to look at the charming tableau being enacted on the bed but stared in frowning concentration at the tips of his own feet.

Although Raymond did his best to hide these feelings, it seemed that nothing could be hidden from Banubai. She was very cold to him. Even when her other visitors had left and she and Gopi had finished their meal, she continued to ignore Raymond. But Asha now became very keen to talk to him. She drew him out of the room and said eagerly, "You see, you see how everything has changed."

Raymond said, "*You*'ve changed."

"That's nothing," she said, impatiently tugging at her coarse cotton sari. "That's just outward—nothing—of no importance at all." She regarded him with clear shining eyes.

"You look very well."

"Look, look! That's all you can think of. What can I say to you? You don't understand anything, only the outer person."

Raymond did not try to defend himself. He thought that perhaps it was true, perhaps he really did not understand anything. Gopi had also said so.

Anxious to change the subject, he said, "I've been seeing Lee."

Gopi came out of Banubai's room. He said, "She is calling." And Banubai herself called from inside the room in rather a testy voice, and when they went in she looked at them suspiciously and asked Asha, "Where did you go? What are you doing?"

"Just think," Asha said, "Raymond has met Lee."

Both Gopi and Banubai were interested. Banubai asked, "Is she still with—that person?" She addressed herself to Asha as if Raymond were not worthy of being spoken to.

"Is she?" Asha asked him. "Still with that Swamiji of hers?"

"Oh, yes."

"And is she happy with him?" Banubai asked.

Raymond hesitated for a moment, then he said, "I think so. Or rather, *she* thinks so. So I suppose she must be."

Banubai was interested, but she still didn't address herself directly to Raymond. Instead she continued to use Asha as an intermediary. "How does she think herself to be happy?" And when Raymond could not think of a definite reply quickly enough, she went on impatiently, rapping out her words— "How? In what way? Like someone who is satisfied and has found what she is looking for?"

Raymond tried his best to answer truthfully. It was not easy for him, since he couldn't really tell what was the truth from Lee's point of view, or from Banubai's either. He spoke with English slowness and caution. "She *may* have found what she was looking for. I couldn't be sure. Yes, perhaps she has."

Banubai flung up her hands in exasperation. "Such things are not may—they are not perhaps! They cry out like a trumpet! With a royal sound! A godly sound! They cry out yes! And again, yes!" Her hands remained raised in the air; she looked and sounded like a prophetess. To Gopi and Asha she was an inspiring figure but Raymond found himself embarrassed again.

Banubai leaned forward keenly. She said, "You can see Asha and my little boy, how they are with me. There is no need to ask are they happy. There is no may here, no perhaps." This time she addressed herself directly to Raymond and she looked at him directly too. And again, as he met her penetrating glance, he was reminded of Swamiji, and it seemed to him that like Swamiji she was good at reading other people's thoughts.

She seemed at any rate to have read his. She behaved as if he were no longer there. She began to engross herself in her prayers. The beads slipped through her fingers, her lips moved, her eyes filmed over. Asha made a respectful sign to Gopi to lead Raymond away. Gopi too looked very respectful and he tiptoed up to Raymond and took his arm to lead him outside.

"What do you think of her?" Gopi asked as soon as they were outside, but answered himself: "She is a great spiritual person. You know what she is doing now? She is going into samadhi. She is in direct communication. Her spirit is merging with the One. She is a saint," he said, aglow.

"I don't think she thought much of me."

Gopi waved this aside: "Saints are different from others. You cannot interpret their actions. Of course she likes you, what do you mean? She loves you."

"Oh, does she?"

"She loves everyone. She is my mother. She is everyone's mother."

A Reading in the Ashram

Lee was sitting cross-legged on the floor of her hutment, meditating. She didn't take any notice of Raymond. Margaret was lying on a bed and she also took no notice of him. However, since she did not appear to be meditating, he spoke to her. He said, "Aren't you feeling well?"

She answered in a distinct voice, spacing her words: "I—am —not—ill." She said it as if it were a gramophone record she had put on for the benefit of people who had been bothering her with such questions.

When Lee had finished, she got up off the floor. She greeted Raymond with "When did you come?" but obviously she wasn't interested in an answer, so he didn't give any. He said, "Asha wants to see you."

That too failed to interest Lee. She was about to leave the hutment when Margaret called out to her, "Where are you going?"

"Why don't you just rest," Lee said and went out. Raymond stayed by Margaret's bed. He put out his hand to feel her temperature but she pushed him aside.

"I'd like to bring a doctor," Raymond said.

She began to cry; tears rolled down her sick face. She said, "Get out, leave me alone."

Raymond caught up with Lee. He said, "She's very ill."

"That's what I keep telling her." She went on walking. Raymond caught her arm and said, "Wait a minute." She didn't want to but she stopped still. Raymond said, "We'd better get a doctor out from town."

"She doesn't want to see anyone. She says she's all right."

"Don't be ridiculous."

"I know, but she gets so angry. She's terribly irritable. Actually, I think it's her stomach. She hates the food here; even the smell of it makes her sick."

She looked past Raymond toward the tree where Swamiji sat. Swamiji waved to them and Lee wrenched her arm free and hurried toward him. There was a cluster of disciples sitting around his cot, and Evie was reading to all of them from a big book which lay open in her lap. Lee made her way through the circle and went up to Swamiji's cot. She touched his feet, crouching down like a good and humble disciple, but he had eyes only for Raymond. He beamed with pleasure and said, "So you have come to pay us a visit." He waved some disciples aside to make room, but Raymond wouldn't sit down. Swamiji looked at him in his keen way and asked, "What has happened?"

"He's worried about Margaret," Lee said.

"Yes, she's not feeling up to the mark these days," Swamiji said regretfully. He turned to one of the women sitting round his cot and asked, "Did you give her those powders?"

"She couldn't keep them down," Lee reported.

Swamiji clicked his tongue in pity. Then he beamed again at Raymond: "You have come very auspiciously. I thought and thought about you all last night and wished oh, if Raymond would come. And today you have come. You must have heard me calling you. So it is true, you see—I have very special powers." He laughed.

Raymond was still standing. His Adam's apple went up and down in agitation. "I could get a doctor out here or I could take her back to town with me."

"Let him hold it," Swamiji said to Evie. She took the book from which she had been reading and gave it to Raymond. It was the same bulky manuscript they had brought to the hotel.

"There it is," said Swamiji. "Our first fruits. Our first child." He and Evie both smiled with pride and so did everyone else there. "We are now in your hands," Swamiji said. "We have placed our hearts and hopes in you. It is all up to you now." He waved his hand to express the abandonment of all care for the manuscript.

But Raymond stood holding it as if he didn't know what to do with it. He looked down at it; actually he felt like flinging it on the ground and maybe stamping on it. Swamiji noticed his preoccupied look and gently took the book away from him.

"Come," he said, "leave it with me for a little while longer. I feel," he said with his smile, "like the father giving away his daughter to a husband's home—only one moment longer, he begs, let me hold her in my arms for this one last time." He ran his hands over his manuscript and some of the disciples breathed "Ah" in blessed contentment. He passed the book back to Evie and asked her to continue her reading. She did so joyfully.

"On Friday morning after breakfast we were all sitting under the tree. We were discussing an incident that had happened the day before which had had a very bad effect on some of us. A stray dog had been found lying injured near the ashram. It was in a very bad state and cried and cried and touched our hearts to pity. Lee especially was very much affected. She wanted to have it put out of its misery. But Swamiji would not allow it. The dog howled all night. She went again to Swamiji and begged for his permission but again he would not grant it. He said the dog would be dead in the morning. And so it happened. But Swamiji saw that Lee was still very much upset, so he explained the whole matter to her. He said, 'Everything must be experienced to the end. This is true for a dog as for a man, as for a bud on a tree. Everything must unfold and ripen. There is sunshine and gentle breezes and there is rain and bitter storms. We must accept and enjoy, or accept and endure, as the case may be. Because we need both enjoyment and endurance, both sun and storm, so that we may ripen into our fullest possibility. Isn't it wonderful that even a dog should be allowed to grow into such ripeness! And if for a dog, then how much more for a human being!' "

There was a murmur of appreciation from the listeners. Swamiji too appeared to enjoy and approve of the thoughts expressed. Evie looked as if this reading had done her good in her innermost soul, and her face was radiant with love and bliss. She looked so gentle, so good, so full of kindness for all created beings that Raymond was stirred to appeal to her.

"I really think she ought to be in a hospital. I could take her back with me now—I have a taxi waiting—or if you think that's better I'll bring a doctor out—"

Before he had finished speaking, she had turned away from him, still with that smile of goodness and love, and fixed her gaze on Swamiji. Everyone else was looking at Swamiji in the same way. Raymond left them to go back to Margaret.

Lee came running after him and when she had caught up with him she said, "How can you behave like that?" She was angry and started shouting at him: "Don't you realize what an honor he was doing you! And you stood there holding it as if it were—just nothing. I felt so ashamed of you. And he's an angel, a saint—he really *is* a saint—his feelings were deeply hurt but his only thought was for you, that you shouldn't be embarrassed—"

Raymond remained cold to this outburst. He said, "I think we ought to worry more about Margaret than Swamiji's or my feelings."

"She's all right! Just leave her alone!"

They had reached the hutment where Margaret lay on her bed. Her eyes were shut and she breathed like a person in pain. When they came in, she opened her eyes and made an effort to sit up.

"You're all right, aren't you?" Lee said to her. "I mean, apart from your upset stomach—everybody gets that."

"Why don't you come back with me?" Raymond appealed to Margaret.

"She doesn't want to!"

"Let her speak for herself."

"I don't want to," Margaret said. She struggled to get up. She sat on the edge of her bed. She had been a plump girl but now her skin hung loose. It had turned yellow.

"You've got jaundice," Raymond said.

"Don't talk rot," Lee said. "It's her stomach. You should try and eat something," she encouraged Margaret.

A shudder ran over Margaret and she made a retching sound. She scratched at her thighs in an impotent, hysterical way. "I feel so itchy all the time."

"That's jaundice," Raymond said.

Lee said, "It's those damn bedbugs. You should see what I go through all night. Lie down, Margaret, he says you should rest."

"He said that?"

"Yes, he said tell her to rest and get quite well and then she shall come and be with me again."

Margaret shut her eyes again, perhaps to overcome her pain, perhaps to think this message over. After a while she said, "You're lying."

"Truly, Margaret, that's what he said. I swear."

"He didn't. You only want to keep me away from him." She looked at Raymond. "She'd do anything to keep me away from him. She's so jealous. She and that Evie both." She fell back on the bed as if in despair and burst out crying.

"You're being very unfair, Margaret. You know that's not true, you're just saying it. It's *you* who're jealous because you don't realize that in his love for us we're all the same—"

"Oh, shut up," Raymond said, and he even pushed Lee out of the way. He sat down on the edge of Margaret's bed: "Please come away with me. The moment you're all right again I'll bring you back. I promise." She made no move. "Or I can bring you back straightaway, if you prefer that. We'll just see a doctor and then we'll come back. It's easy."

"You're making her feel worse," Lee said.

Raymond got up. "Then I'll have to bring a doctor here."

Lee followed him out. "Swamiji doesn't like doctors."

"He doesn't?"

"He believes in the ancient form of Indian medicine like it's written in the shastras. I believe in it too. We all do."

Raymond got into his taxi which was waiting on the dirt track outside and drove away.

Universal Synthesis

Raymond had meant to find a good doctor as soon as he got back to the hotel, but there was a message waiting for him that delayed his plan. The message was from Gopi and asked Raymond to meet him immediately in the discotheque; it was very urgent. Besides this message, there were also two letters for him, one from his mother and the other from Miss Charlotte. He told himself that he would read his mother's letter later at his leisure and opened his leather portfolio to keep it inside: but as he did so, he saw another of her letters lying there. It had arrived two days ago but so far he had forgotten to read it. He shut the portfolio again and, thrusting Miss Charlotte's letter into his pocket, hastened off to obey Gopi's summons.

He found him sitting in the discotheque with Babloo and Babloo's friends. They were the only customers, for in spite of its attempts at a modern atmosphere, the place had not proved popular. They were discussing a news item that had appeared in the papers that morning. It concerned a popular film star against whom a charge of bigamy had been brought. Babloo and his friends discussed hotly to and fro. Some were against him, some for him, but all were united in passionate involvement. They spoke of him as a person they knew well and the details of whose life were as familiar to them as their own. They knew about the fabulous house he had built on Juhu beach and his white Mercedes sports car; they discussed how much he got for each film and that most of it was in black money to evade the income tax; twice a week he went for a body massage, and last year he had been involved in a brawl with a rival star and had slapped his face at a great glittering première party in a Bom-

155

bay hotel. All this they spoke of with excitement. Raymond enjoyed listening to them. They were youthful and fervent and their eyes shone beneath their brushed-up puffs of hair. They reminded him of Gopi as Gopi had been when he had first met him. But now Gopi appeared very different from them. He wasn't taking any interest in their conversation but leaned back in his chair and stretched and yawned rather arrogantly. Finally he nudged Raymond under the table and made a sign to him that they should leave. He got up first.

His cousin Babloo stopped talking and looked up at him. "Where are you going?" There was something imploring in his eyes that said don't go. It touched Raymond and he would willingly have stayed. But Gopi said, "See you later."

"All right." Babloo dropped his eyes, tender and hurt. How often Raymond had seen Gopi look like that and how it had always wrung his heart!

Without another look at his cousin, Gopi steered Raymond outside. "They are so boring," he said.

"Do you think so? I like them."

"That's because you haven't heard them one hundred million times before."

Gopi said he had to speak to Raymond very urgently. Raymond told him how he must get hold of a doctor to take to Margaret. He wanted to do it at once, but Gopi said wait, they would go home and ask his uncle about a good doctor, but first Gopi simply had to speak to him, he had been waiting for him most impatiently. They were standing in the busy street and Gopi looked round for somewhere to go. They found a tea-stall and went and sat inside the booth attached to it. It was a steamy, dingy little place with only two tables in it.

Although Gopi had been so impatient to speak, now he was shy. He bent his head and scratched his finger on the wooden table. "Yes," he said at last, "they took me to see that girl. You know," he said, impatiently, even angrily.

"The one they want you to marry?"

156

Gopi looked round as if he didn't want anyone to overhear. There wasn't anyone except the proprietor, who sat with his back to them, engrossed in frying.

"They want to do it quite soon," Gopi said. "Very soon."

"I see."

"What do you see? Why do you say that?" Gopi said, relieved to be able to vent his nervous irritation. He turned round again to throw another suspicious look over his shoulder. "They took me for tea there."

"With her family you mean?"

"They are a nice family. The tea also was very nice. They had pakoras and samusas and all sorts of other things. A cake also." He stared down at the table and scratched at the dirt ingrained in it. "They said the girl had baked the cake." His voice had become husky but next moment, as if ashamed of this, he added, "Of course they always say that. They say it to show you how well versed she is in household affairs." He laughed with false cynicism.

But soon he was quite serious again. There was a brief, thoughtful silence.

Then Gopi said, "I must tell Asha."

"Yes," Raymond said.

"She will be very happy. She often says she wants to see me well settled. Naturally, every mother wants this for her son." He said sharply, "And she is like a mother to me now."

So as not to have to look at Gopi, Raymond looked at his watch. "Shall we go to your uncle's house now and ask about a doctor?"

"I want you to go to Asha first and tell her."

When Raymond said nothing, Gopi urged, "It's best if *you* tell her." He didn't say why but leaned across the table and lowered his voice intimately: "Don't you want me to be married?"

"Of course I do."

"And well settled?"

"Of course."

"Then?"

Raymond began to climb the stairs to Banubai's room, but on
the first gallery he met Asha, who told him he couldn't go up
now. "She's in her mood," she said, looking up reverently toward Banubai's door. Raymond didn't know what she meant,
but he was relieved not to have to unburden himself of his
message in front of Banubai. "I'd like to talk to you," he told
Asha.

"What about?"

"It's—something quite private really."

"About Gopi?" she said at once, with a nervous catch in her
voice so that Raymond could not pluck up enough courage to
begin. Instead he said, "I have to find a doctor—it's for Lee's
friend, she's very ill."

"Oh, my God, Lee is very ill?"

"No, her friend Margaret."

He explained the situation. Asha said she would go with him
into town to fetch a doctor she knew of. She was ready to start
at once. So then Raymond had to say, "There's something else.
. . . It *is* about Gopi."

Asha's hand flew to her heart. "Come in here," she said. She
drew him into the little room which housed the University of
Universal Synthesis. There were two mattresses on the floor, on
one of which the founder-president lay asleep. Some clothes
hung from a nail on the wall and there were piles of old newspapers and pamphlets.

Her eyes scanned Raymond's face. They kept scanning it
while he told her the news till at last she flung her hands in front
of them and rocked herself to and fro. When she uncovered her
eyes again, her first question was, "What about her?"

"Who?"

"Her, her—that saint, that mother!"

Suddenly a very sweet sound came from the top of the house.
It was Banubai singing. She had a high voice, clear like a flute.

With what joy she sang, how she trilled and soared! Tears rolled down Asha's cheeks. She said, "She is singing to her Lord Krishna."

Their host sat up. He was surprised to see two guests in his room and fumbled for his spectacles to see who they were. When he couldn't find them, he gave up and instead listened to the singing from above. He loved it. He was an old man with sunken stubbled cheeks and suffering from cataract, but he was smiling in a childlike way. He said, "Beautiful, beautiful."

"She is in such mood today," Asha told him. "She got up this morning and said He had come to her in her dreams. He said, 'Come, Banubai, today we'll play.' She followed Him but He hid behind a tree. She called 'Where are you?' but He only laughed at her and then He hid behind another tree. The more she followed Him, the more she called to Him, the more He hid himself and laughed at her. Sometimes He played little snatches on his flute to torment her. Oh, He was so mischievous! He had a good game with her!" She smiled through her tears, but next moment she turned again to Raymond and wrung her hands. "How will I tell her?"

"But you say she's Gopi's mother—mothers are glad on such occasions—"

"Yes, his mother but also so much more! It's true, she has made him her son, she loves him like a mother but the Lord has many aspects. . . . What is the use of telling you these things, you understand nothing."

"I know I don't. Everyone keeps saying so."

"And also you are cold and unfeeling."

Here their host leaned forward to intervene with gentle wisdom. He touched Raymond's knee with his forefinger, and then held that forefinger up for attention. "Not unfeeling," he said, "but rational, rational. For the Westerner the mind comes first, then the heart. With us it is topsy-turvy, or vice versa. It is the aim and basis of my university to unite these two tendencies of the human constitution, to educate the mind in the language of the heart and the heart in the language of the mind. This synthesis achieved, then we shall truly have a fully rounded human being."

"And once I thought you cared for him too. Now I see you don't know what love means. If you did, you couldn't come here like this—"

"Like what!" Raymond cried.

"Banubai is right: she told me Raymond is a cynical person. She said she got bad vibrations from you. I told her oh, no, Raymond is a very feeling person. He loves Gopi the way English men often love boys. I told her about poor Peter, Rao Sahib's tutor who tried to kill himself, and I said you were just like Peter. But she said no, he doesn't feel love in his own heart and he sneers at the love in other people's. It's true."

Raymond did not relish this analysis of his character but checked himself from taking offense. He said gently, "How do I sneer? Why do you say that?"

"You don't believe that I've changed. You sneer when I say I'm his mother."

"I don't *sneer,* surely not."

"But you have bad thoughts."

Instead of defending himself against this charge, he suddenly said, "You really think I don't care about losing Gopi?"

She didn't hear him. The sweet sounds had started again from upstairs. For a moment she listened to them with delight, then she sighed. "I must tell her." She got up to go, leaving Raymond behind as if she had forgotten all about him. He could see her ascending the stairs with a heavy tread. Considering his mission here accomplished, he was anxious to get away and find a doctor to take to the ashram. But when he attempted to get up, the old man gently pressed him down again. He wished to give him more details about the University of Universal Synthesis: he loved talking about his scheme, and it did not often happen to him that a new visitor came to listen.

It was a fully worked-out plan, noble and beautiful in its

conception. Students and teachers would come from East and West and from all other parts of the world. Each civilization was to have its own department in which to delve deeply into its source and meaning. Then the different departments would meet and discuss together, and in this meaningful interchange a deeper understanding would be reached not only of other cultures but also of one's own, thereby transcending insularity with a true world-view by means of which peace, harmony, and understanding would be achieved forever.

The old man spoke with such controlled fervor that it was a pleasure to listen to him. At the same time Raymond also listened to sounds from above: Asha must have reached Banubai by now and imparted her news. Raymond waited, he didn't know for what. But nothing happened except that the singing continued to gush forth as pure as the waters of a mountain stream.

From an exposition of principles the old man passed to the more practical aspects of his scheme. A site was to be selected in some cool and pleasant hill station and an architect in full accord with the aims of the university was to be appointed. The ground plan would be laid out in the shape of two perfect circles intersecting each other, thus providing on the physical plane a symbol of that wholeness and unity that was to be achieved in the realm of the spirit.

Raymond expressed his wholehearted appreciation. The old man was pleased. "We shall begin as soon as funds become available." He pressed a pamphlet into Raymond's hand and, while Raymond leafed through it, turned aside modestly to refresh himself on a piece of dried-up chapatti. Raymond read that grants of five hundred thousand rupees each were expected from various industrial corporations as well as from international and government organizations. Private donations would also be encouraged. He turned to the front of the pamphlet and read its dedication: "To the Soul of Mankind." He was

161

still straining his ears toward the upper part of the house. But the singing continued undimmed.

A Letter and Some Visitors

Raymond's taxi was waiting for him outside Banubai's house. When the driver asked him where to, Raymond said he supposed they had better go back to the hotel. Since his other sources had failed him, he intended to ask at the reception desk for a suitable doctor. He leaned his head against the greasy car covers: he was feeling tired and dispirited, and it seemed to him that too many things were happening and that there was nothing he could do about them, and in any case it was too hot to do anything.

The traffic was so dense that the taxi had to crawl along. Raymond could not help looking out of the window though he would have preferred not to see anything. There was one street in particular that he wished they could have avoided—the one populated by people who had come to the holy city in order to die there. Some of these were quite close to their goal and lay prone on the street; others could still sit up and even eat a meal. Raymond saw one young man, half naked and entirely emaciated, bend over a tin plate and greedily stuff rice into his mouth while his eyes glowed and his fingers trembled so much that most of the rice kept falling back into the plate.

Raymond remembered Miss Charlotte's letter, which was still unopened in his pocket. He took it out and looked at it, with relief, with pleasure. Miss Charlotte's handwriting was round, small, firm like herself.

". . . Some of our old people are really stubborn and we have quite a job to persuade them to move. Naturally, everyone likes their own home, although I must say in some cases it isn't always very much of a home. There is one old dear in Kanpur, a Mrs. Grenfell, she has been in India all her life, whom we found living in the most pitiful condition all alone and in what used to be a stable. Some of these people have such stories to tell of the past, they really are an embodiment of history and I wish one could get it all down just as they tell it. Altogether it has been a most interesting trip, and I have been doing more than my share of combining duty with pleasure!

"I have been to Agra too to meet Mr. Tompkins, such a nice old gentleman who first came to India fifty years ago to be an assistant in Phillips' (a very smart gentleman's outfitter; it closed down in '47). Now he lives in the servants' quarters of a local hotel and every day he takes up his place in the veranda of the hotel and sells ivory bookmarkers and other curios to tourists. We are sending him to Madras and he is quite happy to go because he doesn't like the north Indian winters. It is curious, isn't it, the way elderly English people find it so difficult to stand the cold here although it is nothing compared with the cold at home. But I think it is because the blood gets very thin in this climate. Of course while in Agra I paid several visits to the Taj Mahal, by day and by night although as luck would have it there was no moon. Can one ever, ever get tired of it? Each time it is more beautiful. I also took a little trip to Fatehpur Sikri and it was an especially happy time to go because an anniversary festival of Salim Chisthi was being celebrated and there were some moving religious festivals. So you see I have been quite indulging myself, and now I intend to indulge myself a little more and hope to pay you all a visit in Benares. Please tell Lee and Margaret too that I look forward to meeting them again and hearing all their news. I shall be staying at the Benares mission, or I should say what used to be the mission but now it has been taken over by the local church. . . ."

At the reception desk Raymond was told that some people were waiting for him. The hotel clerk—a smart young man from Kerala who had learned to speak English with an American accent—looked at him strangely as he delivered this message, as if he did not altogether approve of Raymond's visitors.

163

Raymond found them waiting for him in the lounge, sitting side by side on a sofa. It was Swamiji accompanied by Lee and Margaret. There was no denying that they looked odd in these surroundings. Not Swamiji—his dignity and poise could assert themselves anywhere—but the two girls: Margaret was in a handspun cotton sari and Lee in one of her long peasant skirts. They both looked bedraggled.

Raymond rushed up to them. "How are you? Are you better?" he asked Margaret. She didn't look better.

She waited for Swamiji to speak. He said, "You were worried about her, so I brought her." He spoke simply and frankly, as one who hoped he had done the right thing.

Raymond took them to his room and at once telephoned for the hotel doctor. He tried to persuade Margaret to lie down on his bed. She refused, but not in the surly manner in which she had spoken to him in the ashram. She was gentle and kind.

Swamiji also urged her. "Lie down. Take your rest. You are tired from our journey."

Then Margaret lay down on Raymond's bed. Obviously it was a relief to her. She still looked sick and yellow, but all the same there was contentment in her face. She lay there and her eyes were fixed on Swamiji as if she were grateful to him for the good care that was being taken of her.

Lee sat slumped in a chair. She was so silent and listless that Raymond suspected there was something wrong with her too. But when he hinted at this, she brushed him aside scornfully.

The hotel doctor, diagnosing infectious hepatitis, said Margaret must be removed from the hotel immediately. He was terribly anxious that no rumor of this sickness having been allowed to enter the hotel should reach the other guests. He hurried off to report to the manager. Raymond said, "We'd better take her to the hospital."

"Oh, no," Margaret said at once. They all looked at Swamiji but he made a gesture to show that the whole matter rested only with Raymond. Margaret didn't say anything more but she seemed anxious and frightened.

"It'll be best for you," Raymond urged her. "You'll get well quickly and then you can go back to the ashram."

"Lee will stay with you," Swamiji said. He told Lee, briskly, not looking at her, "Evie will bring your things."

Lee said, "Why should she go to the hospital? It's just hepatitis. She can easily get cured in the ashram."

"Who told you that?" Raymond asked.

"I've met lots of people who've had it. Almost everyone gets it in India. It's just a routine thing."

Margaret confirmed this. She said, "I'll get better much quicker in the ashram."

"But the doctor, the doctor!" Swamiji implored her.

"You don't believe in doctors," Margaret said.

"Who am I to believe or not believe? I'm a completely ignorant person. We must put our trust in Raymond who is well versed in the miracles of modern science."

Just then the manager came to the room and called Raymond outside. He was a pale, flabby Swiss and was very agitated. He said that Margaret must be asked to leave immediately, that she should never have been allowed to enter the hotel at all. He said he had a sacred responsibility toward his guests to protect them against the terrible diseases that stalked the land. He had been in India for thirty-five years and knew more, more than enough about them. It was his life's task to see that every drop of water in the hotel was boiled, and to make personal inspection of every lavatory in it—yes, even the *servants'* lavatories, that was doubly important, for it was through the servants that so many of these fateful, filthy germs were carried. He implored Raymond to remove his dangerous visitor without a moment's delay. He also implored him to take immediate injections himself as a safeguard against the disease. He described cases he had seen—of people swelling up, they went into a coma, their livers were eaten away—oh, he could tell a thousand terrible things, and remembering them, he cried out in fear and clasped his white, white hands. Raymond, trying to calm him, assured him that Margaret would be leaving at once.

And indeed, when he returned to the room, Raymond found all three of them ready to leave. Margaret had got up from the bed.

"Do sit down again," Raymond said. "Let's decide first which hospital."

There was a silence. The two girls looked stubbornly at the floor. Then Lee said, "We're going *home.*"

Swamiji twinkled at Raymond who, however, remained quite grave. "Is this wise?" Raymond asked. Lee looked more stubborn. Margaret swayed a little.

"Lean on me," Swamiji told her. When she hesitated, as if not daring to, he firmly took her arm and tucked it under his. Through her yellow sickness, she beamed, she glowed.

She turned to Raymond and in her happiness she spoke to him very gently. "Please don't be worried about me. I'm all right. Truly I am. Swamiji has explained it all to me so beautifully."

"So has the doctor," Raymond said dryly.

"Doctors don't know a thing. These diseases that people get in India, they're not physical, they're purely psychic. We only get them because we try to resist India—because we shut ourselves up in our little Western egos and don't want to give ourselves. But once we learn to yield, then they just fall away."

Raymond asked, "And have you learned to yield?"

Leaning securely on Swamiji, she didn't answer but dropped her eyes in bashfulness. Swamiji laughed and pressed her arm against his side. They walked out of the room together and Lee was about to follow them when Raymond detained her. "What about you?" he asked her. "Have you learned too?"

She shook him off. He watched her walking down the hotel corridor behind Swamiji and Margaret; but whereas they went rather jauntily, she had her head bent and dragged her feet in misery.

An Unexpected Arrival

Banubai had taken the news very well. After Asha had told her, there had been a fractional pause and then Banubai had gone right on singing. Her face like her voice had been full of lighthearted joy. From that time onward, she never spoke about Gopi. There were so many other people who came to her day in day out. She was like the sun and wind that play on all alike. And not only was she universally playful like sun or wind, she was also universally indifferent. It was as if when she no longer saw Gopi she also no longer thought about him. Asha was struck with wonder. Banubai had loved Gopi so much, had so clung to him. And then to be able to forget him just like that—empty heart and mind of him as if he had never been—how Asha envied her for that! Her own case was very different.

She ceased to benefit from Banubai's presence. Other people came and listened to Banubai and went away with their hearts purified and spirits uplifted. But Asha remained sunk in her own oppressive thoughts. She began to feel herself to be a disturbing element and did not spend as much time as formerly in Banubai's room. Instead she wandered moodily by herself around the house. She gazed at people who came and went but saw no one. When they spoke to her, she hardly heard them. But one day someone came up to her and said, "Here I am, sweetheart."

It was Bulbul. At first Asha could not believe her eyes, next moment she was very angry. She said, "Who sent you?"

"Rao Sahib."

"You're a liar."

Bulbul did not contradict. Instead she began to complain about the journey, how hot and crowded it had been in the train, that she had not been able to get a wink of sleep all night nor had she been able to buy anything fit to eat; consequently she was now dying of hunger and exhaustion. Asha took her into an empty little storeroom where Bulbul at once began to make

167

herself at home, rolling out her bedding and untying her bundle to take out the little plaster figures of her gods and goddesses that she carried with her everywhere. She was arranging them in a niche in the wall when Asha said, "You are going back on the next train." However, after Bulbul had begged enough, she consented to allow her to stay for a day or two.

Bulbul sighed and wept—but with joy at being reunited with Asha. She described how miserable her life had been without her. Oh, they had been kind enough to her in Rao Sahib's house, they had given her a nice dry quarter and all the servants were very respectful to her and there was plenty of food and hot tea whenever she wanted it, but what was all that when Asha was not there? Was it possible for a person to be happy even in a palace if deprived of the sight of sun and moon? Bulbul went on like that and Asha let her. Then at last Asha told her about Gopi and his marriage. For the first time Asha gave full rein to her feelings. Bulbul held her in her arms and comforted her as only Bulbul knew how. Now Asha was glad that she had come.

But Banubai wasn't. She had never liked Bulbul although Bulbul always treated her with tremendous respect. Now too Bulbul flung herself at Banubai's feet, striking her forehead on the ground and calling her blessed saint; indeed, she rather overdid it, so it was no wonder that Banubai received her coldly. But Bulbul didn't care about that. She made herself at home in the house and attended on Asha.

Asha was like a sick person and seemed to be sinking under her load of suffering. At last Bulbul could bear it no longer and said, "Let me bring him to you."

"No!"

"You'll die, sweetheart. You'll kill yourself."

"What does that matter. As long as *he* is happy with his bride."

168

A Summons

The men of the prospective bride's family had come to visit the prospective bridegroom's. There were so many things to discuss —marriage settlements, wedding arrangements—but these were being politely kept in the background so as to give the visit a purely social aspect. There was eating, drinking, joking: the two families were looking each other over to see how they got on together. There would be many, many occasions in the future when they would be meeting in this way, at other weddings, at births, at festivals, at funerals. Their life would be forever intertwined at all its stages. So it was important that they should suit each other. And evidently they did—at any rate, they laughed at the same jokes, ate and drank with the same relish; an atmosphere of good cheer prevailed. The women hurried backward and forward with heaped-up dishes, their faces flushed with excitement and happiness.

No one took much notice of Gopi. He hovered on the outskirts of the circle and listened to the jokes and conversation. He was not expected to contribute anything and he accepted this and liked it. These men had taken over his fate and he was content to leave it in their hands. He felt secure with them. They were all of them—from the bride's side as well as his own —prosperous, self-made, comfortable men. They had seen a lot, they had learned a lot, they had cleared a good niche for themselves from where they knew how to deal with things. They were very, very different from his Delhi uncle, who was always weary and depressed and didn't know how to deal with anything. Gopi did not want to think of his Delhi uncle at all. He wanted only to be with these men and let them guide him and do whatever they said he should do.

They were laughing at a joke, and he smiled too—not because he was amused but because he wanted to prove himself in full accord with them. He was so engrossed in them that he failed to notice a plucking at his sleeve. The plucking was repeated, increased; a moist little voice whispered "Babu." He turned and saw the servant, a meek, worried, much scolded little boy. He looked more worried than ever, his whole face was creased like an old man's. "Babu," he said again. The smile faded from Gopi's lips, he removed his arm and said in annoyance, "What do you want?"

"Babu, there is someone calling you."

"Who?"

The boy's eyes darted around nervously; he was terrified. He had to swallow several times before at last he dared to whisper, "A woman."

Then Gopi was terrified too. He got up at once and followed the boy, who led him into an alley at the back of the house; at the end of the alley stood a horse-drawn cart and inside it there was indeed a woman waiting for them. Gopi's first feeling was one of immense relief that it was not Asha; but this relief did not last long when, from amid the folds of sari which she wore like a shroud, he made out the familiar figure of Bulbul. She took a coin and threw it to the boy; at the same time she hissed a warning to him and hissed it again till he nodded to show he had understood; then she allowed him to run away, which he did without once looking back as if afraid of what might be following him. Bulbul made Gopi climb up into the carriage with her. She touched and patted him and laughed with pleasure. But he only wanted to get rid of her as fast as possible. He said, "Why have you come here?"

"To see you," she answered; she pinched his cheek and smiled. "Pretty, pretty." He jerked away indignantly and that made her laugh again. "What, are you shy with your Bulbul?"

"Are you mad coming here? My God, what trouble you will get me into." He looked around him in fright.

But the alley was completely deserted. Bulbul's cart was parked at the end of it, abutting on to an abandoned building site. This too was deserted except for the owner of the cart and horse who squatted there on his haunches. He showed no sign of interest in them, only in his cigarette butt at which he pulled and puffed through his cupped hands.

"I told a lie," Bulbul confessed. "It is she who has sent me. Only she said don't tell him I sent you. How she cried and cried and begged and begged, 'Bring him to me! Bulbul, bring him!' "

Gopi turned away from her and scowled.

"If you had seen her, if you had heard her!" When Gopi gave no sign of relenting, she edged up close to him and whispered in his ear: "Have you forgotten? All those lovely times we had . . . in the hotel. . . ."

Gopi drew back. He felt repelled by Bulbul's nearness, by her breath on his ear, by her smell of betel, spices, and musty unwashed clothes. And he didn't want to be reminded of the hotel.

"That's all finished now," he said.

"Not for her."

"For her also. It is all philosophical now. Philosophical and spiritual. You don't know anything." He made as if to jump down from the cart but Bulbul held on to him. She had skinny, tight hands that held him like a vise.

"You think that bald old witch knows better than Bulbul?"

"Don't speak of Banubai like that! You are not fit to speak of her. She is a saint."

Bulbul spat betel juice in a practiced stream. Again Gopi tried to jump down, again she prevented him. "Come with me, we'll go to my sweetheart. She is waiting for us."

This time, by being quite rough, he managed to free himself. He jumped off the cart and hurried away down the alley; he longed to be safe inside his uncle's house again, enjoying the party with the others and smiling at their jokes. Bulbul was like a bad dream.

She was calling after him in a loud voice. He was afraid that someone might hear and come out and find them, so he had to stop. She had got off the cart and was coming after him as fast as she could, clutching a painful hip.

"What should I tell her? When will you come?"

171

They were quite close to the little back gate leading into his uncle's house. Gopi had to get rid of her fast. He said, "Soon."

"When?" Suddenly she broke into a wail. "How she will be waiting, how she will be looking out for us! Oh, I can see her before my eyes! She is suffering, suffering!"

Gopi shushed her desperately. "I'll come—as soon as I can."

"Tonight?"

He nodded.

"I shall wait for you. I shall be standing at the end of the road —you know where?"

"Yes, yes."

"Not the river—"

"I know."

"By the wall. If you don't come—"

"I'll come."

"If you don't, I will be here to fetch you. I shall come right into the house and I shall ask, 'Where is Gopi?' "

"Go now—"

"At seven o'clock. By the wall."

Before leaving, she tweaked his cheek again—affectionately but also quite hard, like a warning.

Lee

He was very nice to Miss Charlotte. He insisted we should bring a chair for her to sit on instead of on the ground with the rest of us and he called her madam and apologized for the heat and discomfort. Afterward he talked a lot about his admiration for Jesus Christ and how really all religions are one and God is one. Miss Charlotte didn't say much. She looked funny sitting there perched up on her chair with her hands folded in her lap and her ankles crossed. She was wearing one of her awful frocks. Whatever Swamiji said, she said "yes" and "quite" like a polite guest agreeing with the hostess. She was prim in the same way Raymond gets prim and terribly polite when he's embarrassed or put out. Actually, the two of them sitting there seemed to sort of belong together—if only because they were so different from the rest of us. Raymond didn't get a chair but the way he sat on the ground was quite prissy and awkward (he's never learned to do it properly, he doesn't know what to do with his legs). He was also the only one besides Miss Charlotte who was not wearing Indian clothes. Their faces were different too, I can't quite say how but they didn't have that *look* that everyone else in the ashram has, Evie and Margaret and all the rest whether they're Indian or foreign (but especially foreign). I suppose it comes from meditation and all of us feeling the way we do about him.

Then suddenly, while he was talking about Jesus Christ, Miss Charlotte asked about Margaret. Swamiji pointed at her and said, "Well, how does she look to you?" but Miss Charlotte didn't answer that, instead she said that these diseases could be very insidious and it was impossible to tell when they might not flare up again or what they might not secretly be doing to you from inside. Margaret didn't like Miss Charlotte talking like that, and she interrupted her to say that she was quite all right, that she had taken some Indian powders which had cured her completely. She said she felt better than she had ever felt in her whole life before. And when she said that, she looked at him, and really there was a glow in her face that I know has never been there before. But he told her to be quiet and not to interrupt Miss Charlotte. So Miss Charlotte went on to say—she spoke calmly like always but there was something stubborn in her now too—she said that it was true these Indian powders were often very efficacious, but on the other hand it happened that the disease could get a deeper grip than the patient suspected. Experience had unfortunately taught her that this was not unusual with Westerners coming to India and unaccustomed to its food or water or climate; and that in their case it was only the most powerful antibiotics that had any effect. Margaret said she didn't believe in antibiotics. Miss Charlotte went

173

on as if she hadn't heard her, she said that she really must warn Margaret that not only were these diseases extremely danger- ous but even, and not all that infrequently, deadly. Miss Char- lotte did not pull her punches when she said that word—it came out really like death and all it meant, so that everyone was quiet for a moment. But then Margaret cried out—she sounded a bit frightened now—she cried she was all right, all right, and it wasn't only the powders that had cured her but her own happi- ness too and being in spiritual harmony. Yes, said Miss Char- lotte, spiritual harmony was fine, was very good, but we did live in physical bodies too and we couldn't achieve much if we failed to look after those.

Swamiji applauded her. He said he liked to hear such good sense spoken, and that the trouble with all of us was that we tried to live on too high a plane: higher than we deserved, he told us, affectionately but meaning it too. Now, he said, what he would like to do was to put ourselves entirely in Miss Charlotte's capable hands and whatever Miss Charlotte said should be done about Margaret we should follow her advice. Miss Charlotte lost no time in taking up his offer and said that she would like to take Margaret back to Benares with her and show her to a doctor there.

"I've *seen* a doctor!" Margaret said. She began to look a bit panicky.

Miss Charlotte argued with her, tried to persuade her. It was just between the two of them, no one else said anything. Marga- ret kept glancing toward Swamiji, as if waiting for him to inter- vene. And because he didn't—because he didn't *order* her to go with Miss Charlotte as he could have done, and as we all (includ- ing perhaps Margaret herself) expected him to do—she became bolder with Miss Charlotte and at last she said definitely, "No, I'm not going, and you can't make me go." Then she got up and left us. And again we all waited for him to do something, to call her back perhaps, and again he didn't. Instead he spread his arms helplessly and said to Miss Charlotte, "Now you can see

with your own eyes what naughty disobedient disciples I have,"
and he smiled at her in his nicest, most charming manner.

She didn't smile back. Her face was flushed, and she was
fumbling to pin up her thin little bun, which had come undone in
her agitation. She told Raymond they had better go back to town
or it would get too late and their driver would miss his meal.
Swamiji got up off his cot and personally escorted them to their
car. Miss Charlotte walked in front and busied herself in talking
to me, so he had to walk behind us talking to Raymond. He was
jovial and laughing, I could hear him, but Raymond was very
quiet. Then I heard Swamiji say, "I think you're cross with me,
Raymond," but Raymond caught up with Miss Charlotte and me
and walked by my side, leaving Swamiji behind. I stopped still to
be with Swamiji but Raymond wouldn't let me, he drew me
aside. He said, "There's something wrong with you too."

I knew he had been watching me all the time. Not in curiosity
but in concern. And that was the way he looked at me now too.
I wanted to get away from him, but also I was terribly tempted
to speak, to unburden myself.

"Lee?" he asked, waiting for me to answer. And his voice was
also full of concern—*personal* concern—caring for me. At that
moment I was ready to open my heart: and how I longed to do
so!

But I was saved from my own weakness. I glanced away from
Raymond and—yes, of course, *his* eyes were on me. For the first
time in how long he showed a sign that he was aware of me. I
left Raymond at once to go and stand beside Swamiji. He gave
no further sign to me—he was busy being polite to Miss Charlotte—but I stood there and felt grateful and was able to say
good-bye to Raymond cheerfully.

Home Is Home

Miss Charlotte did not talk much on the way back in the taxi.
Raymond could see that she was disturbed but also that she was

doing her best to overcome her feelings. She seemed disinclined to discuss the two girls. There was nothing that could be done for them. So Miss Charlotte struggled to resign herself to this knowledge, and after a time she appeared to have succeeded. Her face was again serene and her bun firmly pinned into place. She asked Raymond, "What do you hear from your mother?"

"She is well, thank you."

"I expect," said Miss Charlotte, "she's beginning to look forward now to your return." She spoke with lively pleasure as if she were putting herself in Raymond's mother's place and sharing her joyful anticipation.

His mother wrote practically every day now. Her letters were full of local gossip, about her friends and activities and new books at the library, and also how she was planning to go up to town to have lunch with his Uncle Paul. She tried to make out that she was busy and contented, but between every line he knew what she was asking him. That was why nowadays her letters did not give him as much pleasure as before, and often he put off reading them.

"As soon as I've settled everything in Delhi, I shall be on my way too," Miss Charlotte said. "There are still so many little things—what a job it is to wind up! I'm getting quite impatient."

"Impatient to be off?"

"Yes. I want to go home."

She no doubt felt Raymond's surprise but did not for some time comment on it. They had got to the place where she was staying. It was a British-built bungalow, almost identical with the mission in Delhi, standing stolidly—in spite of age and disrepair—amid the encroachments of an overgrown garden.

Miss Charlotte said, "When your work here is finished, then it is time to go home."

"But you've been here thirty years!"

Miss Charlotte smiled. She said, "Still, home is home. . . ."

An ancient servant, indistinguishable from the ancient ser-

176

vants at the Delhi mission, came out on the veranda to peer at them. Miss Charlotte did not yet get out, for she had more to say.

"I've been enjoying myself this last month, being a tourist. It was a lovely little holiday. . . . Perhaps we'll be going home about the same time? You'll write and tell me, won't you, when you're leaving?"

"Not just yet, Miss Charlotte."

"But soon?"

The old servant opened the taxi door for her and she got out without waiting for an answer. Raymond waved to her and called that he would probably be seeing her in Delhi before she left. He drove to his hotel, where he found Gopi anxiously awaiting him.

Lee

Last night Margaret came to bed very late. I was still awake, lying on my bed and looking up at the corrugated sheet roof. It wasn't quite dark, moonlight came in through the bit of dusty skylight set into the wall. Evie was asleep; and Evie sleeping is always like a person not there at all. She lies absolutely still on her back the whole night through and doesn't even seem to be breathing. She wasn't in the least disturbed by the noise Margaret was making. Margaret is always clumsy and drops and bumps into things, after which she curses to herself. She doesn't usually worry about disturbing others, so I was surprised when she leaned over me and, seeing my eyes open, asked, "I didn't wake you, did I?" However, she didn't care much about my answer. I think she was glad I was awake so that she could share her thoughts with someone. She had a lot of thoughts, I could see. She sat on the edge of her bed and looked up to the skylight and her face, lit by the filtered moonlight, was radiant. She sighed, but with too much happiness, not pain.

"Why aren't you asleep?" she asked at last.

"It's these bedbugs."

She made a sound of impatience. Obviously she thought it was petty of me to be bothered by such things. I remember a time when she herself was very much bothered by them. But nowadays she never complains about anything—the bugs, or the heat, or the food—she doesn't seem to notice them at all any more. I know she's still sick—she doesn't tell anyone, she tries to hide it—but I know her stomach is very bad and once when she was bathing I saw it was distended and also she had a funny sort of rash down the back of her thighs. She looks unhealthy too, there's something wrong with the color of her skin, but somehow one doesn't notice because of this look she has, of contentment and even bliss.

She said, "I was with him. We were working on his itinerary."

I pretended I wasn't interested. I hate her at such moments. I hate myself even more for hating her. She's happy and I'm not, that's all.

"He wants to go to Copenhagen first because of a Mrs. Lund there who's interested in the Movement. Have you been to Copenhagen?"

When I didn't answer, she assumed I was asleep. She lay down too, but I think she didn't get to sleep either for a long time. I've noticed there are whole nights she hardly sleeps, but all the same next day she's bright and active.

I drag myself around. I've never been like this before. Everything is so strange, so dismal; it's as if there's no light in the sun, and those glorious Indian nights, well, they too now are dark and drab to me. Even at the hymn singing we have morning and evening when he always seems to be singling out each of us separately, even then I'm not there for him. Lately I've stopped joining in with the others when they sing. I just stand there silent; I don't *feel* like singing. I'm sure he's noticed—he always notices when anyone doesn't sing fervently enough—but now with me he pretends not to. He ignores me completely. I don't know why. I think about it all the time.

I spoke to Evie about it. Because I couldn't stand it any longer by myself. At first she wouldn't say anything, she thought I was accusing him, so she turned away her face. But when I said I must have failed somewhere and wanted to know what I could do to make it right, she became more sympathetic. I asked her had he ever been like that with her—had he cut her out the way he was doing to me—and she said no; but she said it in a hesitating sort of way as if there were more she could say only she wouldn't because it was some secret thing.

I said, "He never speaks to me. He doesn't look at me."

She asked me to be patient. She said she knew what I was going through because she'd gone through the same. I interrupted her eagerly: so he had been like that with her too at one stage? But she became all shy and trembly and said no, not like that but in another way. She begged me not to ask her any questions, she said she couldn't tell me anything more. It was something only between her and him, just as what was happening now was only between me and him. And if I could bring myself to understand that his present neglect of me was nothing but an expression of his care and love for me—if I could only accept that, then not only would my suffering be at an end but I would live in joy at my own submission. When she said that, she lowered her eyes and blushed softly. It was the first time I had seen her express so much emotion. She was even holding my hand and pressing it ever so gently. I didn't like that much, though.

Three Mad Crones

At first Raymond tried to refuse Gopi. He was very reluctant to meet Bulbul by the wall. But Gopi was so frightened and pleaded so hard that in the end Raymond knew he had to go. As soon as she saw him, Bulbul made a questioning gesture and asked, "Gopi?" Raymond shook his head. She said something which he couldn't hear because of the noise. It was the time of evening prayers—always the noisiest part of the day with singing and cymbals bursting out of the temples and prayers echoing up and down the river as the sun sank into it.

Bulbul beckoned him into the house. It was just as noisy in there. Not only did the sounds penetrate from outside, but Banubai was leading a group of devotees in singing hymns. Bulbul drew Raymond into the windowless, pitch-dark little storeroom where she slept at night. She made him sit on the floor close beside her and began to talk very fast; but of course he couldn't understand a word.

The door opened and it was Asha calling for Bulbul. Instinctively Bulbul clapped her hand over Raymond's mouth. "Yes, sweetheart, I'm here," she answered in her sweetest voice. Asha peered into the shadows where Bulbul crouched with Raymond. "Is there someone with you?" Asha asked. Bulbul cackled loudly. "What are you saying, darling, an old woman like me!"

"There *is* someone," Asha said.

Raymond beat Bulbul's hand away from his mouth and struggled to stand up.

"Who is it!" Asha cried.

He identified himself. Bulbul was clutching and tugging at him to pull him down again and he struggled to get away from her and reach the door. But just as he got there, Asha shut it. Now they were all three of them trapped inside.

"Why are you here?" she asked. She fumbled along the wall for the light and found the switch; but there was no bulb. Bulbul lit a candle that stood in a niche with her images and Asha snatched it from her and held it up close to Raymond. "What are you doing here?"

"You'll burn me with that if you're not careful."

"Why have you come?"

"Ask her." He pointed at Bulbul.

Asha's hand trembled. Raymond cautiously took the candle from her and replaced it in the niche. All Bulbul's little clay gods sprang into view, painted and smiling; she had also propped up an oleograph of Ganesh, the elephant-headed god, mounted on his rat.

"She told Gopi you wanted to see him." He looked toward Bulbul still crouching in a corner and with her sari pulled right over her head as if she were pretending not to be there. "She told him all sorts of things. She frightened him no end. . . . I say! What are you doing!" he exclaimed.

Asha had pounced on Bulbul. She dragged her out of the corner. Bulbul was crying out in fear; she put up her arms to protect herself while Asha, flailing her fists, struck her again and again. While she was beating Bulbul, Asha also fired questions at her which Bulbul tried desperately to answer but always her answers were drowned in new questions accompanied by threats, curses, and blows. Raymond was shouting at Asha to restrain her, and then he tried to drag her away, but she was moving so fast and was so strong that it was impossible for him. He clasped his arms around her waist to try to pull her off. He felt her body pulsating with strength and fury; it was like clasping a demon. She dragged him here and there with her as she went on beating Bulbul, but he hung on fiercely. Their voices —Asha's in fury, Bulbul in fear and pain, his own in protest— did not quite drown the prayers rising from the river nor Banubai and her group singing their evening hymns.

At last he felt Asha's tensed-up body slackening and, using all his strength, he managed to drag her away from Bulbul. He got the door open and forced her outside, leaving Bulbul lying face downward on the floor inside. She whimpered and heaved— quite energetically, which was a relief to Raymond: at least she wasn't dead. He shut the door on her and turned to Asha, who stood against the wall, panting and flushed and with her black eyes glittering.

At that moment Banubai's little group of hymn singers came out of her room. They were mostly elderly people. Their faces smiled and shone. As they passed Asha, they greeted her with a serene affection which enfolded not only her but the whole world and every human being struggling in it. One woman, in an excess of love, put out her hand to grasp Asha's—but drew it back immediately and with a cry. "How hot you are! Are you in fever?" She made to touch her again but Asha broke away from her and pushed through the devotees as if they were a flock of sheep.

Raymond followed Asha into Banubai's room. Banubai was displeased at seeing him and even asked, "Why does he come here?" But Raymond ignored this; he was intent on Asha.

"Are you all right now?" he asked her. "What about poor Bulbul? You're not going to—again? Are you? Are you, Asha?"

Asha shrugged indifferently. "She's had her beating."

"You nearly *killed* her!"

"Ha! You think it's so easy to kill Bulbul?"

"Why doesn't he go?" Banubai asked crossly. "Why don't you go?" she asked Raymond. "You don't want to be here. You don't like us."

Now he was forced to attend to her. She was looking at him with a glance that went right through him. There was nothing he could hide from her. Swamiji was the only other person who could look through him in such a way; but whereas with Swamiji Raymond felt that his thoughts met with tolerance, forgiveness, even amusement, it was not so with Banubai.

"We don't want people like you here," she said. "Only those who truly appreciate our culture are welcome."

Raymond wanted to defend himself. But he was not sure that he was entitled to do so; certainly, there was much, much he had truly appreciated, but he had to admit that there were other things he was not capable of appreciating at all. It was these evidently that Banubai was referring to.

"For two hundred years you tried to make us believe that you are superior persons. But now the tables are turned. Now that your culture is bankrupt and your lives have become empty and meaningless, you are beginning to learn where truth has been

182

hidden and stored away throughout the centuries. Even your scientists have learned this lesson."

Unable to find an adequate reply, Raymond said, "I've enjoyed my stay here very much." He added courteously, "I've learned a lot too."

"You're not capable of learning. To learn from us you have to be—wide open! And full of humility. There was a German gentleman who came to me. A very cultured person, he had studied in all branches of science and philosophy and had many German degrees. But after all his years of research and learning, in the end he learned only one thing: that he knew nothing. He came to me with these words: 'I know nothing.' When he said this, he folded his hands to me and touched my feet. I loved him for this attitude. I was very gentle and kind to him. I laid my hand on his head which he had shaved to be like a good Hindu. I said, 'We will do our best with you.'"

Bulbul came in. She crept in cautiously, as if she were afraid of being noticed. Asha was sitting on the floor and Bulbul also lowered herself to the floor and somehow managed to get lower than Asha and to crouch at her feet. Asha allowed her to stay there.

"You're not here to learn," Banubai told Raymond. "I don't know why you are here. Can you tell me? Please tell me."

Raymond thought seriously and honestly. But he could not find a satisfactory answer. He watched Bulbul touch Asha's feet; when Asha did not pull them away, she became bolder and began slowly, tenderly to press them. Why was he here? Raymond thought. He didn't know and, moreover, it seemed to him that Banubai was right and that really he didn't want to be.

"Someone with your materialistic outlook has nothing to take from us. I ask you in all humility, please go home. You have already done us enough harm." Raymond, taking her to be referring to British imperialism generally rather than to him personally, felt no need to defend himself. But she went on to say, "Look what you did to that boy—what's his name—"

183

"Who?" Asha cried at that.

"That boy who used to come here."

Asha stared at her incredulously. "You mean Gopi?"

"So many people come, I can't remember everyone's name."

She lay down on her bed and turned her face to the wall. They could hear her prayer beads begin to click. Raymond felt Asha looking at him with eyes that were deep and brooding. She made him uneasy; he asked her, "What does she mean?"

Asha continued to look at him in the same way. "Perhaps what she says is true."

"What, *what* is true?"

"Perhaps it is you who have taken Gopi away from us."

Raymond almost lost his temper. He said, "Don't be so damn silly."

"Banubai sees further than others."

Raymond felt as if he were locked up in a room with three mad crones. There seemed no sensible reason why he should be there. It was then that he decided not to wait for Gopi's wedding but to leave as soon as he could.

A Boat Ride

For Gopi it was not so much Raymond deciding as life sweeping them apart. Of course it was sad—what could be sadder than the parting of friends?—but it was inevitable and so had to be submitted to. There was even some charm in thus submitting and suffering. Gopi sang a beautiful lyric to Raymond which went as follows:

> You have gone away
> And although the moon is still silver, the rose blooms, and
>   the song of the koel is sweet
> There is neither moon nor rose nor song in my heart.

Raymond liked it very much. What he liked best, however, was not the lyric itself but the expression in Gopi's eyes and the smile that lingered on his lips as he sang. The setting was also very beautiful. They were being rowed in a boat on the river. This had become Raymond's favorite diversion in the holy city. As soon as he was out on the water, he felt as if all the squalor of the city—the stale puddles, the rotting vegetables, the people waiting to die on the sidewalks—was all suddenly purified and washed away. Yet how could that be? How could that water purify anything? Crowds of people, many of them diseased, were constantly dipping into it—and not only living people but even the remnants of dead bodies which (on account of poverty and the high cost of wood) had not been burned up completely. But Raymond, especially with Gopi sitting opposite him singing his lyric, found it easy to ignore these facts. It was a clear day, cooled and washed after a shower. The steps leading down to the river were almost empty at this time of day (the crowds would come later), and there were hardly any other boats about. Gopi sang, they glided, Raymond gave himself over to enjoyment. He would have been happy to go on like that for many hours, or till Gopi got bored. He hardly dared move for fear of breaking the mood and was so absorbed in his contentment that he failed to notice where the boat—drowsily rowed by an old man chewing opium—was taking them.

The steps leading down to the river from Banubai's house were also empty at this time of day; even the widows were sleeping somewhere curled up in some hospitable corner where they were in no one's way. Asha sat alone on the steps and looked out over the river. She was in a classic pose of sad reflection with her elbow propped on her knee and her chin on her hand. Probably she saw Raymond and Gopi before they saw her, but she may have at first taken them for a vision or a dream drifting across the empty space between sky and water on which her gaze was fixed. Next moment, however, she had jumped up and was waving and shouting.

Reluctantly their boat was made to row toward her. Before they got too near, Raymond threatened Gopi. "I'm *not* going

185

in. I'm *not* going near that Banubai again." But it appeared that Asha had no intention of asking them in. Instead she jumped into their boat, landing with a thud on her feet and swaying dangerously so that they had to steady her.

Raymond held her left arm, Gopi her right. Her left side remained normal—but the right! Her sensation transmitted itself to Gopi, who dropped her arm and refused to meet her eyes that turned toward him loaded with meaning and message. But he too was shaken. He sat down on the seat again, leaving Asha to Raymond. Raymond helped her to sit down. He was solicitous, but he was aware of what was going on and was affected by it. He stole a look at Gopi. Then, to help everybody, he began to make conversation that was of no interest to anyone. He pointed out the balcony of the Man Mandir Ghat and said what a pity it was that the building had been restored with inferior brick and plaster. When no one else said anything and the difficult atmosphere persisted, he went on to speak of the observatory and to compare it with the other four observatories (at Delhi, Jaipur, Mathura, and Ujjain), all of which he had seen. He was prepared to go into further detail, but Asha said, "Why are you talking so much?"

"Oh, all right," Raymond acquiesced good-naturedly. Then he said, "Perhaps you would let me off here."

"Why should you go?" Gopi said. "It's our boat, yours and mine. *We* took it."

"Why did you stay away from me when I called you?" Asha asked.

Gopi's eyes went blank. There was no sound in their boat except for the oars creaking and striking the water and their boatman breathing rather painfully. Raymond said he thought they ought to land now, the old man was getting too tired.

"I was waiting for you," Asha said. "And Banubai too."

Gopi stirred uneasily. "How is she?"

"Of course she is sad that you haven't come. . . ." She trailed off. She thought of Banubai, serene as always, undisturbed.

186

Banubai had even forgotten, or pretended to have forgotten, Gopi's name! "It's easy for Banubai," she said. "She is a saint. But I—"

"He really is tired," Raymond said.

"He's getting paid," Asha said. "I've been here so long now, I've done everything—meditation, prayer—and you see how I look, look at me, and I sleep on the floor and no meat, no drinks, nothing nothing. . . . But I don't mind! It was easy, not difficult at all. I like it. What is there to give up? It's all nonsense. I don't want it or need anything—except one thing only. Not what you think! Even that, though it's the hardest of all. But I keep thinking of you. I try and meditate and I see your face and I remember so much—"

Here Gopi interrupted her. He had been shrinking into himself, pushing his arms between his knees and glowering at the bottom of the boat. He didn't speak now but, by as discreet a sign as possible, indicated Raymond's presence to her. Asha was not put out. She said, "He feels the same way."

Raymond looked away. His lips quite disappeared, he set them so tight.

"When you love someone," Asha said, "only this beloved being fills your soul. You can struggle and turn whichever way you want, it's all useless. Why don't you help me?" she appealed to Raymond. "Explain to him. He is young and unfeeling, he doesn't know a thing."

Raymond said firmly, "I think our boatman is getting very tired." He made gestures to the man to take them to the landing stage. Gopi confirmed these with a few brisk words of command in Hindi. Asha said they were both very cruel. She spoke in despair.

"Asha, he's getting *married*," Raymond said.

"And I? What do you want me to do? Should I lie down and die? Oh, I wish I could. If only I could."

Suddenly she struggled to her feet and made to throw herself over the side of the boat. The water at this spot near the steps was quite shallow, but nevertheless Gopi cried out and hung on to her to save her. They struggled together, she cried, "No, let me go. I want to go." He wouldn't and at last managed to dissuade her. Both sat trembling side by side.

Their boat bumped onto the steps and the boatman jumped out to secure it. Raymond got out too and paid him. He waited for the other two, who still sat there together.

Lee

Sometimes the ashram seems quite spooky. It's so much in the middle of nowhere. All around there is nothing but miles and miles and miles of flat land and flat sky the same color as the land. No trees or anything green, just a few scrubs withering away in all that dusty expanse. Quite often there are dust storms and great columns of dust rise up and sweep across the country-side and sometimes you feel when they have settled down again that the ashram will have disappeared, leaving no trace. And at night, when everyone's asleep, it's spooky inside the ashram too. You think of all those people sleeping and you know that though they're lying quiet on their beds they're having fantastic dreams. They can't not have them because all day their efforts are concentrated on meditation and getting in touch and all sorts of spirits are being called up, even some evil ones that have to be exorcised by means of the good ones. And you can't just lay all that energy to rest, it goes on even when you're sleeping and it's hovering over all those beds and over the whole ashram so that you can almost see it in the shape of some very fantastic pictures. And there's also what's going on inside my own hut-ment, where I'm shut in with Evie and Margaret, both of them sleeping and both—I can't help feeling sometimes—so strange, so strange. I mean, Evie lying there like *nothing*, not even breathing, and Margaret on the other hand breathing very loudly and in an unhealthy way so that I think not only of the dreams she's having but also of what's going on inside her body.

I keep remembering what Miss Charlotte said about diseases that rot you away from within, and it seems to me that that's what's going on inside the hutment, inside Margaret.

But all the same I'm not really basically frightened, not deep inside me, just sort of superficially. Because in the middle of all that spookiness there is something good and radiant that scatters it like a light scatters shadows. And I think of it literally like a light: it really seems to me there is something like a column of light over the hutment where he is. And all I have to do is to concentrate on that and then I feel everything is all right—no, not all right but marvelous, marvelous! As long as he is there, I don't have a thing to worry about.

Still, I do worry and that's why I'm so often awake at night. I know it's egotistical of me to worry this way and that I have no right to. What does it matter whether he takes any notice of me, whether he looks at me or talks to me or whether he completely ignores me as he's been doing —what difference does it make, since the only important thing is that *he is there*. He exists, and shouldn't that be enough and more than enough and an abundance for me? The fact that it isn't goes to show what a low stage of development I'm at. All the same, it does seem to me that sometimes he takes pity on me. Not in the day but at night when I'm lying awake on account of him. Suddenly when it gets very bad, it seems to me that he is in fact thinking of me the way I am of him. Then I feel—oh, quite all right, and I don't want anything more, no further sign from him. I don't get one either and next day it's like it's been all the other days so that I begin to doubt again and think that what I felt in the night was only my imagination.

But last night . . . Suddenly I was sure that not only was he thinking of me but that he was calling me. I don't know how I got this idea, how it was transmitted to me. Did the light hovering over his hutment become a signal as from a lighthouse? No, it wasn't like that—it wasn't something from outside but as if there was this beam beckoning from right inside me, from my own heart. I got up at once.

It was a strange night. There was a full moon but it wasn't bright, it was dimmed-out and pale like the pale shreds of cloud floating across it. The sky was all torn up by these clouds shifting and sailing rather fast as if they were being driven and making everything up there look very disturbed; and on the earth it was disturbed too with little hot winds blowing through the air and blowing up puffs of dust that skimmed the ground and rose and whirled around in spirals and then sank back again. The dust got into my hair and teeth and nostrils as I crossed the open space round which all the hutments are grouped. Swamiji's hutment is on the opposite side of mine. As usual, there were two disciples outside his door; I couldn't make out who they were that night but I saw they were both asleep, lying in a rather contorted way on their cots. But he was awake as I knew he would be. He wasn't lying down but sitting up in his usual lotus pose. He recognized me at once even though the only light was from the dimmed moon; he didn't seem very surprised to see me, though he pretended to be.

"Oh-ho!" he said. "Just see who has come for a visit."

"I couldn't sleep," I said; actually, I mumbled. One part of me —the superficial, conventional part—felt I owed an explanation for my sudden appearance, another part knew I owed nothing of the sort.

"Why not? Have you done something bad? It is people with bad conscience who can't sleep. Remember *Macbeth* by Shakespeare." This seemed a good joke to him and he laughed.

"You know perfectly well why I can't sleep."

I was really getting annoyed by his attitude, and that he should be so relaxed and casual when I was—well, the way I was.

"No, why not? Tell me."

He spoke with a sort of fake "genuine interest" that made me quite mad. I began to shout. I didn't care about waking the

190

people sleeping outside the door, I didn't think of them. And he seemed not to care either if anyone overheard us, for he didn't try and stop me but let me go on and say what I wanted. I reproached him for everything he had done to me over the past weeks, I demanded explanations, and I pleaded for justice. He heard me out. Once when he thought I had finished, he began to say something, but when he saw I hadn't he stopped and said, "Oh, sorry," and let me go on. I became more and more worked up, and yet it was such a relief, after all this time, such a relief to be able to say these things to him.

When I had said everything, I stood there trembling and as if a great torrent had rushed through me and swept away bridges and boulders. After a time he asked quietly, "You have finished?"

It was very, very still in the hutment. I noticed that the slight snoring sounds that had come from outside had stopped; the two disciples must have woken up and now they too were holding their breath so as not to disturb whatever was going to happen next. I stood awaiting this. I think we all knew what it was going to be. Probably I had known before I came.

Now I was sitting on his bed with him. He was stroking me but it was as if he were doing it wrong, like stroking a cat's fur the wrong way so that the thrill consisted mainly of distaste. But I think he did it that way on purpose. He was saying, "How stupid you are, what a stupid little fool"; he said it in quite an affectionate way but that was only the beginning. He soon stopped being affectionate. He said terrible things and he did terrible things. I wanted to cry out and ask him to stop but my voice got stuck in my throat and came out in a funny whimpering sound. It was hot, stifling hot in the hutment. I didn't feel as if I were a person any more, only this awful sensation like an electric shock wriggling in the dark. *He* was the only person there. He was terrible, terrifying. He drove right on into me and through me and calling me beastly names, shouting them out loud and at the same time hurting me as much as he could.

It went on for a long time. I was exhausted but he seemed able to summon up unending waves of new energy so that he rose on them and grew stronger and stronger. I loathed him. He revolted me both with what he was doing and the vile words he was saying. The strange thing was not only did I suffer but I got bored too because it went on so long and wouldn't stop. I even began to think my own thoughts. These took me back to the time I had been with Gopi up in the hotel room overlooking the mosque. How happy that time now seemed to me, how idyllic and good. I remembered the sound of the phonograph coming up from the café downstairs and the sounds from the mosque and the market. There had been a smell of incense, or had Gopi worn a dash of some sweet scent? But next moment the memory was wiped out in a flash as Swamiji drove home again: he shouted abuse and lay panting on top of me. The hutment was dense with a greasy hot smell like of a goat, and the only sounds were my funny whimpering and his animal breathing.

When he had finished, he turned me out without another word. And I must say I was too glad to get away to want any further conversation. I got out so quickly that I caught the two disciples by surprise; they were both sitting up on their beds with their ears tuned toward the open door and their mouths dropped open. When they saw me come out, they flopped down at once and made a ridiculous attempt to pretend to be asleep. As if I gave a damn for them. I dragged myself across the compound, feeling wounded and torn; my clothes were literally torn. The dust storm had worked itself up more and the columns of dust were denser and rose high, filling the air and obscuring the moon, which was already dim enough. Now a pack of jackals began to howl, and I joined them, though not very loud but again in the same whimper I had heard coming from myself in his hutment; only now it wasn't so much in pain as in rage and disgust.

192

Bulbul Sings a Folk Song

After her boat ride, Asha's thoughts began to work along a line that pleased Bulbul very much. Asha spoke often now about Maupur and their home there: she spoke nostalgically, and Bulbul too was filled with nostalgia for this place where both she and Asha had been born and had grown up. Bulbul said, "Let's go, sweetheart," with a sigh of longing, and Asha also sighed in the same way though next moment she said what was Bulbul thinking of, why should they go there, and called her fool and idiot. Bulbul was quiet then, but she was happy; she knew that an excellent start had been made. The days passed and they kept coming back to the subject of Maupur. They also spoke about Gopi. One day Bulbul quite simply brought these two subjects together by wondering how Gopi would like it in Maupur. She said she thought he would like it very much.

Outwardly, Asha's life with Banubai continued unchanged. She still cooked her meals for her, slept in her room at night; sometimes they still laughed and had fun together. But they were no longer close—or rather, Asha was no longer close to Banubai. Banubai was as she always had been, there was no change in her, she was there; but whereas formerly Asha had drawn strength from her being there, had as it were illumined herself from Banubai's flame, now she was turning away from her as if she no longer wanted or needed her.

She even began to feel uncomfortable with her. This was tolerable during the day when many people came to see Banubai, but at night, when they were alone together, and she knew Banubai to be lying there wide awake in the dark, then sometimes Asha had a queer sensation. Not of reverence, but something else. Once it became so overwhelming that she could not bear to stay with her but had to get up and leave her. She stood outside the door. She kept listening for some sound or movement from inside, but there was nothing. Yet she knew Banubai was awake: wide awake as always. Sometimes Asha suspected

193

that Banubai never slept at all but lay there all night in the dark, utterly silent and yet giving out a sense of tremendous activity as if she were busy spinning endless filaments of light and spirit.

Asha went into the little storeroom where Bulbul slept. Bulbul was making ugly breathing sounds through her nose; Asha hated these sounds which always accompanied Bulbul's sleep but now she was pleased to hear them. She touched Bulbul's prostrate body with her foot, and when Bulbul didn't stir, she did it again and harder. Then Bulbul gave a cry and started up. "Who is it, what?" she cried into the darkness.

"Idiot."

"Oh, it's you, sweetheart. How you frightened me. I thought it was that witch Banubai."

Asha stretched herself on the floor beside Bulbul. She was still full of odd sensations. Bulbul got up and began to fuss over her. Asha did not resist but allowed her to do everything she wanted. There was no pillow good enough for Asha's head, so Bulbul offered her own lap. She stroked Asha's temples, lovingly brushed the hair from her forehead: slowly, under these ministrations, Asha began to feel soothed. Her eyes closed. Bulbul began to sing. She started off with the lullabies that she had sung when Asha was a baby. "Sleep, baby, sleep, you have eaten bread and sugar, now sleep." Then she sang a folk song about a girl looking out from her father's fortress to see if her lover was coming over the ravines. Bulbul's voice was hoarse and grating and rather wicked; with relish she sang of the awaited lover, describing his round strong arms and his thighs which were also round and strong. Asha's eyes opened and closed, closed and opened; a delicious drowsiness swept over her and yet she didn't want to sink into it because what Bulbul was singing was even more delicious.

"Again," she said when Bulbul's song had ended.

"Go to sleep, darling."

"No, again."

So Bulbul sang that song again.

Lee

Asha didn't ask too many questions and didn't seem much surprised either when I said was it all right for me to stay there. She said okay and made Bulbul drag away my bundle and bedroll and dump them somewhere. She did ask once or twice about the ashram, but when I wasn't inclined to answer she didn't insist. I think it wasn't so much out of tact but because she wasn't all that interested. She wanted more to talk about herself.

Because she looked different I thought she would be different —that being here and living with a spiritual person, she would have changed. But she hasn't. She does nothing but talk about Gopi and how unhappy she is because he's going to get married. She has this fantastic plan to take Gopi away with her to that place she comes from and keep him locked up in the desert fortress or palace or whatever it is she has there. I said, "But if he's going to get married?"—and her eyes went hooded the way they do when she has tragic thoughts and she said she only wanted him for herself for a short brief while before that, to snatch a last morsel of happiness before old age and despair closed in on her forever.

I don't know why I don't like Banubai more. I can see she's very advanced spiritually, but I don't feel right with her. She's not the right person for me, that's all. I know I could never accept her as my guru. Well, that's not surprising because it's not that easy to find a guru, and there are people who spend their lives looking for one and never succeed, or only after years and years. For each particular person there's only one particular guru, and you have to look for him and look for him and when you've found him—then you're his and no one else will ever be right for you again. At least that's what people say. But I don't want to believe it. And even if it's true—all right, then from now on I'll do without anyone.

At first Banubai used to ask me about him. When I evaded her questions, she looked at me, into me, the way he's the only other one I know can look into people. I tried not to let her see anything, I lowered my eyes away from her; but I knew she could see more than I wanted her to. I didn't like that; and there was something else I didn't like and that was the way she seemed *pleased* that something had happened to take me away from him. And after a while when I didn't say anything and didn't answer any of her questions, she began to say things about him. Nothing outright but she insinuated—she said she had heard this and she had heard that, she hinted at all sorts of nasty stories that I didn't want to hear about so that whenever she started on them I got up and went away.

She began to dislike me. In the beginning she had been very friendly to me and had even made quite a fuss over me, always insisting that I should sit near her and she would put her hand on my head and say I was her new little daughter. And all the people smiled at me. It made me feel a fool; and I was also uncomfortable with her hand on my head. So I was glad when she stopped favoring me, though now she began to go in the opposite direction and she was sulky with me and turned away her face whenever I came into the room. Once when there were a whole lot of people there she even attacked me, though in an indirect way. She talked about foreigners who come to India because they are bored in the West. They pretend to be in search of spiritual values, but because they don't know what true spiritual values are, they fasten themselves on harmful elements who only help to drive them deeper down into their disturbed egos; and so not only do they themselves suffer bad consequences but also all sorts of poisonous influences are released, polluting the air breathed in by truly spiritual Indians. She didn't look at me while she was talking, but of course people guessed very easily whom she was referring to. Some of them gave me sidelong glances and I felt everyone was edging farther away from me where I sat in a corner by the door so that

196

I could not help feeling that perhaps I really was a polluting influence.

Asha told me not to mind. She said saints were always moody people, you never knew from one moment to the next how they were going to behave. But I didn't want to stay there any longer. And Asha said no, why should I, and then she had a marvelous new idea, she said come on, we'll all go to Maupur. Well, I didn't particularly want to go to Maupur, but where else could I go? There wasn't anywhere. She kept urging me and urging me and she said Raymond too would come with us. All four of us—she and Gopi, Raymond and I—would go and we'd have a house party there. She became very enthusiastic about this idea and began to describe the place and the marvelous time we'd have there. Bulbul came in on it too, also very enthusiastic, she kept babbling on and on (of course I couldn't understand a word she said) and she made gestures in the air with her hands as if she were drawing fantastically beautiful pictures there, scenes of splendor and delight.

Gopi Is Restless

Gopi didn't know what was happening to him. He no longer slept as well as he used to; or rather, he slept all right but not dreamlessly as before. Moreover, they were not good dreams. He could never remember what they were about, and perhaps they were not about anything but were more in the nature of sensation. This sensation was one of heaviness, a physical oppression as of a weight laid on him; and when he woke up there really was a weight, right on his stomach, and he realized it was all the food he had eaten the day before—which he had had to eat because of guests coming and going, and to oblige his aunt and the other women who were cooking so hard and urging and urging to take, to eat, to eat his fill in order to build up his strength. There were always jokes about building up his strength which he would soon be needing in plenty. Gopi pretended to enjoy these jokes, as he pretended to enjoy the food, but really he didn't. He didn't enjoy anything. He felt during the day as he felt in the night—as if there was something too heavy lying on his stomach.

Whenever Babloo proposed an outing nowadays, Gopi agreed at once. Babloo was pleased, but not for long, for when they got to their place of entertainment Gopi remained bored and silent all the time and was soon in as great a hurry to leave as he had been to come. Babloo and his friends were hurt and insulted; but when Babloo reproached him, Gopi shrugged him off as if he didn't care for him at all. He couldn't explain anything to himself, what was there he could explain to Babloo? So he explained nothing but lived on day by day under his weight of oppression and hoped that something might happen to relieve him of it.

Perhaps he was expecting Bulbul—at any rate, he did not have a shock when she turned up. This time she did not come to his uncle's house but lay in wait for him outside the discotheque. Gopi remained cool. He told Babloo to go ahead and join his friends and that he would be with him soon. "Go on," he said, rather sternly, discouraging Babloo's curiosity and watching him till he had disappeared inside. Then Gopi was ready to follow Bulbul wherever she might care to lead him. He expressed no surprise when she took him into one of the disreputable houses that surrounded the discotheque. They were shown into a room where a great heavy woman lay on a bed smoking a hookah; there were also quite a few other people, most of them untidy young women in rather showy clothes; a man sat in a corner tuning a musical instrument. The fat woman seemed to be a friend of Bulbul's; she greeted her heartily, even deferentially, and was also kind to Gopi, smiling at him with tiny little teeth stained red by betel juice.

The room, although very small, was further subdivided by a curtained screen. Bulbul took Gopi behind this screen, where there was nothing except one bed with a colored quilt on it.

Bulbul told Gopi at once that Asha wanted him to come with her to Maupur. Gopi replied that it was not possible, he was getting married soon, and what would he tell his relatives? But the way he said this it was not so much an objection as a problem which he was presenting to Bulbul in order that she might solve it. And she did solve it quite easily (it was not difficult for her at all). She said he need only tell his relatives that he was going on a short tour with his English friend Raymond and would be back well in time for the wedding. Then Gopi said that Raymond was going back to England, but that too Bulbul did not feel to be an insuperable obstacle. On the contrary, she seemed quite confident that things could be arranged with Raymond in a satisfactory manner. All this took place not in a secret whisper but in raised voices—there was no other way, on account of the noise of music and female talk on the other side of the partition. Gopi kept his eyes fixed on this partition and ever afterward he remembered the curtain, which was green with large pink and lilac roses on it.

Raymond's Plans

Raymond said it was a crazy idea and anyway he couldn't come, he was going home. Asha said reproachfully, "How can you go?"

"How can I go?" Raymond repeated with a laugh. "It's high time I did."

"And Gopi?"

"Gopi is getting married."

"Raymond, Raymond, how can you be so cold?"

Raymond knew there was no point in defending himself against the charge of coldness. Self-control, a certain stoicism he had grown up with and used all his strength to develop—these too came under the heading of coldness and were equally reprehensible.

She pleaded, "Only a little while, a few days, that's all."

"But then it'll have to end anyway."

"So let it end."

"And then?"

"Then—nothing." She made a throw-away gesture with her hand. He didn't know what she was throwing away but it looked like her whole life.

A few days earlier Raymond had written to his mother. He had given her the date of his return. He had also suggested that why didn't she meet him somewhere halfway? For instance, in Teheran or Istanbul. His mother was a wonderful traveling companion. She liked the same things he liked. He had enjoyed every trip he had taken with her, and there was no doubt in his mind that he would enjoy this one too. Later, he had another good idea and at once sat down to write another letter. This one was to Miss Charlotte, and he invited her to join his mother and himself. Miss Charlotte and he would leave from New Delhi and Mother would meet them in the Middle East. He urged Miss Charlotte to come; he said he knew she and Mother would get on famously—perhaps too famously, he joked, so that he himself would end up feeling left out.

After Asha, Gopi also came to ask Raymond to go with them to Maupur. He said it would be a very interesting cultural tour for him. When Raymond said he had already committed himself to a cultural tour with his mother and Miss Charlotte, Gopi urged him to postpone that and not to miss this unique opportunity to see more of India. "Perhaps you will never come back to us again," Gopi pointed out, making a sad face, and perhaps he was really sad at the thought, but Raymond could see that he was also pretending a bit and his feeling was not so pure now as it had been that day on the river when they thought they were saying good-bye forever.

"What about your wedding?" Raymond asked.

Instead of answering the question, Gopi said, "If you cared for me at all, you would want to come. You would want to be with me." He lowered his voice and it became soft and wheedling. "We shall have such a nice time, you and I."

"And Asha."

Gopi was silent.

"Gopi, you shouldn't go."

"But why not?" Gopi made innocent eyes. "Only for a little holiday before my wedding. My family are very happy. They say yes, go. Go with your friend Raymond." He scanned Raymond's face. "You will come? Say yes. Say yes, Gopi, I shall come and we shall have a nice holiday together. Say it."

"No! I won't!" cried Raymond.

"Just think—perhaps it is for the last time. Perhaps you will never come back to India. Or if you come, many years will have passed and you will be an old, old man, with white hairs, and I shall be fat like my uncle."

"Ah—don't," said Raymond, putting out his hands as if to ward off something.

"Yes, with my stomach like this—and my chin *here.*" He tucked it in. They both laughed.

Raymond Changes His Plans

"You see," Swamiji said, "Lee wants to do only half."

He had come by himself, unattended by Evie or any other disciple. He had told Raymond quite simply that he would like Lee to come back. He also told him the reason why Lee had run away; that too he said quite simply and smiling a little at Lee's foolishness. Then he said, "You also, Raymond, want to do only half. But with you it is the other half."

"Are we discussing me now?" Raymond asked. He found himself talking in the somewhat bantering tone he usually adopted with Swamiji. He was rather glad to see him; he always enjoyed his company, sometimes in spite of himself.

"Thank goodness we don't have to discuss you, Raymond. You are not like those girls. They would like to sit all day and discuss about themselves." The way he said that made Raymond laugh, and Swamiji smiled too and continued, "For them their own personality is the most important subject in the world. But—poor girls—what personality do they have worth talking about? They are like little mice, quite undeveloped. And when I try to develop them, they run away from me." He smiled ruefully, one hand outstretched as if appealing for justice and reason.

Raymond said, "It seems you're the injured party."

"Certainly! I am injured. Very much injured. Please consider my position. Lee came to me, she wanted to be my disciple. I said, very good, Lee, I will take up this burden you have put on me. We are two people signing a contract together. It is signed and sealed. Very good. Then one of the parties decides that he or she no longer wishes to abide by the terms. In such a case, is it right willy-nilly to tear up the contract, to say finished, I don't like it, go to hell? Is it right, Raymond? I leave it to your judgment entirely."

Raymond said, "I believe she wasn't aware of everything there was in the contract."

"Oh, I see. She wasn't aware. Then answer me one more question. When we find ourselves born into the world, we are here whole and entire, isn't it? We are not just spirits but also minds, not only minds but also bodies. It is so, there can be no question or argument. Then what would you say to a person who, on discovering this incontrovertible fact of nature, says no I don't want it to be so, I want to be only one or the other? You would say such a person is deficient in his understanding; you would say he is weak up here, poor fellow." He said, "Everything must be full, whole, round, Raymond. It must be one."

"Have you been to see her?"

"She is not ready for me now," Swamiji said sadly. Then he brought his face close to Raymond's. His eyes were bright as with fever, he ran a broad, pale tongue swiftly round his lips. "But I want her to become ready for me again. She must come to me as she did at first: with her hands joined, begging for me to take her. And I will take her, and we shall start again from the beginning. But this time we shall go further. I will take her far, very far, right to the end if need be—and this time, Raymond, this time there will be no running away."

Raymond didn't tell Lee about this visit but he did tell her that, if she wanted to go to Maupur, he would postpone his departure and go along with her.

part III

MAUPUR

The Retreat

Asha had taken it for granted that they would have the New Palace to themselves, but when they arrived they found that Rao Sahib was already installed there with a retinue of retainers and helpers. Election time was drawing near, and he was very busy. He drove around the district in a jeep decorated with the flags of his party and a giant photograph of himself and addressed election meetings and met voters. All day party workers went in and out of the palace, which had become Rao Sahib's headquarters. It was known as the New Palace to distinguish it from the Old Palace which was in the heart of the city. The New Palace had been built around 1910 and looked large and imposing with a vast marble entrance hall decorated with marble busts of Edward VII and Queen Alexandra, but it had in fact very little living accommodation so that the arrival of Asha and her party was a distinct inconvenience.

Asha took them all away to another house. It was some way out into the country and had been built by Asha's father in the thirties as a kind of private retreat. It was, in fact, called The Retreat. Asha's father had been fond of Western pleasures such as whisky and cabaret artists, and the drawing room had been modeled on a nightclub featuring a bandstand and a bar with a jazzy mural over it. He had had great hopes of the place but, although he had lavished a lot of care on it, it had not yielded as much pleasure as he had anticipated. This was mainly due to its unfortunate situation in the middle of the desert. There was no water and the sun beat down on a landscape inhabited by jackals and vultures. Struggling hard with tube wells and electric generators, Asha's father had managed to lay out a garden, and in his lifetime there had been a few weekend parties which his guests claimed to have been as good as anything to be enjoyed in London or Paris. But after his death there wasn't anyone to take an interest in the place and it fell into disrepair and the garden died.

Since the country was too rough and sandy for a car, Asha had to take her guests there in a jeep. They passed no signs of habitation on the way, and so it was a shock suddenly to see the house rearing up: a building in the thirties style, with futuristic cantilevers jutting out in sharp geometrical shapes. It had been plastered to resemble raw concrete, but the outside had not been repainted for a long time and had suffered much from the climate. The inside, however, was an agreeable surprise. Contradicting the austere style of architecture, the furnishing was of an Edwardian opulence; and although no one had lived there for many years, the servants had done their best to keep it all up—perhaps in the hope that one day the good times would start again.

Each of the guests was shown into a separate suite of bedroom, dressing room, and bathroom. Raymond's suite was mainly red: red-shaded electric candelabras set into the walls, red plush curtains, and a slippery red velvet bedspread over the double bed. His bathroom had elaborate imported fixtures, but when he turned on the large majestic taps only a trickle of brown water came gurgling out. He heard Gopi calling him in an excited voice from the next room. When he went there, he found a suite almost identical with his own except that everything was in yellow. Gopi pointed out the attractive features of the room which included a set of old *Punch* drawings framed around the walls. Gopi looked at them and liked them but asked Raymond to explain them to him. They were English jokes of the thirties—mainly of a sporting or political character—and though Raymond tried to explain them, he did not feel he was able to make himself very clear; nevertheless Gopi said they were funny and laughed at them. He was pleased with everything and kept asking Raymond, "Aren't you happy that you came? Aren't you grateful to me that I brought you?" He threw himself backward on the yellow double bed and bounced up joyfully on its springs.

Lee

At first I thought it was a bit like the ashram. Perhaps because, like the ashram, the house is stuck out in the middle of nowhere with nothing growing for miles around as if it's all been killed off by the sun. But of course it's very, very different. I always felt good in the ashram but here I feel—not good at all, for many reasons. One of these is Asha and Gopi. They're together all day. They sit down there in that drawing room with the bar and the bandstand. They both seem to like being here, though they don't do anything except just sit. Oh, yes, sometimes they play cards. Asha's started drinking a lot again, and Gopi drinks with her to keep her company. I think he's beginning to like it too. In the afternoon they're both in Asha's bedroom and there's no sound from out of there hour after hour. I don't know if they're asleep or not. I'm also in my room but I can't sleep because of the heat.

I think of him though I try not to. Now it's not only that I don't want to think of him because it hurts me to do so. But also I feel it's not right to think of him. Not here. If I think of him here it's almost as if I'm desecrating—not him so much but what he's always been for me, what he's stood for. And what I still believe in. How wrong, how bad this place is for me! To think that I've traveled and traveled and come all this way and now I've ended up here.

As soon as it's cool enough, I go out of the house. I walk through what's left of the garden—which I think was quite elaborate at one time but now there's only some broken statues and overgrown zigzag paths—till I'm out in open country with nothing there except all that dry land. It's as flat as the land around the ashram, but before it reaches the horizon there is a band of hills with woods where wild animals live. I see the sky and the stars in it. Then I feel better, and I can forget the house and everything in it and I can think the same thoughts as in the ashram. I know if only I'm patient enough and do everything he said to do and be what he said to be, then in the end I shall overcome myself. But how difficult that is.

How can I not think of him! Sometimes I see him so clearly with his forehead wrinkled up under his cap and he's smiling and beckoning with his eyes and teasing me.

Asha at Home

Asha said, "You know what I think? I think you're in love with your Swamiji."

Lee stared straight in front of her. Raymond also pretended not to have heard. Only Gopi responded: he sniggered in a rather unpleasant way. He and Asha had been drinking for several hours and their faces glistened with heat and alcohol.

"So what's wrong," Asha said. "Why don't you admit it? It's nothing to be ashamed of."

Lee said, "I think you're very boring." She got up and wandered out of the room. Raymond would have liked to follow her but forced himself to remain. Asha and Gopi went on drinking —not just out of boredom but with real thirst: only they couldn't quench it because their drinks were warm, the ice kept melting away in the heat. Unfortunately also the electricity had failed again and the electric fans were not working, so Asha had called a servant to stand behind them and wave a large black-and-pink Japanese fan to and fro.

"Why does she run away like that?" Asha said. "So what if she is in love with her Swamiji. It can happen to anyone."

"She's frigid," Gopi said.

"Who taught you that word?" Raymond said sharply.

Gopi reared up; he was offended. "I've known it since long," he said, and then allowed his indignation to mount. "You think I don't know anything. Only you know. Only you are very clever."

"Not at all," Raymond said. "Especially not in these things. And I think you're nicer without that too. Thank you," he told the servant who bent more closely over him to cool him with the fan, "I really don't need it."

"This side," Gopi commanded. "Harder. Faster. I think everything we've been told about people in the West is a lie. It's all just propaganda. You don't know anything about sex—none of you know, you're all frigid."

Raymond told Asha, "You're giving him too much to drink."

He went away. He went out into the garden. The sun beat down and the light was electric sharp, but it was a relief to him to be here rather than in the house. There was a garden pavilion which was built as a hexagon with an emphasis on form and with the remains of its pink plaster peeling off in chunks. Raymond sat on the triangular bench inside and thought about what to do. He could send a telegram to Miss Charlotte and to his mother to reinstate their postponed trip; they could leave quite soon— it was only a matter of air bookings and hotel reservations. They would stay in international air-conditioned hotels, for Mother would prefer comfort to local color and so would Raymond himself.

He looked up and there was Asha coming toward him down one of the overgrown paths. Ever since their arrival in Maupur she had been getting herself up in her own version of the local peasant costume. She wore a voluminous skirt striped in black and gold with a loose blouse of shot silk and a festoon of heavy silver necklaces.

"Come in," she told him. "The electricity is on again."

"I prefer to be here."

"It's too hot."

But she sat down next to him on the concrete bench. She seemed inclined for confidences. She said, "Papa used to love coming here. This house was his dream. . . . And now Rao Sahib wants to sell it."

"Oh, does he," said Raymond, wondering who would want to buy it.

"But I will never allow it, never. If there were someone who could appreciate—but it is a local person who wants the land to put up factories. Can you imagine! Oh, I will never allow it, I've told Rao Sahib. Papa planned and did so much work for this place. He had a German architect but most of the ideas were his own. He liked having parties here—very intimate type of parties that he couldn't have in the palace. Papa loved to have a good time. Like me." She looked at him out of the corner of her eye, mischievously, her mouth corner twitching as if wondering whether she could smile; when Raymond gave her no encouragement, she didn't, and went on talking quite seriously. "Of course we weren't supposed to know what was going on and he never brought us here, but we knew. Everyone did. He always had a lot of girl friends all his life long but toward the end he fell in love very seriously. She was quite an ordinary girl, an Anglo-Indian, her name was Kitty. She used to sing in a cabaret in Calcutta, that's where he saw her first. He brought her here and it was for her he had the parties. He would bring a band all the way from Calcutta and they played and she sang the numbers she used to sing in the cabaret. Papa was always afraid she would get bored and wouldn't want to stay—she was quite young and she was used to living in Calcutta; so he would do anything for her, anything he could think of to amuse her. But she did get bored. Poor Papa."

212

Raymond said, "Gopi's going to get bored too."

"He is very happy here."

"How long do you intend to keep him?"

Asha's face clouded over; the necklaces on her bosom heaved.

"You said just a few days."

She shook her head. Tears shone in her eyes like jewels.

Raymond said, "Why not let him go now, before he gets bored like Kitty and runs away."

"Kitty didn't run away."

He knew he was going to hear some dreadful story. He didn't want to. Already it was so oppressive in that dead garden. Some heavy dark birds hung motionless from the sky. He asked, hoping to ward off the story, "Is there any wildlife around here? Sometimes—at night—it sounds like it."

"Those are hyenas. Perhaps there may be a stray tiger, but this is not really hunting country. If you want to shoot, you have to go farther to Sagarvan. That's very good country. Do you want to go?"

"Not really."

"No, I think you're not the sporting type. Like Peter. I told you about Peter, Rao Sahib's tutor? Once Papa took him hunting. When they came back, Papa was laughing and laughing. 'What sort of an Englishman are you?' he asked him. Peter couldn't stand the sight of blood."

"I don't like it either."

"You're very much like Peter. I told you before." She hesitated. Again he felt her to be on the verge of some undesirable revelation. Meanwhile Gopi had put a record on the gramophone and the "Donkey Serenade" came out into the garden. It sounded gay and tinny.

"It was here, in this house, in this garden, that Peter tried to kill himself."

Raymond said, "Asha, I don't think I need to hear this."

"It was all Kitty's fault. You see, she got so bored she was ready to take up with anyone. And that boy was quite handsome

—the one Peter was in love with, the clerk from the guest house. When Papa was away, Kitty would send for him and he came and they had a good time together. And Peter followed him and waited down here in the garden. All night sometimes."

Gopi sang with the record. He didn't know the tune, and his attempts to reproduce it sounded bizarre because he had transposed it into the Indian scale. Sometimes he laughed at himself for the strange sounds he was producing.

Raymond said, "You really shouldn't make him drink so much. He's not used to it."

"If you take him away, I don't know what I shall do. Can you imagine being alone here?"

"You don't have to stay here."

She said, "It's the same everywhere. In Bombay too. Those sounds you say you hear at night, so often I hear them in Bombay. Of course I know it's the sea really but to me it sounds like here and then I think I am here."

Progress

Raymond had to go into Maupur to post letters to his mother. Afterward he was reluctant to return to The Retreat, and he walked around Maupur although there was not very much to see. It was quite an ordinary little town with a bazaar and a railway station. On a craggy mound overlooking the town stood the remains of what had once been a fort. From here Rajput chieftains had marched out to fight—sometimes against other Rajput chieftains, sometimes against Moghul princes, and sometimes against Mahratta generals. That particular clan of Rajputs had died out—those that had not been killed in battle having been poisoned by their sibling rivals—but had been revived through the female line by the British. That had been the beginning of Rao Sahib's own family history. They had not lived in the bleak old fort but in a palace in the town with many little dark rooms and passages. This palace had also fallen into disuse, and the bazaar had grown around it and encroached on it closer and closer so that now there were little stalls selling electrical goods spilling right into the palace courtyard.

Raymond went to visit Rao Sahib in the New Palace on the outskirts of town. As usual, Rao Sahib was cordial but he was also very busy and kept having to greet new visitors. He was cordial to everyone and anxious to show that he liked them. His visitors were leading citizens, self-made men with little businesses, and they were pleased to be there in the palace and looked around them complacently. They spoke reassuringly to Rao Sahib and promised him all the votes they knew they had in their pockets. In return, Rao Sahib redoubled his attentions to them, and a nice atmosphere of mutual good will was built up. They spoke of different areas of interest and the most powerful men to be courted in each area. There was particular mention of one man —a shopkeeper who had made money partly through his shop in the bazaar but mostly through his money-lending activities —and everyone stressed how important it was to make sure that he was on their side. He had given promises, but in a town as small as this it was not difficult to hear that he had given promises to the other side as well. On the spur of the moment, Rao Sahib decided that he would personally go and call on the man at his house. They all piled into Rao Sahib's big Mercedes. Raymond went along too, although the car was already very crowded and there were several people crammed together on the front seat, getting in the way of the chauffeur who was ill-pleased and somewhat contemptuous of them.

The house they went to was in a very narrow lane, and they had to descend several steps to enter it. Now they were in a cool, dark room which was bare except for a white sheet spread on the floor and bolsters spaced at intervals. Their host emerged from behind a greasy curtain and declared himself over-whelmed by the honor. However, he did not appear to be overwhelmed at all but quite self-possessed. He was a thin old man with a dyed mustache and a rather merry face. They all sat

215

in a circle on the sheet, and although conversation was sparse, there was no sense of awkwardness. A lot of activity was going on behind the greasy curtain which trembled in excitement, and soon refreshments appeared and were passed round and pressed upon the guests. There was spiced tea in tumblers and a variety of fried delicacies that looked harmless from outside but released a stuffing of fire in Raymond's mouth as soon as he bit into one. Conversation became more lively under the influence of these refreshments, although it remained an expression of pleasure in one another's company and still no mention was made of the election. And indeed, Raymond began to see that it would have been bad manners to mention it.

One or two anecdotes were related, and here their host showed himself particularly talented—at any rate, the guests were very appreciative and they laughed and repeated his punch line to each other. He was pleased and stroked his dyed mustache and twinkled with his bright eyes. And he stroked and twinkled in the same way when he turned to Rao Sahib and said, "The boy is waiting to come and speak with you." Everyone craned forward a bit, and Raymond realized that for the first time something of importance had been said. Their host smiled and turned up one hand in a gesture of resignation. "Nowadays, young people—" and there was a murmur to say that times were changing fast. Then Rao Sahib thanked God from the bottom of his heart that they were, and their host smiled depreciatingly as if it were a compliment paid to himself.

Later Rao Sahib and Raymond sat together in Rao Sahib's drawing room in the New Palace while Rajput bearers served them with Scotch whisky. Rao Sahib was excited, even exalted. He talked freely to Raymond. He said how the country stood on the threshold of great changes and what a privilege it was to be able to play a part in them. He was sincerely grateful that he had been born in these times when it was not rank or wealth that counted but one's own character and abilities. Here he was modest. He said he knew he was not a man of very outstanding ability but there was one quality he had in abundance and that was his sincere desire to serve. Under the influence of whisky and excitement, he spoke with more passion than usual, and his rather sad eyes—large and full like Asha's—shone the way hers did.

He spoke warmly of all his visitors that day, but especially of the man whose hospitality they had enjoyed. Rao Sahib admired him very much, for, although the son of a poor widow, he had worked his way up by his own efforts and made himself rich and powerful enough to be a leading citizen in the district. And that wasn't all—no, the story of progress went further—for this man had sent his son to college in an adjoining state and from there the boy had gone to America; and now he had returned and was starting a chain of workshops all over the district and making money hand over fist. "Soon," chuckled Rao Sahib, "he will be buying me up"—and indeed, already he was making an offer for The Retreat.

"Yes, I've heard," Raymond said.

"She told you?" Rao Sahib shifted a little uneasily. "Unfortunately Asha doesn't understand what is going on in the country today. She has no conception of progress."

"I suppose not."

But Rao Sahib had. He told Raymond about the young man and his plans for The Retreat. Not that he wanted the house—he was going to tear it down—but he was buying up all the land around there in order to start workshops manufacturing spare parts for mechanized drills. He was a very go-ahead young man.

Lee

At first I thought they were a mirage. They looked like a mirage suddenly appearing on the horizon. The sky, the air, and the earth were all dust colored, and those two were the only figures on the landscape. Evie and Margaret. They were both in white saris. Slowly they came toward me; they were dragging bedrolls behind them across the dust. They had traveled a long, long way. We hardly greeted each other. Of course I knew why they had come and who had sent them. After the first shock, I wasn't even surprised any more. I took them into the house.

There was something very strange about Margaret. She seemed . . . not there, somehow; disconnected. I think she didn't know where she was, and I also think she didn't recognize me. Her hands were trembling in a peculiar way. But Evie said it was just exhaustion and all she needed was sleep. They both slept throughout that day and through the night. How they slept! Then, the morning after that when I went into their room, I found Evie awake and dressed. She sat on the edge of the bed with her hands folded in her lap. I don't know if she was just waiting or if she was meditating. Margaret was lying on the bed and at first I thought she was still sleeping. But she was breathing in such a strange way and moving her arms as if she were trying to get at herself, trying to remove something from herself and not succeeding. Evie said again it was all right, that Margaret was just exhausted; they had had a very difficult journey because their train had started late and they had had to spend a night on the station platform, and when finally they got on, their carriage was very crowded—of course they had traveled third class—and they couldn't get any place to sit although toward the early hours of the morning Margaret had been able partly to stretch out on a luggage shelf. The bus that had taken them to Maupur had also been overcrowded and it had broken down twice. After that, they could not get any transport to take them to The Retreat and they had had to walk these last miles. So, naturally, they were very very tired—who wouldn't be?

Evie told me all this shortly and rather impatiently, as if it were something irrelevant and she had far more important things to communicate to me. Of course I knew what they were. And I wanted to hear them, there was so much I wanted to hear from her; but when she said, "You know why we've come," then it was like I was afraid to hear. I quickly went back to talking about Margaret, and asking about her health and how she had been all this time. Again Evie answered impatiently— she said Margaret had been fine, nothing wrong with her at all; but looking at her, I felt that there *was* something wrong, she was not sleeping normally. "She's tired," Evie said.

"But she's been all right, quite all right?"

"Yes, yes." Then she added, "She wasn't quite well on the journey but of course I told you—it was strenuous." I wanted to ask exactly how had she not been quite well but before I could do so, Evie went on: "In the ashram she's been so well! So happy! Just her usual bit of tummy trouble but that's nothing. She forgets about it every time she's near him." When she spoke of him, I burned and blushed and she saw me and smiled into herself. She said softly, "You know how it is . . . how we all get . . . near him."

At that moment Margaret began to make strange sounds. She was talking, I thought it was in her sleep. I shook her, I called her name. She didn't hear me and she didn't wake up—her eyes were not quite shut, the lids had lifted slightly showing her pupils fixed in a frightening way. I tried to make her sit up but she was heavy like a sack partly filled with stones. I called to Evie in panic.

"It's all right," Evie said, soothing and gentle.

But I knew it was not all right. I rushed out of the room and shouted. Servants came running, doors opened. Asha came out of the drawing room downstairs not only with Raymond and Gopi but Rao Sahib was with her too and one other man whom I didn't know.

Bob

That morning Rao Sahib had brought the prospective pur- chaser to The Retreat. He brought him straight into the draw- ing room, where Raymond and Asha and Gopi were playing cards. For Raymond it was a desultory game which he was

219

playing in the hope—unfulfilled—of relieving his boredom; but for the other two it was completely serious. Asha was winning and she was exultant. She slammed down her winning card with an exclamation of triumph, and at the same moment Gopi flung his remaining cards on the floor and stamped on them. She laughed, and he accused her of cheating. They both turned to Raymond as referee, both shouting and outshouting each other so that he couldn't make out what either of them was saying.

None of them heard the visitors enter. Raymond saw them first, and it was only when he got to his feet that the other two interrupted their quarrel. The person Rao Sahib had brought was interesting enough to make them forget their card game for a while. He was a young man, well set up and very well dressed in stylish American clothes. Although he had just crossed the desert in a jeep, he looked entirely crisp and fresh. He moved so swiftly and with such decision that he seemed to cut through the air. He shook hands all round the room, pumping arms up and down with genuine pleasure. When Rao Sahib introduced him as Harish Chandra, he said, "Please call me Bob," and flashed a broad American smile. But his teeth were whiter than an American's.

He sat at his ease on one of the velvet banquettes. His eyes swept round the room: evidently he took it all in—the bar, the bandstand—but if he thought anything odd, he gave no sign. He said "Nice place" and flashed another smile, this time directly at Asha. He took in Asha too in the same way as he had taken in the room. Then his eyes roved on and stopped at Raymond. He shot out his finger. "English—right?"

"Right."

"I can always tell." He crossed one leg over the other and was pleased. "I was over there on my way back from the States. I visited London and Oxford. I liked it. Oxford is very impressive. Very traditional."

Rao Sahib gave a conspiratorial smile toward Raymond. "Mr. Raymond and I are both on the other side. Light Blue. Cambridge," he explained. "The light blues and the dark blues are traditional, should we say rivals, Raymond?"

"I suppose we could," Raymond joked back.

"Is that so," Bob said with polite interest. "I've heard they're both very fancy places. I was three years at N.Y.U. In business administration. That's a fine course. Some very fine people there." A bearer offered him a tray with a tall glass of water on it. He drank it off at one draft. He drank it in the Indian way, laying back his head and pouring the liquid down his throat without allowing the glass to touch his lips; the way he held the glass rather daintily between two fingers was also very Indian.

Again his devouring glance went around the drawing room. This time he lingered for a moment on Gopi, but Gopi was of no interest to him and his eyes swept on not only through the room but through the French windows and out into the garden, estimating its size and possibilities. He said, "I guess there isn't too much water."

Rao Sahib began to explain about the tube wells that had been sunk in his father's time but which had since fallen into disrepair. He said, "You see, no one has been using the place."

Asha said, "Up till now."

Rao Sahib silently implored her. She ignored him.

"A man is coming tomorrow to give an estimate for the tube wells. Of course prices have gone up terribly since Papa's time but that can't be helped. I want to get the garden nicely laid out by the winter because many friends from Bombay and other places will be coming to stay with us."

Rao Sahib was embarrassed, but Bob was already tactfully looking away. He fixed his attention on Raymond, who began to feel aware that Bob was calculating how he fitted into the setup. Suddenly Raymond noticed that he was still holding the cards with which he had joined in Asha's and Gopi's game. Blushing, he made a movement to lay them aside, then checked the movement and blushed more.

Asha said, "It can be very beautiful in the summer too. Once

I get the generators replaced we shall be fully air conditioned and not have to suffer in this beastly heat. What is modern science for? To make people comfortable. That's more important than going to the moon or blowing each other up with atom bombs and such like." She challenged them to contradict her —but at that moment Lee's cry for help was heard.

Lee

They carried Margaret downstairs and put her in Bob's jeep and Evie and I climbed in with her. Raymond sat in front with the driver and with Bob, who was wearing large sunglasses. It was a horrible journey through miles of sun and dust. Whenever I looked up—which I didn't like to do because of the glare—I saw huge black birds hovering in the sky. They were flying so slowly they didn't seem to be flying at all, but they remained with us all the time. I thought how Margaret and Evie had done this journey on foot two days ago, dragging their bedrolls behind them through the dust, and I wondered if these birds had been following them that time too.

Margaret remained the same. We made her as comfortable as possible but it was a rough journey at the back of the jeep. All of us were being rattled and shaken from side to side, and Margaret more than any of us because of being utterly limp: more like a thing than a person. We tried to keep at least her head steady, and it lay in Evie's lap with her eyes glinting from between her lids and her mouth dropped open and a trickle of saliva at the corner. From time to time Evie bent down to whisper something into her ear. I could guess that this was the secret mantra given to her by Swamiji. I knew that Evie firmly believed that it would get through to Margaret, that it would pierce her coma and reach her. I don't know if I believed it or not. I wanted to, but it was difficult under present circumstances. Also it was unnerving to see Evie doing this to Margaret's lolling head, and to hear her calling to her so firmly, even severely. I could see Raymond biting his lip trying to control himself, but finally he turned around and snapped at Evie to stop doing that. Evie looked at him in surprise for a moment and then she smiled in a wan, kind way—sort of in pity for Raymond and his lack of understanding.

It was good Bob was with us because he got things organized very quickly at the hospital. At first we drove to the wrong block, which was very nice and modern but quite empty from inside and smelled of bat droppings. Later we learned that this block had been built with foreign aid, but when it was finished there wasn't any money left for furnishing and equipment, so now they were waiting for more aid. Meanwhile, they carried on in the old buildings. These were very old and rather grim, built partly of stone and partly of brick; inside they needed painting and plastering very badly. The walls were full of those stains you see everywhere in India which at first you think are blood but afterward they turn out to be betel juice that people have spat out. But in a hospital of course they may really be blood. There were an awful, awful lot of people. Not all of them were sick, I knew that—for each patient there were always many members of his family in attendance. I had learned that even from Miss Charlotte's little clinic; but all the same it was difficult to imagine that there could be anywhere in the world enough staff to cope with so much sickness. There certainly weren't enough beds. Everywhere, in all the corridors and along the verandas, patients were lying on the floor so that one had constantly to step around and sometimes over them.

Bob arranged for a little storeroom to be cleared for Margaret. It was a tiny oblong box and there was just room to put a bed. She was carried to this bed and she lay on it with all sorts of tubes stuck into her. From time to time people came to change the tubes and to make her bed and clean her. She only lay there, breathing in a peculiar way. Sometimes she made sounds but they didn't mean anything. Her face didn't mean anything either; it was no longer Margaret's face. There wasn't any Margaret left really, only this body in a coma being fed with tubes. The doctor said her liver was completely destroyed and that this process must have been going on for a long time.

Evie and I stayed with her. At first Evie still tried to get through to her with her mantra, but obviously it was hopeless. So then Evie lost interest in her and began instead to concentrate on me. We were together day and night, cramped together on the floor of that hot little box, and day and night she spoke to me of him and everything he had done for us and everything we must do for him in return. When I asked her to stop, she smiled in an indulgent way and went on all the same.

She wanted me to meditate with her. I tried to but it was impossible for me to concentrate. Outside the door patients quarreled and some laughed and some groaned and some cried out; rickety trolleys were pushed rattling and shaking through the stone corridors. Inside our room there was Margaret lying up there on her bed gurgling sometimes and mumbling sometimes but otherwise quite still with colorless liquids silently flowing into her. None of it bothered Evie. She sat in the lotus pose and meditated. Then it was like being with two people who were not there—she and Margaret both. Flies settled freely on their faces. Sometimes I chased them off Margaret and all the time I was chasing them off myself. I got irritated, frantic even, and longed to escape.

The only ventilation in that storeroom was from a tiny open grill; someone had hung a piece of sacking in front of it to keep out the heat and glare. When I felt very desperate, I stood on a box and pushed aside that piece of sacking to look out. I looked beyond the hospital grounds—crowded with patients, visitors, cycle rickshaws, and people selling bananas and peanuts—toward the remains of the fort that stood overlooking the town. I liked doing this especially at dusk when the sky went soft as silk and with the strangest lights in it and how beautiful it looked stretched out behind the rugged walls of the fort.

I didn't want to turn back into the room but sooner or later

Evie always called me. She made me sit beside her. She spoke gently with me then, knowing I was in a gentle mood from looking out at the sky like that. She said, "We'll go back together, you and I, won't we, we'll go back to him where he's waiting for us." When I didn't answer, she persisted. She pressed my hands, she laid her cheek against mine. She was so sweet with me. She said, "We'll go soon now. As soon as Margaret's dead." She added in a joyful voice. "How happy he'll be to have us back! He'll tease you no end, you look out. How he'll tease and joke! You'll see." She clapped her hands, laughing.

Raymond and Bob

Raymond hung around the hospital, waiting for news. Whenever he entered Margaret's room, Evie became hostile, and when he talked to her, she pretended not to have heard. So he did not go in very often; anyway, there was no room. He had sent a telegram to Miss Charlotte and hoped very much that she would come.

Meanwhile he spent his time with Bob. Bob led a full and busy life. He dashed around the town and its surrounding districts in his jeep and made contacts and inspected land and set up deals. He sat in meetings with peasant landlords in their dark little rooms smelling of incense and cow. He told them that they could never hope to enter the modern world unless they radically changed their ways and adapted themselves to modern business methods. They listened with interest while sucking their milky tea. Often he threw up his hands and told them they were hopeless and, climbing back into his jeep, thundered away in a cloud of dust. Everyone liked him. He had grown up here, spoke the same language, ate the same food; his father was one of them, and so was he, and they were proud of him because he shook hands like an American and wore those clothes and dark glasses and was going to be very rich.

But sometimes Bob was in a relaxed, pensive mood. Then

Raymond and he climbed up the hill to the remains of the old fort and they sat there and looked out over the town. They usually came in the evening when the day's heat was over and the dust had settled. Everything that had been bleak during the day was transfigured by the evening sky. Bob became quite sentimental at such times. He pointed out all the landmarks of the town—the maze of the old town huddled around the maze of the Old Palace, the New Palace set in a park with peacocks, the old Civil Lines area with decaying British bungalows turned into municipal offices: and stretching around and beyond everything, so immense and unending that the town seemed no more than a handful of houses flung there in a moment of aberration, the brown and gray desert swelling a little now and again into brown and gray mounds.

Both Raymond and Bob often looked in the direction of The Retreat. Raymond thought of Gopi in there, but Bob had quite other thoughts. He had big plans for development in that area. He explained how he would be setting up workshops for the manufacture of spare parts which before could only be imported from abroad. He told Raymond about the process of manufacture and Raymond liked listening to him, although the details were usually too technical for him to understand.

But one day Bob said, "Seems she doesn't want to sell."

Raymond said, "You see, the place has such associations for her."

"I know." Bob nodded maturely. "I guess I can build around it, but of course there'll be a lot of construction work and it may not be the best place for those parties she's planning. . . . Is that boy always there with her?"

Raymond saw Gopi as Bob must be seeing and judging him. He blushed and spoke quickly. "He's just on a visit. He'll be going back soon—as a matter of fact he's getting married quite soon." Encouraged by Bob's kindly interest, he grew bolder. "He's marrying into a family in the sugar business. I believe it's quite a prosperous concern, and Gopi has plans for expansion. He would like to try out some new ideas."

"Nothing like new ideas," Bob said, taking a deep breath as of sensuous enjoyment.

Another time they walked around the fort within its massive crumbling walls. There were only a few pillars and gateways left inside, besides a temple and an empty tank and some subterranean passages. Bob knew the place well and pointed out spots where momentous events had happened— the cave in which he had found and killed a cobra, the broken-off steps from which one of his friends had fallen and broken his ankle and had had to be carried all the way down the steep hillside. He also tried to tell Raymond something of the history of the place; but here he was rather vague. Although he was proud of all that had happened, he had only a general picture of brave women who had flung themselves onto the funeral pyre while their brave men rushed down the hillside to meet the enemy.

"They always wore saffron when they went off to fight," he said. "Because they knew they were going to die. They were a fine set of people. Of course they were all Rajputs. Rao Sahib is a Rajput."

"Yes, I know."

"A very fine person. . . . My family are banias."

Raymond had read about the Rajputs and their martial spirit and heroic exploits, but there was not much to be read about the banias, who lacked these inspiring qualities. Bob also could not tell him very much.

"I guess we've always liked to make money. That's where I get it from." He laughed and threw a stone into a well. "I'm going to make a lot of money. Just wait and watch."

Raymond regarded him with affection. He had not before met anyone like Bob. There was something very new about his combination of vigorous speech and movements with his deep dark eyes and delicately turned wrists. Bob kept himself very fresh with deodorants, and though he still liked occasionally to chew betel, he was careful to rinse his mouth afterward with a hygienic mouthwash.

"In business of course you need contacts. You know, influence. Next elections I'll be getting a ticket."

"You'll be standing against Rao Sahib then."

"A very fine person," Bob said again. "If you stay around, Ray, you'll see some changes. I wish you would. I'll give you a job. What do you think of that? I need you, Ray. I really can use you. I mean it."

Raymond felt flattered but had to say truthfully, "I don't think there are any jobs for me."

"Listen, I'll tell you something. It's terrible but I can't spell."

"You don't need to spell."

"Are you joking? Do you know how many letters I have to write a day? *A day.* And that's only letters. And who'll write my speeches once I'm in Parliament?"

"Not me, I fear."

Bob playfully punched his arm. "You don't want to stay."

It was true, Raymond didn't want to stay. He wrote many letters to his mother; sometimes he wrote twice a day. They were beginning to think that perhaps they wouldn't meet in the Middle East after all but in Europe. What about Italy? The proposal had come from Raymond and his mother had enthusiastically assented. Now often, when driving with Bob through this town of stone and rubble scooped from out of the desert, he thought of the Mediterranean. He longed for it.

Brother and Sister

Bulbul was telling stories to Asha and Gopi. It was one of their favorite occupations. They turned off the lights in the drawing room and Gopi lay at one end of a velvet settee and Asha at the other; their naked feet touched and sometimes they caressed each other's soles.

Bulbul's stories were all of the old times, of things that had happened in the Old Palace or, even further back, legends from the times of the fort. Bulbul was richly endowed with memories, for her family had been here as long as Asha's. As far, that is, as she could be said to have a family. She came from a long line of singing and dancing girls none of whom had ever married but had handed down their traditions from daughter to daughter. Bulbul herself had been too ugly to be a singing and dancing girl, but she still had her connections in those circles. Sometimes she disappeared from The Retreat for several days, and went to stay with her cronies in a certain quarter of the town or to visit very old women with dyed hair who still lingered in outhouses inside the Old Palace compound.

Today she was telling a story of a hundred years ago concerning a widowed sister of the Rao of that time. She had been a woman of strong appetites who had to have many lovers to satisfy her. As she got older the lovers got younger, and there was a lot of scandal. But she did not care one jot for that nor for the warnings of her brother the Rao. To enable her to carry on her intrigues undisturbed, she had constructed a secret passage that led straight from her rooms to the back alleys behind the palace. It was not, however, very secret, as many people knew the way. "It is still there," Bulbul said.

"Where?" asked Gopi, pulling away his foot, which Asha was tickling with her toe.

"Behind a picture," Bulbul said. "The picture is of Rao Birendra Singh and it is in a beautiful gold frame but it is not really a picture but a door."

"Don't do that," Gopi told Asha, not wanting to be distracted from the story.

"When the widow would not listen to her brother but went her own sweet way, then the Rao decided to teach her a lesson. He was a man of very strong temper, everyone trembled before him. Only his sister defied him. One night, when he knew she had a lover with her, he came to her quarters and, pounding on the door, commanded her to open. She did not lose her head but quickly let her lover out of the secret door. Then she told her maidservant to open up for the Rao Sahib. So when he burst into the room with his attendants, there she was playing chess with her maid. When she saw him, she rose to welcome him and modestly covered her face with her veil." Bulbul showed how, with a very graceful movement. "The Rao Sahib gave a sign to his attendants and quick as a flash they opened the secret door and pursued the lover down the passage. Then all the cries and pleas for mercy were in vain. He was dragged back into the room and there right there in front of the weeping princess the Rao Sahib—oh, he was a terrible, terrible man—drew his dagger and with his own hand he"—Bulbul made a dramatic downward movement and a sound as of a dagger whistling through the air—"he cut it off."

"Cut what off?" Gopi asked.

The two women burst out laughing. Asha extended her hand to show him, but just then the light was switched on and Rao Sahib asked, "Why are you sitting in the dark?"

They all three had a shock—from the sudden light and also because they had not been expecting him. He apologized for the disturbance; he said he had been passing nearby on his way back from a village which he had visited for electioneering purposes. He was dressed in his electioneering clothes consisting of a plain dhoti and kurta such as the villagers wore; but his was made of very fine new muslin. He also had a big orange turban tied around his head.

Asha made a fuss over him and settled him comfortably. "How hard you work," she said, soothing, admiring.

"We drove over two hundred miles today."

She clicked her tongue. "It's too much."

"Oh, but Ashi, I like it! I never get tired at all." His cheeks shook with pleasure. "Those villagers are a wonderful lot of chaps. Of course they are still bound by old traditions but at the same time they are very open—you know, ready to listen and learn. We had some thumping good discussions."

"That Bob or what does he call himself was here again today."

Rao Sahib lowered his eyes. The glad expression went from his face.

230

"I'm not selling," Asha said.

"Can I talk to you?" Rao Sahib pleaded.

Asha firmly grasped Gopi's hand. "We are going to live here."

But after a time she consented to go out into the garden with Rao Sahib. In the moonlight the garden looked not dry and dead but as if it had mysteriously begun to bloom. Asha's Rajasthani skirt rustled as it swept along the paths. She lingered by a group of statues and ran her hand over a noseless maiden with a headless bird on her shoulder: "I'm going to get them all repaired." After a while she added, "And the fountains too."

Rao Sahib said, "You know he has acquired all the land around here."

"Not this land. Not Papa's house and garden."

"He has called for bids. He will be starting work very soon."

"Let him," Asha said. It was indeed difficult to imagine this future event. Like the garden, the surrounding landscape was transformed by moonlight and appeared as silent and silver as the moon itself.

"He is a very go-ahead person," Rao Sahib said. "Such people are urgently needed. There are so many new developments that from now on it is work work work for all of us."

She loved him. She kissed his cheek. She looked into his eyes that had never changed from the time he was her baby brother.

"Listen, Ashi, I'm going back to New Delhi in a day or two. I want you to come with me. . . . Don't say no, just listen to me. You know how many committees Sunita is on, how much work she does. And she is always looking for helpers, for really sincere people that she can trust and rely on. . . . Why are you laughing? What is there to laugh at? If you really put your mind to it, you can do it. Really, fundamentally, you are a serious and capable person. I have often said so to Sunita. If only you will put your shoulder to the wheel."

"What wheel?"

"Of course if you are going to keep laughing . . ." he said in an offended voice.

"No, I'm not." She straightened his great orange turban that had slipped sideways. But she could not help laughing again, though she struggled against it.

Now he was really offended. He turned and left her to go back into the house. She went after him, asking him to wait and listen to her. He did so. Now she was quite, quite serious.

"You are sure you are going to win this election?"

"Of course."

"How do you know?"

"They are all on my side."

"Who?"

"All of them. Everybody. All the people in the town and the villages. . . . You don't know what it's like—to feel such *affinity* with the people—such a sense of—what's the word. . . . Are you crying?"

"No."

"I think you are."

She burst into tears. She said, "Because of you."

He comforted her as best he could. He was very nice to her, very gentle, as to an invalid or someone sick in mind.

Lee

Miss Charlotte arrived the day Margaret died. At first no one realized Margaret was dead, and it wasn't until the nurse came to wash her—she had already begun to do so—that she noticed her breathing had stopped. Then they disconnected all the tubes and covered Margaret with a sheet. Everyone was quite businesslike about it. The event had been expected. Evie and I too had been expecting it. Evie said we would leave in the evening.

But when Miss Charlotte came into the room, everything changed. Miss Charlotte embraced and kissed me and made my face wet with her tears. She got down on her knees by the side of Margaret's bed and began to pray. Her lips moved, tears continued to flow down her face. Then the body on the bed was not only someone who had died and had been expected to die —but was Margaret! Margaret!

I remembered so much then, so many things. I saw Margaret looking at herself in the fitting-room mirror and hating herself in her bridesmaid's dress. I thought of her mother and her sister Penny who hadn't understood her and hadn't wanted her to come here. All the same she had come and she had been happy because she had been truly in the process of finding herself. I admired and loved her and would not allow her to be dead. It couldn't happen! How could it? She had only just begun and so much was left for her still. Perhaps in the end she wouldn't have stayed here—she might have gone back, not as the same person but changed and probably stronger and better. Now she wouldn't ever go back. I wished it had been possible to shake Margaret and say come on, get up, it's all a mistake. It *was* a mistake. Yet Miss Charlotte was praying humbly and with her head bowed as if it was a mistake that could be accepted. Evie had also gone down on her knees. She wasn't praying, but two polite tears made their way down her cheeks. She was watching me from the corner of her eye.

In India, because of the heat, dead bodies have to be disposed of quite quickly. The hospital authorities were hovering around a bit—and not without reason, for already a smell I didn't like to identify was beginning to pervade the storeroom where we had spent so many days. The flies that had been living with us all those days had suddenly multiplied and they clustered together and buzzed over the bed. Miss Charlotte asked about a Christian cemetery. Bob and Raymond went to make arrangements, and Evie slipped out at the same time. I thought she had gone with them. Bob had blocks of ice sent in and these were placed around the bed in containers to preserve the body till everything was ready for its burial.

Miss Charlotte said we would have to wash Margaret. The basin of water and flannel the nurse had brought in to wash her when we thought she was still alive had remained, and Miss

Charlotte said they would do. She pulled back the sheet. I was ready, even eager, to help her although I had never done anything like this before and felt quite helpless. Miss Charlotte was very gentle with me; she gave me instructions and was as kind and loving to me as to Margaret whose limbs she tenderly lifted to do what had to be done. It was not in the least morbid or unpleasant—quite on the contrary, there was something satisfying to me in being able to do this for Margaret. I know Miss Charlotte felt the same.

Evie came in and said, "They're here now."

"Who, dear?" asked Miss Charlotte. She was brushing Margaret's hair and admiring it as she did so; she drew the brush slowly down those long strands. "Isn't it pretty?" she said, smiling down at it. Margaret's hair had always been her best feature and it was still as it had been—strong, fair, healthy, and alive.

Evie also admired it. She extended her hand to touch it. "Lovely," she said; then she said again, "They're here."

"Who?" I asked this time.

She lowered her eyes and smiled sadly, as if wanting to spare us something.

"Who?" I asked, with suspicion now.

She made a gesture toward the half-open door. I went to see. There were some coolies standing out there, holding a plank. On the plank, neatly folded, was a red cloth and a strong coarse rope. I recognized all these things at once. I knew them from long ago—from that time when I had stood outside the house in the strange town and they had brought the girl's body out. On a plank like this one, tied to it with ropes and covered with a red cloth. Sometimes I still wondered about that girl and whether she had been murdered or not.

Evie came out too. She said, "People have been very kind and helpful. The wood's been bought and there's a brahmin priest waiting for us."

I said, "Margaret's going to have a Christian burial. Raymond's gone to arrange for it."

Evie was patient and silent. The coolies also stood there patiently waiting. They wore the usual tattered coolie clothes but they were sturdier than the usual coolies. One of them was very short—almost a dwarf—but he had strongly developed shoulders and stood there on legs that were somewhat bandy as if from heavy weights pressing down on them.

"You can tell them to go away," I said and began to turn back into the room. Evie held me. She said, "You know she would have wanted it."

I freed myself from her and rejoined Miss Charlotte. Margaret was ready now and she looked so nice with her eyes shut and her hands folded and wearing a white nightdress. She reminded me of those sculptured figures you see on stone tombs in some cathedral or a village church. Sometimes these figures are of the person who is buried inside the tomb but sometimes they are of angels that have come to take care of his soul. Margaret reminded me of both, of angel and of peaceful dead.

Evie followed me inside and said again, "She'd have wanted it."

"How do *you* know?" I said.

"Hindus are burned, not buried."

Miss Charlotte, who had been looking at Margaret, now looked at Evie. So did I. Evie said, "She was a Hindu." She was speaking aggressively now and as if she were fighting us. "Becoming a Hindu is not like becoming a Christian. You don't have to take formal baptism or anything but freely assent to the Truth within you."

Miss Charlotte said, "We must think of her family too."

"What family? She didn't have a family. He was her family."

"Who's he, dear?"

"Swamiji."

I made a wild, sweeping gesture to drive away the flies that were settling on Margaret's face. I was furious—really furious—yes, with the flies, but beyond them with other things too.

"You know it's true," Evie said to me. "The relationship with the guru is the highest there can be and it cancels out all the others. Margaret accepted that and so did you. Didn't you?" she said and she tried to look into my eyes in the hypnotic way he always did.

I turned away, shouting, "Don't speak about him!" I was full of bitterness and rage. It was he who had brought us here to this room. I detested him and not only him but everything connected with him, all the roads that had led us to him—literally those roads: the trains and buses we had traveled on, the makeshift places where we had slept crowded in together with deformed, diseased people, the water we had drunk, the food we had eaten at wayside stalls, putting it into our mouths without giving a thought to what hands had touched it! And squatting in filthy places that no one was low enough to clean so that excrement festered in the heat, feeding up flies. Those very same flies that were now settling on Margaret's dead face. Again I raised my hand and brandished it to chase them away. I told Evie, "You can go back to him right now if you like. You don't have to wait for the funeral."

Miss Charlotte was again on her knees by the side of the bed. It was a relief to me to join her and also to join her in the prayers she was saying out loud. I stumbled a bit behind her because I was not sure of the words; but I liked to say them. I didn't want to think of anything else but them, and only to keep on kneeling there till Raymond came back to say it was time to take Margaret away.

Raymond Writes to His Mother

" . . . Maupur was a civil station but it can never have been an important one. I suspect it was the sort of place where civilians who weren't doing too well were sent to be out of the way. They must have lived very lonely lives out here, cut off from the rest of the population and dependent only on one another for company. There were probably just two or three of them, like the magistrate and the superintendent of police and a doctor if they were lucky. They had houses just outside the city limits, the usual kind of Anglo-Indian bungalows, dark solid structures with a lot of outhouses. I don't know why they always give me such a gloomy feeling. I think of English people locked up inside these cavernous windowless rooms and battling from in there against heat and disease and all the other things. But of course that's all over now and the houses have been requisitioned by the municipality and cut up into municipal offices.

"The station was never big enough to have a church of its own but it does have a British cemetery. It's just behind the bungalows on a rocky incline full of big stones wedged into the soil. There aren't very many graves—about two dozen perhaps—and they are irregularly placed up and down the incline and of rather haphazard shapes, and some of them have sunk into the ground so that they are practically indistinguishable from the stones. This makes them look very old but in fact none of them goes further back than the 1880's and there are a few from the 1920's and '30's. As always in India, at least half are of children. Where the cause of death is given, it's usually cholera or smallpox. But there is one army officer—Captain William John Douglas—who 'succumbed to injuries sustained at the hand of a native assassin,' and a young woman, Emily Jane Dove, who died in childbirth.

"The soil is so hard and rocky that we had to employ several men to dig it and by the time they were ready it was evening. I've tried to describe these Indian evenings to you before, but I don't think I shall ever succeed. Perhaps one has to live through an Indian day really to appreciate the evening that follows it. I'm afraid Margaret's coffin was rather rough, it was really only a box nailed together by a local carpenter with Bob standing over him to make him hurry up. All through the funeral the birds were flying about in the rather hectic way they do in the evening just before descending into their nests. They were mostly sparrows, indistinguishable from our English sparrows and chirping away in the same silly cheerful way. They kept making me think of the garden at home. The light fading away in the sky and leaving it very soft and with a moist quality in it also reminded me of home. There were a few hardy though stunted trees growing on that mound, and one of them was covered with a fuzz of young leaves that were a very delicate green except where the last remains of the sun shone through them and made them gold. Miss Charlotte spoke the burial service. She has a clear high voice like those voices you hear in church singing above the organ.

"Mother—I'm sorry—I've changed my mind again. I don't want to meet you in Italy or anywhere else. I want to come home. We'll take our trip some other time—truly, I promise—but just now I want to be at home in Hazelhurst. I've asked Miss Charlotte to come and stay with us for a while. I know how much you'll like her and she you. I've spoken to her a lot about Hazelhurst. Last night after the funeral I was telling her about everything—our walks, the pond and the almshouses and Mrs. Teddington's tea shop—and she said she felt she knew the place already and loved it as I do.

"This morning while I was packing Gopi came in. You remember, I've mentioned Gopi to you before, he's the boy who's come on some of my trips, and he's here in Maupur too. We've become quite good friends although lately, ever since we've come to Maupur—"

Here Raymond broke off. There was no point in writing this to his mother. It would be of no interest to her, since she had not been kept up on the progress of their friendship. She didn't know Gopi and so didn't know how he had changed and how this change disturbed Raymond. Gopi had sat on the edge of the big double bed and watched Raymond put his clothes into his suitcase. Raymond liked packing: he folded everything beautifully and then placed each garment carefully in position and smoothed it with his hands. Gopi watched him in amusement and after a while he laughed out loud and asked, "You know what I think?"

"No."

"I think you would be a very nice wife for some lucky man."

Raymond could never do anything about his blushes, but he went on stoically packing. "Yes," Gopi said, "sometimes you are just like a woman. Look how neat you are and tidy! I am sure you can cook very well too. . . . Show me that. Why haven't I seen it before?"

He held out his hand for the pajamas Raymond was putting into his suitcase. Gopi unfolded them critically, felt the material, held them up against himself. Raymond had seen him do this so often with clothes, but whereas once Gopi had been gleeful—full of joy and excitement—now his hand and eye were coolly critical. Evidently the pajamas passed his appraisal, for he said, rather casually, "Can I have them?"

"Of course," Raymond said, keeping his eyes lowered.

"Thanks," Gopi said; then, as if wanting to give Raymond some pleasure in return, he showed him the studs on his kurta: "Have you seen these? She gave them to me. Do you know what they are?"

Raymond gave a fleeting glance. "Rubies, I think."

"Do you like the way they're set? They are very old. They belonged to her great-uncle. You can't get workmanship like this nowadays. What's the matter? Don't you like them? Then why aren't you looking?" He seemed really hurt not to have his new acquisition admired.

Raymond looked up from his packing—not at Gopi's ruby studs but at Gopi himself. He said, "What about your wedding?" Of course he knew that Gopi would scowl and turn away but he persisted. "Don't you think you ought to go back now? I think you ought."

Gopi had got up off the bed. He went and stood with his back to Raymond and admired a picture on the wall. This showed a very plump couple on a sofa. They were in amorous pose though fully clothed in silk and green brocade. In the background was a tall vase filled with arum lilies. "It's beautiful," Gopi said.

"It's perfectly horrible."

Gopi said, "You don't understand anything. It's historical. It's Shahjehan and Mumtaz Mahal."

Raymond suppressed a cry of irritation. Then he said, "You told me you would just stay a short while and then go back."

"I like this room better than mine. When you've gone, I will ask them to change over."

"You said you'd leave at the same time I did."

"Oh, Raymond," Gopi said very sweetly, "I wish you weren't going. I shall miss you very much."

And he looked at him as sweetly as he spoke. Gopi was a very handsome man now. He had filled out somewhat and, though still slender, he seemed broader, more manly. The ruby studs on his kurta were open in a studiedly casual way, revealing his olive skin matted with hair in which nestled the end of a fine gold chain he wore around his neck.

"I'd have stayed for your wedding," Raymond said stubbornly.

Gopi made a patient, gentle gesture with his hand. He sat down on the velvet bedspread again. He said, "It is fate."

"Whose fate? What are you talking about?"

"My fate. Your fate. We meet and then we part."

"Yes but what about your wedding?"

"That's fate too."

"It's not, you know," Raymond said energetically. "There's nothing to stop you from taking a train and going back and getting married and going into the sugar business. Nothing at all, so you needn't sigh like that."

"I thought you were a sensitive person, Raymond. Come here. Sit near me." When Raymond did so, he affectionately straightened his collar. Raymond sat bolt upright and frowning. "Why are you cross with me, Raymond? I don't like it. I'm so fond of you. I think we shall always be friends. Even when you go away, we shall write to one another. I'm not very good at writing letters but I shall try for your sake."

His voice as he spoke became softer and softer. Raymond felt as if it were stifling him. The overfurnished red room and the soft velvet bedspread on which they were sitting also had a very stifling effect. Raymond cleared his throat rather brusquely. "You won't write. You'll mean to for a while but you'll keep putting it off and in the end you'll just let it slide."

Gopi laughed: "I'm very lazy, everyone knows it. But I shall try, I promise. And I shall certainly be thinking of you—so much."

"But I shall try not to think of you at all. How can I think of you," he cried in reply to Gopi's hurt look, "if I have to think of you here in this place? I don't want to think of you like that. I can't. It's too awful."

Raymond was shaking. He was tremendously upset. He didn't know what to do. He felt like imploring Gopi, even getting down on his knees to do so or indulging in some other extravagant gesture. Gopi on the other hand remained very calm. He patted Raymond's shoulder and smiled at him in a way that was both sad and understanding. He seemed much older than Raymond at that moment.

Raymond didn't write any of this to his mother but tore the page off and continued on a new one.

"I forgot to tell you that Miss Charlotte has very kindly—and very efficiently—got rid of my flat in Delhi. She found someone to rent it and buy all my furniture, an American professor and his wife who've come to study (I think) Buddhism. They took the whole place over just as it was, including Shyam. Only there was some trouble with Shyam. I don't know exactly what happened, but the upshot of it was he was sacked. He's been after Miss Charlotte to find him another job and she has been trying, but as she also has jobs to find for her own old servants, I'm afraid she hasn't succeeded. Shyam sent me a long, long letter —written for him I know by the letter-writer who sits outside the post office—all about the turpitude of the new American tenants and asking me to get him a job with the High Commission. But I can't. I just can't. Anyway, there's no time. If there is anything you can think of that you want besides the shawl and the raw silk, please send a cable—care Intercontinental Hotel, New Delhi—because a letter may not reach me in time before I leave."

Lee Travels

Asha had suffered all night. Although of course everyone has to die, and they are doing it every day and one gets used to it, the idea of a young girl—a young foreign girl—with all of life still before her being destroyed in this way pierced her deeply. She couldn't sleep and even her pills didn't work; in the end she had to send Bulbul to Gopi's room and at last, toward the early hours of the morning, she managed to fall asleep in his arms.

After all that, naturally the next day she was too exhausted to be able to get up. She remained in bed and Bulbul propped her up with pillows. The gold curtains remained drawn for a long time, keeping the room in dusk, but when she felt stronger, she asked Bulbul to open them. She had a wide sweeping view from her bedroom, which was the principal room in the house and had been the one occupied by her father and his cabaret artist friend. She could look out over the dead garden and, beyond that, across the whole wide landscape lying broiling in the sun, up to the wooded hills from where the tigers sometimes roared. Asha lay for a long time staring out although nothing moved out there except the birds of prey circling around and around in the dun-colored sky.

After some hours she became aware of a procession of vehicles moving from the direction of the town toward The Retreat. When they came nearer, she identified them as a jeep followed by several lorries. They came nearer and nearer and finally stopped at some distance away from the garden. Bob was the first person to jump off the jeep. He moved around in his quick decisive way, accompanied by a man in a solar hat. The lorries began to be unloaded, raising clouds of dust. Most of them carried materials and machinery, but one was filled with laborers and their families, who jumped down and scattered over the ground and soon made everything look quite lively. Asha watched all this calmly for a while, continuing to think her thoughts, and then she called Bulbul to draw the curtains shut again.

Lee, coming in to visit her, felt quite at home. It seemed to her that she had spent a lot of time with Asha in Asha's bedroom. The bedrooms were in different places, but the general sense of luxurious disorder was always the same. This particular room was more luxurious than the others, for Asha's father had spent a lot of money on it. One wall was taken up entirely by a tapestry which gleamed with golden threads. Asha, lying in the center of the bed, also seemed somehow to be golden-tinted, but no doubt that was an illusion brought about by the curtains and walls and their reflection from within several mirrors.

"I'm ill," Asha said. "I couldn't sleep all night. I keep thinking about that poor sweet girl. And her poor parents. What will they say when they get the news? Oh, poor people."

"Miss Charlotte sent a telegram."

"I loved the way Miss Charlotte said the Christian prayers. It made me feel—yes, really, all religions are the same, don't you think so, Lee? Darling, please don't open the curtains, the glare is hurting my eyes and I have such a headache, it's from not sleeping."

"There's Bob out there."

He was kneeling on the ground looking at something being measured. The man in the solar hat was kneeling beside him, explaining to him from a blueprint. The laborers and their families were beginning to make themselves at home. The children ran around playing games, and some of the women had started cooking fires and others were feeding their babies.

"Shut it, darling. Please."

Lee did so and turned back into the room. She was restless and moved about, picking things up and putting them down again rather irritably. She ignored Asha's request to come and sit beside her on the bed. Asha looked at her with concern. "Are you all right? You look pale. Naturally, it's the strain. How terrible, terrible it has been for you. Oh, dreadful. For all of us." Asha shut her eyes for a moment. Then she said, "Promise me you will take rest and care. . . . Have you written to your parents? How happy they will be. Of course I shall miss you, we shall all miss you, but really I'm glad."

Lee said, "Why?"

"It's for the best, Lee darling."

Lee looked at the tapestry on the wall. It showed pink and white girls dancing hand in hand on a lawn illumined by sunlight. A couple was dallying. There were also a dog and a huntsman and, in the distance, a deer.

Lee said, "Evie's on the train now. I think she's got as far as Kotah."

"It must be very, very hot there at this time of the day."

"She doesn't care."

"I think it's wonderful the way you girls go here and there." Asha leaned back against her pillows. It drained her to think of the hardships voluntarily endured by these girls. She asked, "Isn't she returning home too?"

"No, why should she. She's got what she came for. So why should she."

"What about her parents and her home?"

"As if she cared."

"And you?"

Lee did not think this worth answering. She was standing before Asha's dressing table. It was cluttered with Asha's usual lotions and scents and some pieces of jewelry taken off and carelessly thrown there. Her husband's photo in its frame had fallen down and was obscured by a box of paper tissues sitting on top of it.

244

"I haven't seen this before." Lee picked up another framed photo. This one showed Gopi; it was just a snapshot.

"Give it here."

Asha pressed Gopi's photograph against her lips, and then against her closed lids and her bosom. She held it there. Lee watched her and felt moved by the expression on her face. Asha's passion was deep and genuine. It made something stir within Lee; she said, "I don't want to go."

"Then stay."

"Margaret would have stayed. My God, she *is* staying."

"The poor, poor girl. Ah."

Lee waved that aside. In her present mood, it seemed to her that Margaret was not to be pitied. Margaret had accomplished something; she had gone all the way. Whereas for Lee now there was only the journey back to New Delhi, where, at the American Express, she would find her ticket home waiting for her. The idea revolted her. She felt entirely reluctant to leave. How could she, now? She hadn't finished yet. She said, in a tone of resentment, "It's all right for Raymond and Miss Charlotte. They *want* to go."

"You stay here with us. We'll have a nice time. We'll enjoy ourselves." However, even as she spoke, Asha was not quite sincere about the invitation she was extending. The prospect of having Lee in the house with herself and Gopi disturbed her. She knew how the days could be very long, very hot, very idle —and Lee and Gopi were both so young, so healthy, they would not be able to help themselves. She pressed Gopi's picture closer to her heart, which was now beating in premonition and fear.

But Lee said, "I don't think I want to stay just in one place. I want to travel, you know, go around the way I used to. . . ." Her old line about losing herself in order to find herself rose to her lips, but she felt it to be no longer appropriate.

Asha said, "What about your Swamiji?"

"What about him?"

"Don't you want to go back to him?"

"No, why should I."

But as if Lee could ever be anything but perfectly truthful! That was everything for her—to be truthful, with others, of course, but first of all with herself. She wanted her whole life to be based only on truth found and tested by herself. So now she stood there frowning, searching into herself and determined to pluck up any weeds of falsehood that might have had the temerity to grow there.

"Of course I want to go back," she said. "That's the trouble. I try not to, but I think about it all the time. About going back to him. Being with him again." Her voice shook but she controlled it at once and said, "No I can't. I mustn't."

Asha looked with attention into Lee's face. She thought at last something was changing there. She had always liked Lee's face, but at the same time she felt it lacked something. Now this lack was being made up with expressions that had not been there before.

Asha said, "When I was with Banubai I thought a lot about higher things, just like you do. Of course there are higher things, we all know that; if we didn't know, where would we be better than animals? Yes, there is something higher and we all want to reach it. Only who are we to say which is the right path?"

Lee pushed the curtain aside and looked out of the window again. She pretended not to be listening but she was. At the same time she was following her own thoughts. She looked past Bob and the laborers and the unloading machinery, toward the town in the distance. The only part of it visible from here was the old fort on its hill, but Lee disregarded it and thought only of the railway station that lay beyond it. She loved this thought: also that of buses, trains, travelers; endless hours of monotonous landscape; heat and dust; unexpected adventures in strange towns. If she went, it would be just like before.

No! She knew at once: it wouldn't be like before. True, the

journey would be the same and the view out of the window; but now if some place they passed looked attractive—or she heard of some interesting monument, or some fellow passenger invited her to stay—she wouldn't be able to get off the way she used to and go wherever she was taken. She would have to say, I can't. Because now she would be traveling in one definite direction and get off at one definite station; and then wait for the bus; and travel in that bus down a long and dusty road; and jump off at what looked like the middle of nowhere and, lugging her bedroll behind her, walk across the fields till she came to a board and some barbed wire. There he would be, sitting under the only tree. "Oh-ho!" he would say. "Just see who has come."